Heart's Kiss

Issue 10
August-September 2018

Lezli Robyn & Tina Smith, Editors
Shahid Mahmud, Publisher

Published by Arc Manor/Heart's Nest Press
P.O. Box 10339
Rockville, MD 20849-0339

Heart's Kiss is published in February, April, June, August, October and December.

www.HeartsKiss.com

Pleaee refer to our website for information on how to submit material for *Heart's Kiss* magazine.

Available by subscription (www.HeartsKiss.com) or through your favorite online store (Amazon.com, BN.com, etc.).

ISBN: 978-1-61242-418-7

FOREIGN LANGUAGE RIGHTS: Please refer all inquiries pertaining to foreign language rights to Shahid Mahmud, Arc Manor, P.O. Box 10339, Rockville, MD 20849-0339. Tel: 1-240-645-2214. Fax 1-310-388-8440. Email admin@ArcManor.com.

Contents

OPENING EDITORIAL

by Lezli Robyn

We might still have nearly two months more of summer, but the staff at *Heart's Kiss* are excited for the fall's cooler weather to arrive; the promise of change is in the air. At the beginning of summer my co-editor, Tina, attended the Romantic Times Booklovers Conference. We were sad to learn it would be the very last of its kind. For decades RT has been a cornerstone in the romance community, offering early reviews and articles for readers to enjoy. RT will be missed, but we hear the conference will continue under another name, Booklovers Convention, in New Orleans next May. We're very curious to see how it will be received and looking forward to seeing the authors in attendance.

Along with fall changes on the horizon, we have new writers to introduce to our *Heart's Kiss* family. Rei Rosenquist has written us a heart-tugging short story, *Running from Love, Already Lost* that had me in tears by its closing paragraphs. It's not to be missed. Another newcomer, Gracie Wilson, thrills us with a delightful flash piece, *Big Trouble,* ahead of our publication of her novella, *Beautifully Imagined,* in our next issue. We are so delighted to share their talent with readers and know there will be more to come from these new authors!

We also have our fan favorites back again and they have written to impress! One of those soon-to-be well-loved reads comes from L. Penelope, who has not only delivered a brand-new installment, *Before I Run,* in the series she started for our magazine, but was also interviewed by yours truly. A review of her newly published St. Martin's Press novel, *Song of Blood & Stone,* also appears in C.S. DeAvilla's review column. We are so thrilled to have her as one of our regular contributors and wanted to go all out to celebrate her release by crowning her as our featured author for this issue.

If you still thirst for paranormal romance, we have more in store for you there. Petronella Glover's titillating mermaid tale, *When the Ocean Calls,* or the futuristic thriller, *Old Scars* by Meghan Ewald, may curb your cravings. Or if it's a historical you're after, then check out *The Piano Tutor* by *USA Today* bestselling author, Anthea Lawson, and discover the fun of a titular hero in hiding for love.

Sometimes readers want it all: a true genre-bending story. I steer you towards Andrea Dale's *Penny Dreadful*; with steampunk, supernatural elements, a historical feel and a steamy plot, this short story is sure to entice. We also have a contemporary romance as our novella this issue, welcoming Alice Faris with her first fiction sale to *Heart's Kiss, Pregnant Girl's Guide to Love*—a hysterical tie-in to her Guide to Love series.

Many of our stories this month deal with scars, physical or emotional, and how the right relationship can help you overcome them. Julie Pitzel also delves into an important issue in our industry today: Diversity; something we must continue to work toward, including in our fiction, to keep it true-to-life and relevant in the market.

Speaking of relevance, we love keeping up-to-date with the buzz in the romance field and what authors are up to, which is why we're ecstatic to publish an excerpt from *New York Times* bestselling contemporary romance author Susan Donovan's latest book, *Breathless,* co-written with Celeste Bradley. It's a little teaser ahead of her exclusive interview with us, which will appear in our next issue.

So even as we wrap up this instalment and prepare to pack up our sunscreen and beach towels, the stories we choose to transfix and transport us into thrilling, loving, enticing, compelling, intellectually-stimulating—and whatever else we read romance for—settings remain with us; we never have to pack

those fictional journeys away. We continue to welcome them onto our bookshelves and into our e-readers. Because fiction is an escape and romance offers a passport to a broad and brave wide world.

Tina and I hope you enjoy this issue and the journey forward.

L. Penelope has been writing since she could hold a pen and loves getting lost in the worlds in her head. She is an award-winning fantasy and paranormal romance author. She lives in Maryland with her husband and their furry dependents. Her novel, Song of Blood & Stone, *was just published by St. Martin's Press. Sign up for new release information, updates, and giveaways on her website: http://www.lpenelope.com.*

HEART'S KISS INTERVIEWS L. PENELOPE

by Lezli Robyn

I was privileged to be able to curl up with my chiweenie, Bindi, and interview Leslye about her career recently. After meeting at a convention where we both were speakers on a panel about romance in speculative fiction, I was immediately impressed by this remarkable woman and invited her to submit to *Heart's Kiss* when I became editor. She is now one of our most popular writers, and with her most recent novel being published by St. Martin's Press, her career is only gaining trajectory!

Lezli Robyn: Hello, Leslye! So delighted to speak to you today.

L. Penelope: And you too, Lezli!

LR: We're two people with the same name, in the one conversation. I'm sure that's not going to be at all confusing for our readers! *grins*

LP: *laughs* Ohhh, that's right! We'll do our best not to be confusing!

socializes for about ten minutes

LR: So, lets get into the questions! How did you get into writing? Were you always wanting to be an author since you were young? Or was there an event that happened, that triggered that desire?

LP: I have always written. I wrote my first short story when I was five years old. I still have it.

LR: Oh, really?

LP: Yep. My mom was a teacher and she had taught me to read early. And so it was part of my identity, all through elementary school.

You see, I wasn't really athletic. I did dance and music, but I wasn't in my element until they put me in the summer writing camps at the local community college for kids.

LR: Ohhh, I would have loved that! My second grade teacher once wrote in my school report that I should become a writer one day, because I had such an imagination.

LP: That was me as a child. I was just lucky that they had these programs close to our home, and that my parents found out about them. They were always supportive of all our artistic endeavors, so I took any writing class they offered in school. By high school, I worked for the literary magazine, and I was editor there my senior year.

Writing was so much a part of me that everyone was asking if I was going to major in writing in college. I was thinking that didn't seem a rational choice when you extrapolate getting a job afterwards. So, of course, I decided to major in film, which was *sarcasm* super practical.

LR: *laughs*

LP: I *did* minor in computer science, so that is something. But either way, I was screenwriting in college.

LR: When did you get back to writing short stories and novels?

LP: I stopped writing after I graduated. I always wrote poetry, even when I wasn't doing fiction, but my reintroduction to it was after I got married and we moved to Virginia. We went to the cinema to see a movie and I saw a flyer for this writing school. I started taking writing classes in Norfolk Virginia, at this writer center down there. Soon I became part of a crew of people—we'd always take the same classes—and it became like an ongoing workshop

That happened in 2008. I started writing short stories again, and a book—which I didn't finish—but that was how I began the adult phase of my writing career.

LR: My writing career started in 2008, too.

LP: Oh, wow. Cool.

LR: Your latest release is reviewed in this issue of the magazine, but I see you have another series—The Eternal Flame sequence of books. Is that self-published?

LP: Yes. It is currently self-published.

LR: You would never guess from the covers. They are so incredibly professional. So beautiful.

LP: Oh, thank you! I love cover design. I wish I could be a graphic designer, so I spent a lot of time finding the right designer.

LR: How did it come about that you were writing two series at the one time?

LP: My first book was *Song of Blood & Stone* and that was originally self-published. And while that was out on edits I had the time to explore this other idea, for the book that became *Angelborn*. So I was able to go back and forth between the two.

They're different genres, and different styles. *Song of Blood & Stone* is epic fantasy, whereas the Eternal Flame series is contemporary paranormal romance, and more of a new adult. One is also third person, one is first person. It really helped me to go from one thing, and then take a break and switch to a completely different world.

LR: That leads into my next question perfectly. Is one series easier to write than the other? Is one more of an accomplishment in your eyes, or are they both your babies?

LP: One is not easier to write than the other. However, the first book of both series were easier to write than the later ones. The next books have become considerably harder, once you are dealing with established worlds and their constraints.

They are both my babies. I love both series. I love *Angelborn*—the whole idea of the series—because it is like a breath of fresh air for me. It allows me think and explore on different levels, which I appreciate.

Song of Blood & Stone, on the other hand was my first book. It's got an award—it's had a starred review from *Publishers' Weekly* while it was self-published. It obviously has accomplishments already before it became a St. Martin's Press book. But it's also very personal to me because I put all my feelings into the heroine, of feeling like I never fit in and of being an outcast. Also the reason *why* she is an outcast is important to me. The racial aspects of the story are ways for me to talk about race in this country, but in a fantasy world.

LR: *Song of Blood & Stone* was originally self-published. How did it come about that St. Martin's Press went on to buy it and publish it this year?

LP: I originally self-pubbed it in 2015—in that year I put out the first two books in that series. It was a year later, January 2016, that I got an email from Monique Patterson, who is an editor at St. Martin's Press. She had been looking for something different and had come across my books. She was attracted to the cover, and the genre, so she'd downloaded it, read it, and then downloaded the second one.

So initially she had contacted me about pitching something new—my next series that I was working on. I pitched her, but she came back and said "I *really* like *Song of Blood & Stone* and I think I can bring it to a bigger audience. Would you consider publishing it through us?" And I was like "Oh, wow!"

Basically, it was out of the blue—a complete surprise.

LR: That is amazing. What are the chances?

LP: I know! I couldn't believe it.

LR: so, then, presumably you took the books down off your website.

LP: Yes, part of the contract conditions was to take both the books down, so they could then be prepped to release through St. Martin's Press.

LR: I can't see any downside to that, especially when you see the treatment they gave your first cover.

LP: Yes, the foil treatment to my *Song of Blood & Stone* cover is beautiful. And they kept my original cover image, which was amazing. That was one of the things she said initially: "We will keep the covers. We love the covers."

Usually when people get these deals the covers are changed. Fortunately, I had done my research and picked a really great designer, so the design was good enough to keep.

LR: I've mentioned this before. The quality of your self-published covers look amazing. They look like a traditional publication.

LP: That was really deliberate. I had set out to create a publishing company and wanted it to be as indistinguishable from traditional publishing. I wanted to put the best product out there.

I had also gone into self-publishing purposely. I had not been rejected. But it's a great experience now seeing how traditional publisher does it behind the scenes. I think it's great to be a hybrid author—to have your foot in as many doors as you can.

LR: Curious. Did you have print editions of your self-pubbed versions, too?

LP: Yes, I did! I did the typesetting myself. I used to run a literary magazine—some of us from the writing group in Virginia had started it—so I gained experience in publishing ebooks and printing paperback copies through CreateSpace.

There should be copies of the first books in both of my series floating around somewhere. You never know, maybe they will be worth money someday. *laughs*

LR: Yes, once *Song of Blood & Stone* gets made into a movie, that's the first edition that will be sourced out on eBay!

LP: *laughs* Exactly!

LR: So, I obviously met you at a science fiction and fantasy convention, and next I will be seeing you at a romance writers convention. Do you think the two fields are very different?

LP: I do. Well, in terms of the professional aspects. I'm in the writing organization RWA, and not in SFWA. I had always wanted to be in SFWA growing up, because I had always loved fantasy and SF, but then the "sad puppies" drama happened and I wondered if it was worth joining. I have never been a big convention-going person, as much as I loved the genre. And I think I feel a lot more welcome in romance circles and groups—at least, amongst romance writers in particular.

LR: Before writing your cupid stories for our magazine, had you written shorts?

LP: Most of the ones I have sold to your magazine had been half-finished for years. I had started pieces of them but never finished because I did not have a publishing goal for them yet, being that awkward length. And I'm very goal driven. I had a thought I might do them in a collection one day, but until then they stayed on the backburner while I was writing and publishing novels.

I had one short story—really short, perhaps around three or four thousand words—in the newsletter, so other than that, I had never published short fiction before your magazine.

LR: We're so happy to buy them from you. They're delightful and sexy romances.

LP: Thank you!

LR: How long does it take you to wrote a novel?

LP: It varies. I am working on a new series I started it after RWA last year. While I have taken a few months off writing, the book is mostly complete in less than a year. I believe in fast drafting, so that is how I finish things without stalling because I don't let myself agonize over small details in that first draft.

I try to do a first draft as quick as possible—so usually in about two months. Then it's months of revision. Then I take some time away from it if I'm having problems and can't think of a solution. It depends on how many problems I'm having, and how much space I need away from the book to be able to look at it anew again with fresh eyes, but usually I can produce a clean draft of a book within eight months to a year.

LR: If you had to pick *one* heroine from all your novels, across all your series, and *one*

hero as your favorites, who would they be? And would you think they'd make a great

couple if their paths had crossed between the sheets of the same book?

LP: Oh, that is interesting. I have four books out, and when you write them, you put the hero and heroine together because they match.

LR: That is what makes it interesting. Because in the real world, we tend not to match perfectly.

LP: Right. That is very true. As romance writers we're effectively writing fantasy, even when we're not writing fantasy. *laughs*

I would put together the most odd couple, for some reason. Caleb is the hero of *Angelborn* in the Eternal Flame series, and I would take the heroine out of the second book of the Earthsinger Chronicles, which is going to be called *Whispers of Shadows & Flame*. The heroine is Kyara and she is an assassin. And Caleb is a half-angel who has come to earth to find his soulmate.

I think that if they weren't with their chosen ones, they might be interesting for each other because while they are opposites he is very compassionate and she is a reluctant assassin, so they could help each other become better people. That would be an interesting pairing.

LR: And lastly, what is next for you, for 2018? What do your readers have to look forward to?

LP: I'm definitely working on the Earthsinger Chronicles. I had three books written before I signed the deal, so I'm just editing through them. I'm working on the final part of book two, which comes out next year.

I'm also working on the that new series I mentioned earlier, that I started writing after RWA in July. Hopefully I will finish it completely by this year and can send it on submission with my agent. It's a YA series, and it features dragons.

LR: Thank you for the call. This has been fascinating and thoroughly enjoyable.

LP: Thank you so much, Lezli! See you soon! [At RWA.]

Copyright © 2018 by Lezli Robyn.

BEFORE I RUN

by L. Penelope

CHAPTER ONE

Mascara caked and streaked around my eyes, making me look like a weepy panda. I gather wads of public restroom tissue paper and nearly scrape off my skin trying to remove the excess makeup. Only marginally successful, I give up. Let's just call it the smoky eye look. I'm not pathetic, I'm fashionable.

Staring at myself in the mirror, I lift the hem of my shirt. The largest scar is a little over an inch long, almost, but not quite in the center of my belly, north of the navel. There are other, smaller scars, but the biggest one always catches my attention. It's angry and red. Not fully healed yet. Slightly raised and puckered and hideous.

I'll never wear a bikini again.

Not that I wore them before that often, but at least I had the option. Sure, I've gained a few pounds since hitting my thirties, but who hasn't? My hips are finally nicely rounded, having lost that flat, boyish look that comes from being tall and skinny. They aren't what I would call child-bearing hips, but then again, they don't need to be. Not anymore.

I drop my shirt back down and force a smile in the mirror, still hanging on to that idea from some article I read a decade ago that said smiling at yourself makes you feel better.

It doesn't.

I square my shoulders and exit the bathroom into the quiet cafe.

Coffee Bar, as the original owner so creatively named it, is part coffee shop, part bar. It also houses a tiny bookshop and a performance space. It's the closest thing that our town has to nightlife or day life or any kind of life, and at ten a.m. Thursday morning, it's basically empty. Just me, Trudy behind the counter, and old Mr. Chee in the corner, dozing off.

Everyone else is at work. Or in school. I used to work in a school until about two hours ago but now I don't.

My best friend Trudy frowns at me. The steaming hot mocha latte she made isn't so steamy anymore, so she dumps it and whips up a fresh one without saying anything.

I smile, this one genuine. It makes my cheeks hurt, but I do it anyway because Trudy is amazing and let me sit here sobbing unintelligibly for the past half-hour while she plied me with caffeinated beverages that I haven't been able to drink.

But when she sets the mug in front of me this time, I wrap my hands around it, relishing the sting of heat against my palms.

Trudy hitches a hand on her hip and tilts her head to the side as if to say, *Are you finally ready to talk?* Only she doesn't actually say anything, and I love her for that too.

I force words from my lips. "So, I quit."

She blinks. "Okaaaay."

"In the middle of class."

"Okaaaay."

"I was just standing there, my lesson plan ready, the bell had just stopped ringing. The kids were rowdy, as usual. I didn't try to coerce them into their seats or yell or anything. I just stood there."

I venture a sip of the latte. Trudy has sprinkled cinnamon on the top, just the way I like it. "This is good."

She rolls her eyes like it's a given, though owning a coffee shop is no guarantee you can make a decent latte.

"I stood there until some of them actually noticed me. A few even quieted down. Some were already asleep. The rest were on their phones."

I stare into the remaining foam. "I just couldn't do it," I whisper.

"Maybe it's just too soon," Trudy says, reaching for my shoulder and giving it a comforting squeeze. "Going back to work this week might have been a mistake. Maybe you needed another few weeks. To recover."

I shake my head. "Another few weeks wouldn't help."

"So, what? You just walked out of the classroom?" She picks up her own mug of something way stronger than I can handle and sips it, scanning the shop just in case a customer has sneaked in during the past few minutes and she's missed it.

"I walked to the front office and told the secretary that I needed an emergency sub. And that I quit. And then I left." I look around. "I didn't even take my purse. It's still locked in the desk drawer. I walked here."

I put down the mug and drop my head to my hands. The bell over the door goes off.

"I'll get rid of them," Trudy says.

"You can't get rid of them, this is your livelihood. I'm not going anywhere. I don't have my keys."

"Oh, sweetie," she says, clucking. I hear her go over to the register to wait on the new customer, but my head is too heavy to lift right now.

Everyone always said that I should be a teacher. It was always: Oh, Charlotte, look how well she organizes the other kids. Such a good babysitter, such a good older sister. She'll be such a good mother someday.

There wasn't even a question when I finally got to college. I'd spent six years after high school working full-time and taking care of my little brother Mat, so you would think I'd have given plenty of thought to my major. And yet I still chose Education.

Teaching high school English had made sense. Until it didn't.

I place my hands on my stomach and breathe deeply. What's that thing they have you do in yoga? Lion breath? I never understood exactly how to go about it, but maybe I should give it another shot. Maybe if I breathed like a lion I could grow some courage.

"How do you feel?"

I startle at Trudy's presence behind me. I sit up and spin around on the stool to face her. "Physically, I'm okay. Not 100% yet, but that will take time. That's what the doctor and everyone on the internet says."

She purses her lips. "If you don't want to go back and get your keys from the school, just take mine and crash at my place for the rest of the day. I'll pick up your bag after I get off this afternoon."

I look around again. The coffee shop side of Coffee Bar is warm and inviting. There's a chess table in the corner, a dartboard hanging on the wall, and even an old school Ms. Pac-Man machine.

"I think I'll hang out here if it's okay with you." I rise, holding my mocha. "Just keep the caffeine coming and put it on my tab."

A hint of worry flashes in Trudy's eyes, but she nods. I head for the dart board, ready to work on my non-existent skills. At thirty-three with no man, no kids, and now no job, maybe I can get on the professional dart throwing circuit. I open the case with the little missiles and start throwing.

CHAPTER TWO

After failing spectacularly to hit anything close to the bullseye on the dart board, I move my attention to Ms. Pac-Man—my sister in feminism, eater of dots, and vanquisher of ghosts. I could use a little of her focus and determination right now. I engage in full-scale combat against those little dots until my big mouthed champion starts getting shit done.

As the level changes, I look over at Trudy, trying to communicate via telepathy that another shot of caffeine would be a good idea right about now, but she's with a customer. My neck cracks as I do a swift double take. And stare. Shamelessly.

I get an eyeful of his profile, all honey gold complexion several shades darker than my own. Short, kinky, brown hair and week-old stubble. Tattoos peek out from under sleeves rolled up to his elbows. My ovaries remind me they're still intact. In fact, I'm pretty sure they just grew big Ms. Pac-Man mouths and started salivating.

I blink a few times to clear my vision, but no, he's real, he's gorgeous, and he's looking right at me.

The 8-bit sounds of disappointment cause me to turn back to the arcade game. I was staring a bit too long and now I'm dead. Of course. My options now are to try darts again or convince old Mr. Chee to emerge from his slumber and play chess with me. Or rather, teach me to play chess.

From the corner of my eye, I see the hot guy head away from the counter. I can't help looking over again to find Trudy smirking, the reason for which soon becomes clear when I realize the hot guy is heading right for me.

His eyes have a relaxed, bedroom quality to them. They're a beautiful, sparkling brown, and I get to inspect them in even greater detail because he's standing right in front of me.

"Charlotte?"

Oh dear God, his voice. He should carry around spare ladies' underwear to hand out to any adult, heterosexual woman he finds the need to speak to. Starting with me.

"Yes? Do I know you?" A question I already know the answer to because I do not have Alzheimer's and that is the only way I would have forgotten him.

He grins, and his smile is everything. "No. I'm Micah. Someone asked me to give this to you." He holds out my purse.

Somehow, I'd missed the fact that the gorgeous species of human male was carrying a large, black hobo bag. I pluck it from his hand and lift it up like I've never seen it before.

"That *is* yours, right?"

Imagine if melted chocolate and molten lava mixed and then a mad scientist ran the mixture through a machine that turned it into sound waves—that's his voice. His mouth curves into a smile, and I have to physically remove my eyeballs from his lips.

"Yes. Mine. Um…. Are you a teacher?" Another brilliant question for which I already know the answer.

"Former student. I was visiting Mr. Crescent in the music department when this woman came up to me and asked me to come here and give you this. Then she disappeared." His brow wrinkles adorably. "Like, really disappeared. Into thin air."

I stare at him for a second, and he stares back then raises his brows. "Maybe she was just really fast?" he says. "Or I could have had a mini-stroke."

"Or fallen asleep standing up?"

He chuckles, making me feel all fizzy. "I *am* sleep deprived."

"I wonder if she was the sub?" Though how could she have gotten my purse out of a locked drawer? Maintenance doesn't even have a key, which I sadly discovered early last year. Maybe she's a part-time sub, part-time locksmith? Or jewel thief. That would explain the disappearing act. Besides, it would take a master criminal to handle some of those children.

He stares at me with bright eyes, and I feel the need to talk. "I'm a teacher. Or I used to be. I quit this morning."

I wince, but to his credit, if he feels any kind of way about my oversharing, he hides it well. "Sounds like a really hard job. I know I could never do it."

"I used to like it. No, that's not true. I never liked it, I just thought I should. But life's too short for shoulds, you know?"

He raises his eyebrows and my face begins to heat. Fun fact: when I get embarrassed, my nose turns red, and when I get embarrassed in front of a hot guy, I go full-on Rudolph. The absolute last thing I want is to turn into one of Santa's little helpers in front of Hot Guy Micah.

"Anyway, sorry. Thank you. I should have thanked you. That was a really nice thing for you to do for a stranger."

His eyes dance. "My mom always said her purse was like her third arm. Wouldn't want a pretty lady out there walking around missing an arm." He smiles again, and I just know it's Christmas in October on my face right about now. But somehow, his smile makes me forget my nose, and my sudden, self-imposed unemployment, and also my good sense.

"Do you drink coffee?" I blurt out. "Trudy makes the best…" Wait, what am I doing? Sanity returns like a tidal wave. "Never mind. I'll let you get on with your day."

I clutch my purse to my chest and turn around, hoping to at least make a smooth getaway. Possibly by tunneling through the laminate floor.

"What do you recommend?" Little vaporized bursts of chocolate lava float past my eardrums. They send a tingle down to my toes.

I spin back around very smoothly, not wobbling at all. "The mocha latte is fantastic."

CHAPTER THREE

Micah stands at the counter ordering his drink. I perch at the edge of a chair a dozen feet away, leaning on the table in front of me, so caught up in the play of muscles across his back as they stretch the fabric of his rolled-up, long-sleeved t-shirt, that I don't hear the bell ring again, or sense the presence of another person until said person is standing right next to me clearing her throat in the most annoying of ways.

Phyllis Jones manages to elevate the act of throat clearing into passive aggressiveness personified. I have no idea how I was her friend for so long.

"*Ahem.*"

If she thinks I'm going to ask her what's wrong, she has another think coming. Then Micah turns around and I want Jonesy far, far away from me.

"What?" I snap, looking up at her. She's as short and curvy as I am tall and lean. Her straight, black bob is the direct opposite of my highlighted, bronze curls. I'm basically the film negative version of her, so why Tanner would date both of us at the same time is a great mystery. Also, why, when she found out, she would continue to date him is another enigma. One that I've almost stopped wondering about over the past few months.

"I heard you quit today," she says. When we were friends, Jonesy's ability to know the latest gossip almost instantaneously had been amusing, now it's irritating. "Tell me it isn't true."

We haven't talked in months and I have no desire to tell her anything, true or otherwise. Of course, Micah chooses that moment to sit down across from me. Jonesy scrunches her pert little nose at him.

"Micah Green? What are you doing back in town?" She flips her hair and shifts her weight to draw attention to her butt.

Oh. My. God. Is she flirting with him?

"Just visiting." His face is neutral-pleasant. At least he doesn't seem to be flirting back.

"Are you here for your brother's birthday party? I heard your mom is going all out. But, I thought you were on a tour?"

I look up sharply. Micah's jaw clenches before he plasters on a fairly realistic imitation of a smile. "We had a little break, so I came home to see the fam."

"Are you in the military?" I ask, raking my gaze over him again. His hair is not regulation and the facial hair is a definite no-no.

His eyebrows shoot up, and Jonesy gives a derisive snort. "Our Char, always so clueless. Micah's the drummer of the band RiotSphere. They were on Jimmy Kimmel last month." She shakes her head as if my ignorance of that particular detail of pop culture is just too sad for words. "He was a couple years ahead of us in school and graduated with my sister."

"Oh," I say, digging my fingers into the surface of the table. "I'm kind of out of the loop when it comes to that type of thing."

Micah shakes his head, as if to say, 'No big deal.'

Jonesy presses on. "And now you're out of a job, sweetie. Did *something happen?*"

Oh, the joys of small town living. *Something happened* when Doris Whitaker accused Philip Harlow of sexual harassment at the middle school two years before. It had been a huge scandal that had kept Jonesy's tongue limber for months.

I purse my lips. "I just realized teaching isn't for me."

"Latisha Parrish told her mother you came to this grand realization in the middle of class." She tutted me. Phyllis Jones had the nerve to tut me. "Those children need proper leadership and role models. That was just irresponsible."

"Well, so is stealing your homegirl's boyfriend right before they have major surgery, but shit happens, amIright?" I tilt my head and attempt to blind her with the wattage of my pearly whites.

Jonesy pales a fraction, then her eyes harden. "I guess some women just aren't the nurturing type. And some of us are."

Ice forms around my chest, and the healing wound in my abdomen aches.

"A classroom is a lot like a family," she says. "I would think you'd hold on tighter to the one you can still have." She places a hand on her hip, eyes glittering with pride as she watches her barbed words hit home.

Any retort I might have made sputters and dies on my lips.

"Well, I think leaving a shitty job is brave," Micah says. "You can't sell your soul for a dollar. We only get one life, you know."

Tears rim my eyes. He's talking to her, but he's looking at me.

"In fact, I think Charlotte here is my hero. Those kids will be just fine. This is a good school system, they'll find another teacher to shape those young minds in no time."

Trudy marches over, expression so placid, you'd have to have known her for a while to see the fury raging beneath the surface. I'm afraid she'll slam the two mochas in her hands down on the table. But she manages to place them gently in front of me and Micah before planting herself in Jonesy's face.

"Will you be ordering anything, *Phyllis?*" she asks, emphasizing Jonesy's hated first name. Those two have known each other longer, but I got Trudy in the split.

"Just an iced tea, thanks." Jonesy feigns obliviousness well. "It's good to see you Micah. Is Pierre here too? Maybe you two could do an impromptu performance. Our little stage is no Jimmy Kimmel, but folks here would love it. Hometown boys made good, you know?"

She's back to fluttering her eyelashes and booty tooching her ample rear. Like she doesn't have a boyfriend. My boyfriend. Whom she can keep because they deserve each other.

Micah's lips firm into a grim line. "I doubt it." Then he focuses all his attention on his coffee like the foam is the most interesting thing he's ever seen.

Trudy practically drags Jonesy away, and I make a mental note to do something nice for her, like buy her a cheesecake.

We sip our drinks in companionable silence, not saying a word until the wicked witch has left the building with her iced mango tea.

"So, you're, like, a rock star?"

He grimaces. "No, I'm just the drummer in a band. Well, I was. Maybe I still am, I don't know." His voice is low and tinged with a sort of hopeless desperation I can relate to.

"You having work troubles, too?"

"Something like that." He looks up, panic in his eyes. "That's not common knowledge."

I give him a reassuring smile. "Obviously I don't have TMZ on speed dial, considering I've never heard of Riot-what?"

"RiotSphere."

"Yeah, that. Never heard of you. But I'm sure you're very talented. So, your secret is safe with me. A total stranger. Who you can completely rely on."

We laugh, and little evaporated chocolate lava molecules enter my bloodstream, because you could record his laugh and make an album of it and it would go platinum.

"Hill Valley is a small place," he says. "So I'm pretty sure I can hunt you down if I need to."

"Hunt away." Something crackles between us and I hope my nose isn't lighting up because I didn't mean it like that. Or maybe I did. Okay, I totally did.

He has a little foam on his upper lip, and I'm about to tell him about it when his tongue peeks out and he licks it away. I stop breathing.

The bell rings again, tearing me out of the intensity of the moment. We both look away, then take sips of our drinks.

There's more ringing, coming closer, but this time it's not from the door, it's from a woman. She's young and Asian with purple platform sneakers that match her purple dreadlocks. Little bells are woven into her hair and they jingle as she approaches. Red, cat-eye glasses are perched on her nose and, from neck to knee, she's dressed like a librarian wearing an oversized, drab cardigan and brown pencil skirt.

"That's the sub," Micah whispers.

"What?"

"She's the one who gave me your purse at the school."

I look at the young woman again. She appears to be barely out of college, almost too young to substitute teach. And definitely not someone stodgy old Principal Faulkner would normally approve of. Though given the amount of notice I gave them, maybe she was the only one available.

As if she can sense us talking about her, she arrows her gaze on our table and breaks into a huge smile. Then rushes over and plants herself in the empty seat.

"Oh, good. You found each other. I'm so happy." She claps her hands together.

Micah and I look at her, then at each other.

"You're Charlotte, right? I'm Delilah." She sticks out her hand and gives me and then Micah firm handshakes. When she releases me, my palm is covered in glitter.

"Did you get stuck with my class?" I ask, wiping my hand on my khakis.

"Oh, they were totally fine. Very spirited." She nods enthusiastically setting off a chorus of chimes from the bells scattered around her person.

"That's one way to put it," I say.

"And here, something else that belongs to you." Delilah produces a notebook, from where I can't say exactly since she doesn't have a bag with her. But when I get a look at it, I snatch it out of her hands and flip through it.

"Where did you get this?" It's one of my journals. I've never taken them to school, they're way too personal, filled with my scribblings, thoughts, and poetry. "This wasn't in the drawer."

She taps her finger on her chin like she's trying to remember. Then shrugs. "I dunno. It must have been."

"No, it definitely wasn't."

Delilah leans in conspiratorially. "Well, it's not like I broke into your house while you weren't home to get it or anything." She winks, and I'm pretty sure glitter falls from her eyelashes.

This isn't my most recent notebook, it's the last one—the one I finished after I got home from the hospital. I flip through the pages, remembering those weeks of pain and the dark places my mind had gone.

A few sheets of paper fall to the ground, and Micah stoops down to pick them up. Even though the whole point of a notebook is for all the pages to be kept together, I still find myself scribbling on scraps, paper bags, receipts, or wrappers and then stuffing them inside the covers of my journal later.

Micah pats the edges of the loose pages, making a neat pile before handing them back to me. I stuff them back into the book and when I look up, Delilah is gone. No goodbyes, and no bells—it's like she just vanished.

Micah and I share a look that at least assures me I'm not the only crazy one. It occurs to me that maybe I should take a peek inside my purse to make sure nothing is missing. I have a good feeling about Micah, but this Delilah chick is another story. I'm not even sure she's a good choice to substitute teach.

"Everything there?" Micah asks, a wry look on his face.

"Yeah, I think so. It's not you I don't trust."

"No, I understand." He grins. "So, are you a poet?"

I regard him warily. He couldn't have seen much in the few seconds it took to pick up those sheets of paper. I have no idea what's even on them. "That would be stretching things a bit far. I mean, I do write poems, but I don't think that makes me a poet."

"What does it make you?"

"A girl?"

He drains the rest of his mocha. "Well, it seems like you have some skills there."

"Oh God, please tell me you didn't read anything."

"Not much, but I caught a few lines that were impressive. 'And through the brush, these tangled wilds we snake along. Our bellies raw from rubbing tracks across the ashen ground.'"

I shift uncomfortably in my seat. "You have a pretty good memory."

"Yeah, sometimes too good." His eyes take on a faraway quality for a moment before he focuses in on me. "You ever do anything with it?"

"With what? My writing? No. Definitely not." I shake my head several times for emphasis. "Teaching English doesn't even count. I just…like to get my thoughts down on paper. It calms me, helps organize my brain."

Micah slides his mug to the side and rests his forearms on the table, leaning toward me. Instinctively, I lean in as well, drawn to him like velcro.

"Have you heard of the Children's International Refugee Project?" he asks.

"Sure, they have billboards up and down the 101." Two months ago, a boat full of children had sunk off the coast of Jamaica, fleeing a brutal civil war that had spilled over into two different Central American countries.

"My mom's on the board of directors," Micah says. "They're producing this charity album as a fundraiser for this latest refugee crisis. They've already signed on a ton of big names to sing covers, but they want a few original songs. RiotSphere had a track go viral and we've been getting a lot of attention, so they asked me. That's kind of the other reason why I'm home. I have to finish this song, and it's due this weekend. They're rushing the album out and want some songs performed at the charity's big gala next week."

I'm hanging onto his words, perfectly willing to have him read the dictionary if it means I can keep listening to his voice. But I'm not connecting the dots.

He flashes that wickedly tempting smile, and I melt. "I think you could help me."

I blink. "Help you what?"

"Finish the song."

My spine straightens. Such a shame someone so beautiful is absolutely insane. "I—I don't…. I'm not—"

"Listen, I don't believe in coincidences. And my life has taught me to seize opportunities when they appear. You appeared—a woman with extra time on her hands and a gift for language that I just don't have. I need help, and I think fate intervened to bring you to me in my time of need."

I heard only a few words from that sentence, mainly: *I, need* and *you*. Stars light up my eyes until my brain puts her foot down. "I've never written a song before, Micah. And I'm flattered you think I can do this, but I just don't think it's possible."

He sits back in his chair, gaze never leaving my face. I start to heat under his perusal. "You know how we got that Jimmy Kimmel gig?"

I shake my head.

"A song I co-wrote with my band member Pierre made its way into a meme. The Grocery Cart Towing Challenge. Kids film themselves sitting in a grocery cart holding on to the side of a moving car and driving down the highway. For some reason, our song plays in the background. So far eight teens have been hospitalized."

"Geez, that's awful. I'm so sorry." I'm pretty sure at least a few of my students—former students—would be intrigued by something so stupid and dangerous.

"I never thought something I created would get used like that. It kind of broke me."

"To the point where you're not sure you want to be in the band anymore?"

"Yeah. I figured, this charity album is a small way to make up for it. A way to create something in the world—to leave a positive mark instead. If I'm remembered at all, I don't want it to be as the guy who created the song a bunch of kids broke their backs to."

Understanding flows through me. "You want to leave a legacy."

"Exactly. And this charity album seems like a good start. I've just never been a lyrics guy. That was Pierre's deal. And he's not on board with giving a song away for free." Pain and anger lace his voice. "I need someone to help."

"But why me?"

He smiles. "I have a good feeling about you, Charlotte. And I trust my gut."

My eyes must be shooting out warning lasers because he holds his hands up in surrender. "Okay,

okay, tell you what? How about you just agree to be my muse? You don't have to do anything but show up. I'll write the song and you just…" He waves his arm around.

"Sit there and look pretty?"

"Yeah. Something like that."

His grin disarms me—like, I can't feel my arms right now—and his chuckle rearranges something inside my chest. "I don't know…"

"Do it for the children, Charlotte. You kind of owe them."

It's wild. Completely crazy. But is it any crazier than quitting your job in the middle of the day? Walking out on a full classroom of juvenile delinquents? I really need to start looking for a new way to feed myself and pay for my apartment and my hair products, but his song is due this weekend.

"Okay," I say.

And because the gods are kind and benevolent, Micah reaches over the table to grab my hands in his and squeezes them. I nearly come off my seat at the contact. A circuit in my chest shorts.

I can always start job hunting next week.

CHAPTER FOUR

We agree to meet at his place, or rather, his mother's place, where he's staying. Since he's been on tour for the past few years, virtually non-stop, he doesn't actually keep an apartment.

Google Maps takes me to a nice neighborhood on a hill that looks over the Bay. There's even a little turnout where you can park and look down on the Golden Gate Bridge and the city of San Francisco just across the water. It reminds me of how much I like living here in the tiny, garden apartment that I can just barely afford on a teacher's salary. Without a job it will be impossible.

I turn into the driveway of an enormous two-story Craftsman in the well-heeled neighborhood and park behind a Mini Cooper out of which—no lie—five clowns come out. I do a double take to make sure I'm not imagining it. Then I take out my camera. Pics or it didn't happen, as the kids say.

One of the clowns stubs out a cigarette on the ground with a giant orange shoe before entering the house.

The front door is open, so I follow behind them, trying to keep my jaw in place. More clowns fill the entryway. There are clowns in the dining room, the kitchen, and on the steps.

Micah appears from down the center hall, and I maneuver through greasepaint and fluorescent wigs and polka dots to get to him.

"Care to explain?" I ask, motioning to the circus surrounding us.

"My mom is auditioning talent for my brother's birthday party."

"Of course she is."

"Come on, it's quiet downstairs."

He leads me to the finished basement, which is indeed quiet. A little kid sits on the giant sectional playing a video game.

"Charlotte this is my brother Jude, Jude this is Charlotte."

Micah's brother is brown-skinned with a laser cut high top fade. He's no older than seven and looks nothing like Micah.

He glances up at me while his fingers move faster than light-speed on the video game controller. "Made it through the clowns, huh?" he says.

I like this kid.

I try to think of something to say that's not an insult. "Your mom has an impressive attention to detail."

Jude snorts. "You could say that again."

"Um, do you even like clowns?"

He shrugs. "Does it matter?" This is a kid resigned to the state of the world. I'm not sure if that's especially prescient or just sad. He goes back to his game—some sort of first person shooter, except the gun in the foreground shoots giant exploding globs of paint. Or something.

"Come on," Micah says, picking up an acoustic guitar and leading me to a door in the back. It's a comfortable guest bedroom painted a dark beige with beige carpeting and a beige bedspread. There's an armchair in the corner and a laptop and notebook spread out on the queen-sized bed.

I sit in the armchair, and Micah settles on the bed.

"So, what exactly does a muse do?" I feel a little nervous, but he looks perfectly comfortable. Today, he's got on a black, V-neck t-shirt and artfully shred-ded jeans. I feel slovenly in leggings and a slouchy T-shirt, but I wanted to keep it casual.

"Just observe. Send out inspiring creative energy, that sort of thing."

"Okay." I clasp my hands as he begins strumming the guitar. He plays a melody, a little plaintive but with a bluesy edge.

I streamed RiotSphere's first album the evening I met him. Their sound is not what I expected. It's old school rhythm and blues-style rock with hip-hop sensibilities. I'm not a huge fan of the song that went viral, "Jesus's Cup Holder," but the other stuff on their album sank into my head and stayed there.

The tune he's playing sounds great, and I begin humming along.

Micah stops every so often to change a chord. He's apparently recording parts of the song on his computer as well.

It's fascinating to watch him work, even though I'm pretty sure he doesn't need me for anything.

Then he starts to sing. "Kids, kids, everywhere, in the water, in the air / Walking somewhere really far, cause they don't have a car."

He nods like he's just come up with something that doesn't sound insipid, meanwhile his expression is completely serious. He scribbles a few words in a notebook, then goes back to his strumming.

I look around to make sure a hidden camera isn't behind me.

"Everybody old or young, needs a place to lay their head / Some will find a cardboard box, some will find a bed."

I think what he's writing down are these actual words. On paper. Like he means to save them and, I don't know, repeat them to another human being.

"Micah."

"Hmm?" He crosses something out then rewrites it.

"Come on. Seriously?"

He looks up, guileless. "What? I told you lyrics aren't my thing."

I shake my head. "Your reverse psychology tricks are so, so sad. I can't believe you would stoop so low."

The innocent expression on his face doesn't fool me. This man is messing with me, and I know it.

"No, your presence is helping, I'm feeling more creative already." He grins. And then he starts singing again.

"A box is not that comfortable, it's better than a stone / And if you're really that tired, a board's better than none."

He pronounces 'none' so it rhymes with 'stone' and I can't really handle anything else.

"All right buddy, I'm going to have to stop you there. You are not only mangling the English language, I'm pretty sure you're ruining several others as well. What is this song about?"

"Well, I want it to really tug at your heartstrings, like that Sarah McLachlan song in those puppy commercials."

"Everyone knows those commercials are really a Turing test to weed out sophisticated Artificial Intelligence from real people."

"If you're not crying by the end, you're obviously a bot planning the destruction of humanity," Micah deadpans.

"Exactly." I lean forward in my chair. "But I thought this charity was for Children's International Refugee Project."

"It is."

"Isn't their acronym, CHIRP?"

"Yeah, and?"

"So maybe the music should be a little more upbeat?" I say. "What if you increase the tempo so it isn't so dirge-like?"

He frowns. "It's not dirge-like."

"It's definitely dirge-adjacent."

His fingers go into position on the guitar and he begins playing, speeding up the melody this time. I pat my thigh in time with the beat and an image pops into my head.

This is how I usually write poems. Something flashes in my mind—usually a fully formed visual that makes me feel a very specific way and then I have to write. I was so determined not to help him in this scheme though, I didn't even bring a notebook with me, so I leap for the bed, grab his and shuffle for a clean page.

I write, ignoring the satisfied smile spreading across Micah's ridiculously handsome face.

CHAPTER FIVE

"Okay, so how about this: 'How long will we look away? The silence it drowns us. If we don't stand up today, tomorrow is groundless.'?"

Micah plays the melody he's still tweaking and sings what I've written. His voice is scratchy and deep. He's not the lead singer of RiotSphere, but he could be. Watching him strum the guitar strings, scribble notations, and fiddle with his laptop, I know he's the real deal. A true talent. It makes me feel even more like a fraud.

"So we have the ongoing metaphor about the ocean and water—"

"That's why you added 'groundless.'" He bobs his head up and down. "I get it. Very clever."

I blush, trying not to let the compliment sink in.

"Maybe that could be the bridge." He plays it again as the bridge of the song and it sounds perfect. It really does seem to be turning into the anthem he wanted. One that will hopefully make people care about the refugee children who have lost their parents to violence and war almost as much as they care about puppies. I want the words to match Micah's music and take root in a part of the listener's soul—I just don't know if I can pull it off. In fact, I'm sure I can't.

"Is this really working?" I ask, rising from my seat on the floor. I usually move around a lot when writing, and I'd already sat on every surface in the room and several spots on the carpet.

"Yeah, it's great. We're nearly there."

I shake my head, unsure. Micah looks at me, focusing his intensity in a way that makes me start to sweat from the heat pouring off of him. I've been able to focus on the work and the words, caught up in the act of creation, but in the lulls, this crackling attraction for him takes over and makes my brain overheat.

"What?" I ask, fanning myself with my hand.

"Let's take a break," he says. "Come on, I want you to see something."

We exit into the basement. I lost track of time while we were in Micah's room, but it's been hours. The TV down here is off, and Jude has disappeared. The house also appears blissfully clown-free. Micah takes me out the front door and we head down the sidewalk of the uncomfortably quiet neighborhood.

"Why did you become a teacher, anyway?"

I wonder if I should tell him, if it makes me seem pathetic, but I decide to go with the truth. "Everyone always told me I should. I guess I believed them."

He leads me down a paved path between the houses. We walk at a steady pace and he doesn't seem to be in a hurry.

"So what did you want to do?"

"That's just the thing, I have no idea. I'm good at taking care of people. I raised my little brother after our mom ditched us."

He looks over at me, eyebrow raised. "Did you know your dad?"

"Oh yeah, he was around, kind of. He's in the army and never met a transfer he didn't like. We lived out of boxes my whole childhood."

I stumble a little on a crack in the path, and Micah grabs my elbow to right me. Embarrassment heats my cheeks, so I just keep talking.

"One Christmas, Mom went to visit her parents in Norway and just never came back. Two moves after that, my brother Mat failed the sixth grade. At that point I just refused to move any more. So me and Mat stayed here while Dad trotted all over the globe chasing a higher rank."

"How old were you?"

"Seventeen. I put off college until Mat was situated and by the time I went, I just majored in Education because I knew I could get a job. I thought I had the temperament for it. It made sense."

"So you're mom's Norwegian and your dad's…?"

"Jamaican, originally. That thing about the work ethic is no joke, at least not for him." I snort. "The Colonel will not be happy when he finds out I quit my job." The shadow of his future wrath hangs over me and I shiver, though the October air is warm.

We emerge from the path onto the overlook I passed on the way in, and a perfect, breathtaking view of the bay and the city and the ocean beyond. We sit down on a patch of grass bathed in late afternoon sunlight.

"So if you could do anything, be anything, what would you be?" Micah asks.

I look over to find that instead of watching the incredible view in front of us, he's staring at me. My heartbeat begins to race until it's chugging along like the little engine that could. I forget his question and wrack my brain, rewinding a few seconds.

"Anything?" I ask. Honestly, after being locked in a small room with this man all day, if I could do anything I wanted, it would be him, but even in its blood-starved state my brain tells me that's not an appropriate response.

"I'd write movies." I frown, wondering who said that. It sounded like me, but I haven't thought of that wild dream in years. It's so impractical, so implausible. But for some reason, my answer makes Micah smile, and the engine in my chest shifts into a higher gear.

"Movies, cool." He nods like this makes perfect sense.

"I don't know why I said that. I mean, people don't just…write movies." I finish lamely.

"How do you think they get written?" he asks, smirking.

"I don't know, artificial intelligence?"

"You mean the ones that make it past the Sarah McLachlan Turing test?"

"They've been warning us for decades of their plan. We really shouldn't be surprised when one of them finally goes ahead and launches the nukes."

His laugh is melodic; he bumps my shoulder. I feel the contact sizzle all the way through my body.

"You can write movies. If that's what you want."

"I feel like I'd need to go back to school or get special training or something."

"I don't know. Not every screenwriter in Hollywood has a degree. I think sometimes they just," he lifts a shoulder, "start writing and see if it's good."

Start writing and see if it's good. He makes it sound so simple, like it doesn't require ultimate confidence, or rich parents, or at the very least knowing someone important.

But Micah's grin is full of confidence. "You're already a really good writer. You totally saved my song."

I bump his shoulder this time and say, "Your song was just really bad. Almost anything would have been better."

His eyes smile at me, then he sobers. "It's okay for you to be good at things." I'm not sure he's even noticed the view; the whole time we've been sitting here, his eyes haven't strayed from my face.

My backbone has turned into a noodle, and I lean against him, more to hold my torso up than for any other reason.

"I'd love to be good at things," I tell him. "I just wish it was as easy as you seem to think it is."

"Oh, I know it's not easy, trust me. But it's not impossible. People do it. You'd probably have to work your ass off and try your best to be in the right places at the right times and network with the right people. But you can do it. There are thousands of screenwriters working today. You could be one of them. If you want." His eyes bore into me like a glittering, diamond-tipped drill. "It's okay to get what you want."

The moment hangs there, encasing his words like glass. His eyes dart to my lips and we're so close. I'm leaning against him, but I didn't realize how little distance there was between us until the bottom drops out of my stomach. I can't breathe or think or anything, I just watch as he erases the few inches between us.

But it's taking too gosh-dang long, and so I meet him halfway.

His lips are warm and full, and he tastes like oranges. No, orangesicle, the subtle difference making itself abundantly clear when his tongue breaches my mouth. He's gentle but demanding. His grip on my waist grows tight.

Large, warm hands skim up my back, and I'm not sure if I'm still upright or have fallen into a gravity pit because I can't feel the ground below me anymore. I'm conscious of pressing my hand to his cheek, feeling his stubble abrade my palm as I drink him in.

Both of his hands move back down to encircle my waist now, holding me like a vise, like he's afraid I'm going to go somewhere. What I should tell him is I'm never going anywhere, not while what we're doing right now is an option. The kiss grows all consuming. I feel off-balance and my lungs need air, but I don't pull back. Not yet. Not until I absolutely have to, and then he's staring at me and the sun has somehow set.

Darkness surrounds us and the kaleidoscope of lights across the Bay makes him look magical. This whole experience of meeting him has been magical.

The honk of a foghorn somewhere on the water vibrates through me, convincing me this isn't just a dream. He's real, but I still feel a little fantastical.

Micah grins.

"What?" I whisper.

"Here's to getting what you want," he says and kisses me again.

CHAPTER SIX

It's been a long time since I've been at an eight-year-old's birthday party. My brother Mat's would have been the last one, I guess, and I'm pretty sure that Dad was at work and Mom bought cupcakes from the grocery store and stuck some candles in one of them.

She wasn't super into the whole maternal thing—at least, not with us. I wonder if things are different with her new family. With the younger half-brother and sister I've never met over in Norway.

The front pathway to Micah's mother's house is bordered in two giant, free-standing balloon sculptures. You can probably hear the voices of laughing, screaming children all the way in Sausalito. I wonder if the neighbors mind, but as I enter the house I realize that the entire neighborhood must be here.

It's a big house, but it's absolutely packed with people. Adult people are the only ones I see as I wade through them, trying to make my way down to the basement where I'm supposed to meet Micah.

I peek through into the kitchen and the backyard beyond. What looks like an entire amusement park has been set up back there. I think I actually see roller coaster tracks, but a wall of bodies quickly blocks my view.

I bump into a few people before I make it to the basement steps. The party continues downstairs, but I'm able to squeeze into Micah's bedroom, half afraid it will be overflowing like the rest of the house.

Fortunately, he's here alone, guitar in hand and headphones on. He grins when I push my way inside and shut the door, leaning against it, breath shaky.

He stands to greet me and before I can get my heartbeat back to normal from the *American Ninja Warrior*-style obstacle course I've just traversed, his arms are around me and I'm sinking into his kiss.

I had almost made myself believe it wasn't real. The mouth-watering scent of him, the way his arms crush me like he never wants to let go. Breathing is for suckers anyway, I'd rather inhale Micah exclusively. I would if he'd let me.

When we break apart, he's looking at me with heavy-lidded eyes. A crash sounds overhead, and the corner of his mouth curls up. "Hi."

"Hi, yourself," I reply. I pull away from him to gather what's left of my composure. "Are you ready?"

He's still looking at me like he wants to treat me like an ice cream cone. I shiver and try to redirect him—I'm not against becoming his personal dessert, but not with the fire hazard going on this house right now and an army of seven and eight-year-olds on the other side of the basement window.

Swallowing, I cross to the other side of the room, putting some space between us. "Are you sure you want to play the song for them? This may not be the ideal venue."

"Jude is into the idea. Plus, the song's for a kid's charity, what better way to make sure we've got it right than to test it out in front of a bunch of kids?"

Screams of delight peal, seeming to tunnel through the concrete foundation of the house. "I'm not so sure we'll have a captive audience," I say.

"Hey, if the song can pull their attention away from the rides and the games and the candy, then we know it's good."

"Yeah, and don't forget the clowns."

"Oh, there aren't any clowns."

"What?"

He shrugs. "Mom decided she didn't want any after all." He picks up his guitar, leaning towards me, but I scurry out of the way. He just chuckles and leads me back into the melee.

CHAPTER SEVEN

The DJ turns down the hip-hop music that had been blasting, masking some of the sounds of the games and rides that fill every corner of the massive back yard. Micah stands on the narrow stage, in front of the turntables, fiddling with the neck of his guitar. I'm off to the side, at the edge of the stage, the only one present really paying attention to him.

That is until the microphone feeds back. I wince and cover my ears as the high-pitched whine goes on and on. One look at his face confirms my suspicion that he's doing this on purpose.

When he moves the mic away from the speaker, the entire yard is quiet. "Happy birthday, Jude! In honor of my little homie's special day, I wanted to see what you thought about this song. It's called, 'Going Under,' and I had a very special lady help me out with the lyrics."

When he looks over at me, I want to sink into the ground, but my heart melts just a little bit as well. His long fingers strum the strings, and he begins to sing the song we wrote together.

I'm convinced that at any moment the noise of the games will start up again, the bright, bubbly sounds like melted lollipops poured into your ears. Or that the kids will start shouting and screaming, running around and ignoring what's going on up on the stage in favor of their normal funtime pursuits.

But when I dare look around, they're all rapt. Focused completely on what's happening on stage.

That's when I notice that almost all of these kids are wearing variations of the same t-shirt, just in different colors. The CHIRP logo is emblazoned on the front. These kids are refugees from the charity. This song is actually about them.

I get a little misty-eyed hearing Micah's smooth voice sing my words. And the tears really start to fall when I see the children hanging onto every word. After the third chorus, some are even singing along. I've never had something I've done creatively be heard by this many people before. It's enough to truly humble me.

When the last chords play, there's silence for an endless moment.

And then the applause begins.

Adults crowd around the sides of the yard and peer out of windows and doors in the house, all cheering. Kids are jumping up and down, clapping and screaming. So this is what it's like to be a rock star. Micah seems to take it all in stride. He thanks them, wishes his brother a happy birthday again, and then jumps off the stage. Where he's promptly mobbed by a gang of very intent, very focused, miniature humans.

They're all talking at the same time, some are speaking different languages, no one seems to want anything other than to be heard. Some attach themselves to his legs, there's a chorus of voices demanding that he play the song again and before too long, he does. The kids eat it up the second time, and afterwards I actually lose Micah in the sea of tiny heads. My chest is completely hollow. I'm pretty sure I'm in love.

An hour later, the party has resumed. Micah has managed to tear himself away from his new pint-sized fan club. A trio of adult women march toward him with a disturbing amount of intensity. I sense "Biggest Fan" vibes coming from them as they pass the bouncy house. Micah grabs my hand and tugs.

"Come on," he whispers, and we make a run for it.

There aren't many places to go since the yard is now a theme park, but soon enough we're crouching behind the pool house, hiding from all the attention.

"Those kids really loved you," I tell him. The adults seemed to as well, but I don't mention that.

"They're great. They've had a hard time, but they're good. No child should have to live like that."

"Yeah that's true. Are you satisfied that the song is up to snuff?"

"It's okay. The lyrics are fantastic at least." He grins. "I'm going to send our temp track to the producer tonight and they'll be recording it on Monday."

"So fast? That's amazing." I hear footsteps and hope that no one finds our little hiding spot at least for a few more minutes. "So you're going to the big gala next week?"

Am I angling for an invitation? Maybe. But I think I'm being subtle about it.

Micah's sunny expression darkens a little. "Pierre is asking about me going back on tour with him. They're leaving on Thursday."

My heart sinks. "Oh." Maybe now that he's done his part for the charity he'll feel like he's made up for all those kids who got hurt.

"I don't know if I'm going or not. I'm still not sure what my future is in RiotSphere."

He takes my hand and holds it in his, then brings it up to his lips and kisses it. My chest flutters, and I'm almost incapable of coherent thought. "Y—you don't want to be a rock star anymore?"

"It's not as glamorous as it seems. We've been touring for the past six years, almost nonstop. It's the only way to make a living. I'm thinking maybe I need to settle down a little more. You know, put down some roots."

"Oh, really? All of this looks appealing to you, does it?" I wave my hand around the cacophony of children screaming around our hiding place.

"All of this wouldn't be the worst thing in the world." His gaze holds on me and it feels significant.

I freeze, and the little glow inside me fades. "Um, well yeah, I could see that. You'll probably make a terrific dad one day."

He must see the change in me. "I mean, not at this moment you know, but maybe.... What's wrong, Char?"

"Nothing. Nothing. I'm glad I could help you with the song. I think it'll be great. Thank you for giving me this opportunity."

He's looking at me like I'm rambling like a crazy person, which I guess I am. But the moment is over, and I have to get out of here.

"I guess I'll see you around. I'd better go." I stand and start dusting off my sundress, straightening imaginary wrinkles.

"Charlotte, wait, what's going on?"

"Nothing, I just need to get home. Start job hunting you know? These curls don't de-frizz themselves. And my haircare product bills alone require a good twenty percent of my income." I laugh, high-pitched and fake and make a beeline through a narrow path I've spotted that leads away from the house. Micah jogs after me.

"Charlotte!"

"I wish you the best Micah," I say over my shoulder as I speed-walk. "I really do. I think you're amazing, and I hope you find a way to leave your legacy."

And then I'm at the gate, fumbling with it through the tears building in my eyes. I lift the latch and race through before he can stop me.

CHAPTER EIGHT

Delilah materializes in the alley behind Coffee Bar and shakes out her dreadlocks. In the dying, golden sunlight they look almost brown. She shudders.

Today she's dressed in what she hopes is a professional outfit. There's no dress code for the Cupid Guild, each agent is left on their own to decide what's best. And professional for Delilah means a sparkly purple tank top, pleated miniskirt, and her knee-high platform boots.

Dress to impress, her matriarch always says. Her assignment has been a tricky one, and she's got to make sure it goes through. Managing the love lives of humans is serious business.

She waves a hand to unlock the deadbolt on the back door of the coffee shop and walks through the back hall, the pretty bells strung through her hair singing the song of her arrival. According to the ping she'd received on her trans-dimensional tablet, one half of her assignment should be seated at the bar, talking to her best friend Trudy, and drowning her sorrows in caffeine.

As she approaches, Trudy turns to stare at Delilah, her jaw dropping open. "Where did you come from?"

Delilah waves cheerily. "Good afternoon. Or is it already good evening? I'm never sure where the cut-off point between afternoon and evening is? How does anyone know which one to say?"

She waits for an answer, but both women just stare at her like she's got something growing out of her head. She's pretty sure she's wearing an entirely human form right now—she double-checked before materializing, but she's gotten it wrong before. She bends to inspect herself in the shiny surface of the espresso machine.

Yup, all human. She turns back to the women.

"I'm calling the police," Trudy says.

Delilah looks around, shocked. "Why? Is someone hurt? Did something get stolen?"

"Who. The hell. Are you?"

"That's Delilah," Charlotte answers. "The sub." She tilts her head to the side and squints. "Or, maybe not."

"I *am* Delilah," she says, sticking out her hand. Trudy doesn't shake it. Delilah frowns. She's sure that's rude. She rounds the bar and takes the seat next to Charlotte. "You're upset about Micah."

Charlotte's eyes are red. Two large, empty mugs sit in front of her, already consumed, while another one rests between her palms.

"You're not going to sleep at all tonight, again, with all that caffeine in your system," Delilah admonishes. "You're very sensitive to it, you know."

The two friends look at each other and then back to Delilah, who rewinds the conversation in her head to make sure she had been speaking the correct language. Human tongues are all so similar, with their limited range of sounds and funny way words leave their mouths. She's pretty sure she'd been speaking English.

"The gala is on Friday, and you don't want bags under your eyes, right? Sleep really is very important."

Charlotte's hand rushes to her face to touch the dark skin under her eyes as if to check for bags.

Trudy finally unhinges her jaw and clamps her mouth shut. Her phone is in her hand, but she hasn't dialed the police yet. "How do you know about the gala?"

Delilah waves a hand. Anyone who was anyone knew about the gala. "So what do you have left to decide on? Hair? Nails? I know you *must* have your dress picked out."

Charlotte sniffs and shakes her head. "I haven't thought about any of those things because I'm not going to the gala."

Delilah scratches her ear to make sure she's heard right. "Did you say you weren't going?"

"Right."

"But why not?"

Charlotte throws her hands up in frustration or desperation or some sort of -ation. "Because I'm a mess. Because I ran away from him before he could ask me. Because he's not the right one for me. No one's the right one for me."

"No, I assure you, he is." Delilah pulls out her tablet and taps on it to bring up their file. "See, you two were evaluated based on 1.5 billion data sets. You're a 98% match."

Trudy squints at the screen of the tablet and frowns. "There's nothing but a video of jellybeans pouring into a jar on there."

Delilah looks down. "Well, yes, that's how it appears to you, because 1.5 billion data sets are impossible for the human brain to comprehend. But trust me, the match is cosmically sound."

"*Cosmically* sound?"

"Yes." Delilah nods enthusiastically. "What's really the problem, sweetie?" She pats Charlotte's hand.

"I'm just feeling like…like not a whole person. Like I can't give him everything he wants, you know? I just—" She shakes her head, moving her hand to her stomach, unconsciously. "I just don't think it will work out."

"Well, shouldn't he get a say?" Delilah asks. Charlotte's head shoots up. "You're worried about children and you think he'll act like Tanner did and leave at the first hint of trouble."

Trudy slaps the counter. "This is what I've been telling her."

"Well, Tanner was a douche knapsack," Delilah says. "Is Micah a douche knapsack?"

Charlotte's wide eyes are round. She shakes her head.

"Of course not. 1.5 billion data points wouldn't match you with someone so shallow, and a cheater besides. If you're really worried about Micah's reaction, why don't you just tell him and see what he says?"

The expression on Charlotte's face makes it clear she hadn't even considered that. "So, I should just tell him?"

Delilah smiles encouragingly. Trudy's eyes widen, staring over both their shoulders.

"Tell me what?" a deep voice says from behind them.

Right on time, Delilah thinks, and snaps her fingers, disappearing.

CHAPTER NINE

I swivel around in my seat slowly, my cheeks on fire. They're probably as red as my nose and my eyes. Of course the first time I see Micah after running away from him this afternoon and dodging all his texts and calls, I look like something the cat dragged in.

But when I meet his eyes, they don't recoil, and he doesn't look mad. Hurt maybe, pained, but not angry.

"Tell me what, Charlotte?" I hear footsteps retreating. I'm guessing that Trudy and the woman, who I can only assume is my fairy godmother, have decided to give me and Micah some privacy. Since he first spoke, it's like no one else in the world exists but him.

He tracked me down here, and I owe him an apology. "I'm sorry for bailing on you like that earlier. I just—"

"Listen, I'm sorry if I was moving too fast with the talk of futures and kids and stuff. I promise I'm not some creep who fell in love with you at first sight

and mapped out our futures in that very moment." He smiles a weird, tense smile.

My mouth moves for a second before being able to form audible words. "In the future you haven't mapped out, you want kids?"

He searches my face. "I don't know. Maybe."

"Because I can't. Have kids." I motion towards my abdomen. "It was all messed up in there, so they had to take some things out." I fidget with my fingers. "I'm actually still recovering from the surgery."

Understanding dawns in his eyes. I brace myself for his retreat. For a cold glaze to fall across him now that he knows the fulness of my limitations. But instead of pulling away, he steps closer. "Is that why you left? Being around the kids…was it painful?"

I shake my head. "No, not exactly. I just— There's a door that's closed now. It used to be open, but now it's shut. And that made me look at my life and everything and just wonder, what am I doing? How am I living?"

I stand up and take a breath. Grab his hands in mine because I need this connection with him, even if it won't last. "You said you want a legacy. I've heard that before. My ex wanted that too, and he found it with someone else. My life isn't turning out how I expected and it's just— I don't want to bring someone else down with me."

He's quiet for a while, his gaze on our clasped hands. I try to pull away, but he squeezes tighter.

He clears his throat. "I was five when I was adopted. Jude was a newborn when my parents got him. We were both born to drug addicted mothers. So it's true, some doors are closed for you right now, but there are plenty of windows. If you want a family, you can have one."

My throat is thick with emotion.

"Listen, it's not like I have my shit together. I live on a bus. I don't even have an apartment anymore. I'm a thirty-five-year-old man living in his mother's basement. I'm not in a position to judge."

I lift a shoulder. "Yeah, but you've been on Jimmy Kimmel."

He laughs a chocolate lava sound that fills up all the empty spaces inside me. "Charlotte Woodson, would you like to go on a date with me? I hear there's some fancy gala happening next week."

I stand up straighter and look him in the eye. "Do we have to wait until next week?"

And then he wraps me tight in his embrace and kisses me until I see stars.

EPILOGUE

Micah and I move slowly across the dance floor, the only satellites in an orbit of our own. His hands wrap possessively around my waist and I don't know how much longer we'll be staying at this little shindig. At least until the performance part of the gala is over and our song is sung by a rising pop star who recorded it earlier this week for the charity album.

But right now, it's just us, lost in the soft music and the magic I feel when he touches me. Then a tap at my shoulder has me pulling away from my happy place and staring into a face framed by purple dreadlocks.

"You were right," I tell Delilah, my voice dreamy. "You and your data points."

She gives a little wave. "Hi, Micah. Of course I was. That was never in doubt. But I have someone else I want you to meet. He's in the bathroom now because I spilled cocktail sauce all over his tux, but it'll come right out." She puts a finger to her chin. "Or else I'll have to emergency requisition him a new shirt."

Micah's eyebrows rise, but he wisely stays silent. I think it's probably best not to pay too close attention to all the things I don't understand in what she says. "I hope this isn't another match, because I'm perfectly happy with the one I've got." Micah squeezes me tighter.

Delilah's smile brightens a few watts. "Oh no, he's your new boss. He's looking for an assistant. Wants help managing his schedule, transcribing meetings, some light copyediting."

A fairy godmother who also helps with job searching, interesting. "Oh, well, thanks Delilah. That was awfully nice of you. But I'm not sure if that's—"

"I also think he said something about dusting off his awards case. Apparently, he's got a shelf full of screenwriting awards. No need to rub it in our faces, am I right? I'll point him out to you when he gets back from the loo."

Little bells echo as she spins around and heads off the dance floor.

Micah gives me a look that's somewhere between shell-shocked (a reaction I'm pretty sure Delilah receives often) and proud. I tuck my head back against his chest and keep dancing.

I could really get used to this whole 'getting what you want' thing.

Copyright © 2018 by L. Penelope.

Called a "legendary erotica heavy-hitter" (by the über-legendary Violet Blue), Andrea Dale writes sizzling erotica with a generous dash of romance. Her work—which has been called "poignantly erotic," "heartbreaking," and "exceptional"—has appeared in 20 year's best volumes as well as about 100 other anthologies from Soul's Road Press, Harlequin Spice, and Cleis Press. Her latest release is novella Kiss on Her List. *She finds passion in rock music, clever words, piercing blue eyes, the wind in her hair, and the scent of the ocean. Visit AndreaDaleAuthor.com for more information.*

PENNY DREADFUL

by Andrea Dale

It started because of the séance.

I never took much truck with spiritualism, not matter how much the rage it is, but we were Thomas's guests at his Lake District house, so it would have been impolite of me not to have participated.

I suspected the medium—whom Benedict introduced as a Gipsy, a claim I highly doubted—had rigged things somehow. Certainly she used that clockwork device with the gears and levers and coils that allowed Jessamine's spirit to manifest.

But Thomas had been truly moved by the experience, and indeed the medium had relayed things that he said sounded just like Jessamine, so if that gave him comfort and closure, I can't speak too harshly of it.

The fact is, the whole experience gave me pause as well, although my revelation came later, after the séance, when I saw the medium and Benedict sneaking out of a room behind the library in the middle of the night.

Unable to sleep, I'd gone down to find a volume to read: my usual solace. I crouched behind a sofa, blocking the candle's flame with my hand and peering around.

I needn't have bothered. They were so engrossed with each other, hand-in-hand as they giggled and raced for the stairs as quietly and quickly as they could. That they were flushed and rumpled made it clear what they had begun in that back room, and what they intended to do very soon.

Oh, how I envied her, with an ache low in my belly, in my breasts. Not because of Benedict—he was too gangly and nervy for me—but their passion. According to the medium when she channeled Jessamine during the séance, Thomas and his wife had been shockingly passionate as well.

I wanted that.

Specifically, I wanted that with Rufus.

Ah, Rufus, with that lock of sandy hair that won't stay in place, those broad shoulders, that silk vest which, no matter how hard he tries, never stays quite straight. Our friendship grew from our mutual interest in reading—of all our group, we were the ones most likely to debate an author's meaning or get lost discussing the latest penny dreadful.

There had been a time when I thought he might be interested in me. When a welcoming kiss on my cheek lingered, when he sat close enough on the embroidered settee our thighs touched, sending a delicious thrill through me.

But although I flirted back, making it clear I shared his interest, in the past months he had become distant, leaving me frustrated.

At the séance I had made sure to place myself between Rufus and François just so I could hold hands with Rufus. When the table shook, I squeaked with faux fear and tried to pull away, just to feel his hand tighten on mine.

I had held that sensation in my mind until I returned to my room. I was far from an innocent, but that touch was about all I could get from him, other than a hug and a swift kiss that failed to make contact when we met at the train station to come to Lake District, or the same in farewell when our little group parted ways each evening.

Now, though, I was also immensely curious to discover what lay in the room Benedict and the medium had emerged from. The door was cunningly hidden behind a Morris tapestry, and despite the time I'd spent in this library, I hadn't noticed it until now.

I had never picked a lock before, but I'd read books that described it. A few judicious pokes with a pair of hairpins, and Bob's your uncle.

What I found inside caused my jaw to drop in a most unseemly fashion.

It was full of things that were considered ungentlemanly and, indeed, outwardly shunned by society. It was available to people of mature age and respected morals…which meant the wealthy.

Photographs of women wearing stockings and shoes and pearls and little else. Photographs of women with men in the act of love. Paintings, etchings, sketches.

There was a gleaming contraption in one corner, all brass and levers and sprockets and something that looked like a short telescope. I examined it for a brief moment and realized it was a device for viewing moving pictures. I'd been to a party once where they'd projected them onto the wall.

And books…oh, the books! Of course they are what captured my attention. Unsurprisingly, all had nondescript leather covers, muted reds or browns or even dark green. Of course they wouldn't advertise what was inside.

I was not completely unfamiliar with such things—I had chanced my hand upon a scrap of salacious writing here and there. I was no innocent and certainly no prude. But to hold whole volumes—to know that so many volumes even existed—was thrilling.

Suddenly it was as if I were outside myself for a moment, watching as my hands opened a book, closed it, and tucked it under my night robe. I didn't know how to re-lock the room, and I hoped that Thomas would not discover the borrowing before I had a chance to return the book—for truly, I intended to do so.

I raced back to my room as fast as my guttering candle would allow, and locked that door firmly. Seating myself in the comfortable wing chair, I prepared to read.

The book fell open, unbidden, to a particular page, and I was so immediately engrossed that I didn't care it wasn't at the beginning. The swoop and dance of the words lit a fire within me. Yes, they always did, but this time was different. This fire burned lower, where the spark had ignited when Rufus clutched my hand. The things I'd dreamed of were there, printed on paper for me to read.

I was no stranger to self-love, and to not have to use only my imagination whetted my desire more swiftly than usual. My nipples beaded, hard beneath the linen and lace of my bedgown. Unwilling to set down the book, I touched them with one hand, first one, then the other. A light caress at first, then harder, pinching through the fabric as desire coursed through me.

Between my thighs, I was already wet. I stood, still reading, long enough to pull my bedclothes to my hips and then sit again, one foot on the seat of chair as well, my legs spread.

As I caressed myself, my fingers skidding in my moistness to find my pearl and finding it needy, I half-read the book and half-fantasized about Rufus.

He would kneel on the floor before me, press his lips to my most intimate parts, the ones that ached for him even now. It would only take a kiss, a few explorations with his tongue as my hands would tangle in his hair and urge him closer until….

If I cried out his name as I came, I could not be blamed for that.

As I floated down from my pleasure, another desire consumed me, so swift and sharp it bordered on pain.

While my friends dabbled in painting and sketching, dallying with the Pre-Raphaelite Brotherhood, my need had always been to write. Oh, I had had some poetry published, and I had tried to write the polite romantic fiction of the time, but it had never been true interest. The scraps of fantasy I had dashed out were ones I'd kept hidden, only for myself.

What I'd realized tonight, in the drawing room, watching Thomas say goodbye to a wife taken far too young, was that my own life could be brief. Life was for the living and shouldn't be wasted.

So with firm resolve in my heart, I sat at the dressing table and began to write my own erotic story. I wrote at a furious pace, faster than ever before, the nib of my pen catching and scattering drops of ink in my haste.

I wrote of Rufus and thing things I would do to him, given the chance, and the things I hoped he would do to me.

There were many, to be sure.

The darkness outside my window was fading to blue, then grey, as I finished my tale.

Then, freshly excited by what I had done, I laid upon the bed and pleasured myself again, before dropping into an exhausted sleep.

❖

A few months later the lot of us repeated the journey from London to Windermere, although François and Lucy and I arrived a day later than the rest.

In the intervening time I had been feverishly writing, and in fact, had sent stories to the publisher listed in Thomas's books (an address I had made sure to copy down). The editor and I had begun a lively correspondence, although he knew me only by the pseudonym I had chosen: Penny Dreadful.

It was a jape I wished I could share with Rufus, for I knew he would laugh with delight, and his blue eyes would crinkle at the corners as he did.

Rufus, dear Rufus, the star of all my naughty tales, was waiting outside my room after I unpacked my valise and trunk.

"Livia," he said, giving me a hug. "How have you been?"

"Much better now that you're back," I said, smiling.

For a moment it seemed as if he would flirt back, but then the wall came up between us, and he stepped back, patting my arm as if I were a child. As if his touch hadn't sent my pulse racing.

And right there was the problem with Rufus. So kind and solicitous and handsome and desirable, and yet so bloody unattainable.

Then, however, he said, "Actually, I've been quite anticipating your arrival," and my heart leapt, only to be dashed when he added, "Thomas and I have been wanting to get your opinion on something."

For a brief moment I wondered if Thomas had discovered my previous nocturnal visits to his secret room, but then I realized if he had, he wouldn't have wanted Rufus there when he spoke of it to me.

We made our way through the rambling old house, which was colder now that it was autumn, to the library, where a cheerful fire greeted us.

To my surprise, not only was Thomas waiting there, but also the medium and Benedict, all of whom greeted me warmly.

"We are together working on a project," Rufus explained once we were all seated. I had made sure I was on the settee next to him, as close as I could muster. Benedict and medium were on the other settee, and they *were* sitting close. I firmly constrained my envy and listened to what Rufus had to say.

"The idea was mine," he went on, "and Thomas has agreed to fund its production."

He handed me a rectangular object, made of brass but with a glass screen. A row of buttons, which looked like they had been stolen off a typewriter, ran below the screen on one side.

The prototype device Rufus called an active reader. About the size of an average book, it would be filled with dozens of volumes of books, the text stored in its mechanism. (I confess I missed the explanations of exactly how it worked, because I had become distracted by the line of Rufus's jaw and a spot where his manservant had missed when shaving him.)

In addition, it would include photographs and artwork and, he hoped, small moving pictures as well, to enhance the stories.

"I wanted to get your assistance in the design and functions," he said, "because you and I share a love of books, and I value your opinion."

I could have kissed him right there for saying those words, if I hadn't thought it might send him screaming from the room.

It transpired that the medium herself had invented the contraption that had seemed to bring Jessamine's spirit back. (Her name is Philippa. I knew she wasn't a Gipsy. But nobody else cares, and neither do I, really. She's quite lovely, it turns out.)

And so, while the rest of our group went on walks in the woods and picnics on the chilly lakeshore and played Whist and Crambo, the five of us spent most of our time in the library bent over sketches and notes.

Thomas handling the funding, provided excellent suggestions. Rufus and I brainstormed things we wished the device could do, and Philippa scribbled down possibilities and made lists. As for Benedict… well, Benedict was mostly distracting Philippa, until we sent him away.

There were flashes of the old Rufus there, the one who laughed without hesitation, who bantered with me, who seemed easy and comfortable. And yet, if I answered him too lightly, moved too close, the old Rufus slipped away again.

A fortnight later, as the train rattled and clanked its way back to London, I pondered Rufus's dozing profile (most of us were on the same train this time) and decided that he wasn't worth the heartache.

If he truly did not care for me in that way, then it was best if I turned my affections elsewhere.

As autumn turned to the depths of winter, my correspondence with the editor of my racy books, Charles, took on a flirtatious tone (certainly I didn't think I imagined it). Indeed, he had a quick wit and was a delight with turns of phrase, something I'd also admired in Rufus (although I wasn't thinking of Rufus anymore, I *wasn't*).

Remembering the lesson I'd learned at the séance, I determined to meet Charles. Of course, he might be old or fat or married, but nothing ventured, as they say….

So, one blustery January day I made my way across the bridge and delivered myself to the publishing offices.

Which, above the door, claimed to be solicitor's offices.

I was standing in the street, confused, glancing between the address printed in the book in my hand (one of my own) and the one above the door, when the door opened.

The man who came out had his head ducked and a scarf woven around his face against the cold, but the way he bounded down the steps, I knew him.

"Rufus?"

His head snapped up, his blue eyes widening first in delight to see me (unless I misread that because I wanted to see it), then uncertainty.

"Livia? What are you doing here?"

"I was looking for a publishing company." I held up the book. "Do you know of them? Run by a man called Charles Gower?"

His finely chiseled jaw wagged as he tried to form words.

Then, like a gust of frigid winter wind on my face, it all made perfect sense to me. How easy my correspondence had been with "Charles."

"I believe," I added, unable to stop myself from being wicked, "he knows me here as Penny Dreadful."

And I watched with delight as realization dawned on Rufus's face.

Finally, he managed to say, "Come inside."

He made tea, bringing it to me in the front office that did look like a solicitor's office—a way to keep up appearances, in case the constabulary came calling. Naughty books still were not entirely accepted; every so often a group of puffed-up matrons would squawk a collective complaint and the politicians would have to declare it a crime. (Not that everyone didn't know where the politicians obtained their own titillating material.)

This was, in part, why he'd devised the plan for the active reader: a way to keep the salacious texts and artwork hidden, but easily available.

He confessed as well, his eyes on the steaming teacup cradled in his ink-stained hands, that this was the reason he had drawn away from me. Once had had begun publishing the racy books, he felt it would be best if we were distanced, to keep my honor from being sullied were he to be exposed. As it were.

We had a good laugh about that, Rufus and I.

Eventually, though, we stopped laughing, and he took me upstairs to the small apartment he kept in case he worked late. It was cluttered with books and manuscripts and pens and dried inkwells. He tried to apologize for it, but I sank my hands in his hair and yanked him to me, and I kissed him and made him stop talking, too.

There should be a word for the joy you feel when you experience something you've dreamed of for so long, and it turns out to be better than your imagination ever provided. That was how I felt to finally feel Rufus's mouth on mine, hard and demanding—we'd both waited too long to be tentative, I think.

I felt that kiss down to the sweet spot between my legs. His tongue stroked between my teeth and met mine, and all I could think was how that would feel between my legs, and I kissed him back, hard and urgent.

I was no innocent and he wasn't my first, but when we'd fumbled past buttons and lacings and stockings and corset and I ripped his vest because he'd pinned it to keep it straight, I had a moment of shyness. I'd wanted him, and now I had him, it was a heady thing that made my head spin, my thighs weak.

Perhaps it was because he'd read my books, knew my thoughts and desires as well as I did.

The silk of my split drawers was damp with my arousal, and his nostrils flared at the scent. My breasts felt heavy, and I cupped my hands beneath them, offering them to him.

He didn't need a second invitation to bury his face in them, tasting the powder I'd dusted there that morning. When he took my nipple between his lips I thought I would faint from the glorious pleasure of it, the sweet tugging as if on a string that led down to my most intimate parts.

As much as I wanted him to taste me everywhere, I wanted to taste him as well. I urged him back onto the rumpled sheets, leaning over him to kiss his throat, his chest, the dusting of hair below his navel, as his hands roamed my body restlessly, caressing and teasing and half-torturing me.

Until, that is, I took his cock in my hands and then my mouth.

"Livia," he murmured. "I've dreamed of you…."

I rose and joined him on the bed. "And I of you. Perhaps you didn't see yourself in my stories…."

"Now I envy the men in those stories," he said. "I hope I can live up to them."

In fact, he surpassed them. He licked me until I sobbed for mercy, flicking his tongue against my sensitive pearl, sliding his fingers inside me and bringing me to my peak again and again.

"I want *you*," I said when I could speak again. "To feel you inside me."

He needed no encouragement. When he entered me, our eyes met, and for a brief flash I remembered the look in Thomas's eyes when he saw Jessamine for one last time at the séance.

And I remembered what I'd learned that night, a lesson that had brought me to this place, to Rufus, to this: Life was for the living.

For the first time, I felt as if I lived.

Petronella Glover is a multi-genre author whose work has been translated into a dozen languages, including the Catalonian Romance language, where she has won two awards for Best Translated Story. A little quirky, very geeky, and unabashedly romantic, she hopes to one day visit the City of Love, find a bustling café where she can sample their hot chocolate and write her first New York Times *bestseller. This is her sixth appearance in the magazine, and you can find out more about her at www.petronellaglover.com.*

WHEN THE OCEAN CALLS

by Petronella Glover

I bent down in the sand to pick up the most gorgeous piece of sea glass I had ever come across. Old, although not as old as the black—or rather, olive—convict-era glass that could wash up on Australian shores, this piece's edges were worn perfectly over the years so that it resembled a see-through pebble of the most amazing aqua shade.

I knew that in reality, sea glass was simply trash, having been created out of glass bottles and other debris that had been discarded into the sea, but it also represented history and the cycles of nature. Glass forms originally by heating sand until its melting point…. So, sea

glass, in a way, is just sand in another form, returning to the ocean, to the beaches it originally came from.

I loved the symbology of that process, of nature welcoming it back by slowly reabsorbing it. I didn't know why, but there was just something about the glass that called to me.

Like the man I had met at the party. He called to me, too—like a siren. He said that he had known my father, so I *suppose* that had been one reason he had interested me—no one had never known my father. Not even my mother, not really—but the way he had danced with me at the party showed that he wanted much more than just to talk to me about my Dad. And I was intrigued.

Perhaps *too* intrigued.

How on earth could I have thought it would be safe to meet him, alone, at the beach the next day, as the sun was lowering in the sky? I didn't even know the man.

I slid the piece of sea glass into my netting bag, depositing it on the beach beside my flip flops and towel. I was at the designated spot for our meeting—date?—but Koral was nowhere to be seen. Now what?

As if on cue, I heard him call my name. "Edie."

I looked up and down the beach. No one.

He called my name again. It was only then I looked *into* the water.

Ah. Of course he would have his shirt off, his dark tan skin slick with water and his sun-kissed hair all tousled and wet. I groaned. He had already been too damn hot on the dancefloor. But now, in the ocean?

I unconsciously fanned myself, telling myself it was the hot Melbourne weather.

"Come in," he told me, with a smile that seemed to hint at siren delights.

I hesitated. Something really drew me to him, but he was effectively a stranger.

"I promise I won't bite," he said, in that charming voice of his. Then quieter, more devilishly: "Much."

I couldn't help but laugh. Throwing caution to the sea breeze, I pulled off my cheesecloth tunic and threw it in a pile with my things and strode into the water. He said not a word as I walked deeper and deeper until the gentle waves were at chest height.

Gosh, it felt so bloody good to be back in the ocean. I had always been a water-lover—mom had joked I must have been a fish in a past life—so it felt amazing to feel my toes sink into the wet sand as I waded forward.

While the Pacific was crystal clear in the piercing warm sun, it was also cold, as usual. I stopped in front of him, smiling awkwardly. Unbidden, my eyes were drawn to his chest, peaking out of the water, specifically at the hair that I was delighted to see made a sexy path down his taut muscles to his belly button and into his burnished bronze tail.

Wait—what?!

His *tail?*

"Before you panic, there's something I need to tell you."

I'm *already* panicking, I thought, not having the ability to speak due to my shock. I couldn't take my eyes away from his tail, glimpsed through the rippling water. It was so exotic. So…beautiful.

He reached forward and tipped my chin up so that I looked up at him. "My eyes are up here," he joked and winked.

The normalcy of his flirt would usually have helped calm me, at least somewhat, but as soon as he touched me something pulsed through my whole body. Like he had given me an electric shock, but somehow more invigorating.

I gasped. What was happening? This can't be real.

He lowered his arm and placed his hands firmly on my hips. He gently pulled me closer to him and deeper into the water, his tail undulating back and forth to hold us upright in the ocean swell, to keep our heads and shoulders above the water.

"Just breathe," he told me, catching my gaze with his cerulean blue eyes. "This is natural. All you ne—"

"Natural?" I exclaimed, my voice breaking in shock. "*Nothing* about this is natural. I'm—I'm…. Oh, what is happening?!"

I felt the fabric of my swimsuit tear apart and, my breath catching in my throat, I looked down through the water to see my legs thicken, somehow—no, they were…merging?! Incredulous, and more than a little dazed by a burning sensation in my thighs so at odds with the cool of the ocean, I looked on in horror and fascination as my feet joined together, contorting and stretching into a position not possible for a normal human skeletal structure.

"That's because you're not human."

I looked up, startled, not just by the merman's statement, but by the fact that he must have heard my mental musing and responded.

Yes. That is right, he replied, except this time his lips did not move, and I heard his words *inside* my mind.

I shook my head rapidly in denial. This telepathy stuff—mermen—only happens in fantasy books, not in real life.

Just because you didn't know I existed before today, Edie, doesn't mean I wasn't alive, he pointed out. *This is how we communicate underneath the water,* he continued. *The magic in my blood—in our blood—makes the improbable possible.*

I was still trying to digest that revelation when a new pins-and-needlelike tingling sensation drew my attention back down to my legs. My eyes widened as blue-green scales rippled into existence across my hips, down my now-fused thighs and shins onto what used to be my feet, which flared into a gossamer webbing substance that unfurled into a turquoise—

Tail! Oh my goddess—*I have a tail.*

My jaw dropped as I reflexively recoiled back from myself, from my new reality, only to see my new, ah, appendage, flex impossibly gracefully; I felt it move as if it already knew how to maneuver in the ocean.

I experienced a rush of exhilaration at odds with my still-present fear. It was almost as if, for the first time, I felt truly—

"At home," the merman concluded, out loud this time, to preserve my sanity, no doubt.

And, stunned as I was, I could feel the calm of the water soothe me; I felt an increasing ease to be *in* the water. I made a conscious gesture to undulate my tail and was surprised to find the scales were tactily sensitive to the rush of water, rather than just being a hard form of armor.

"They are both," Koral said quietly.

The merman flexed his hands on my hips, and, all of a sudden, I was aware again of his touch. He tugged me closer still until my chest pressed up against his torso. Sliding one hand around to the small of my back, pinning me to him, he raised his other hand to stroke the side of my face.

"Your tail will be just as sensitive to touch as your face is—if not more so," he pointed out as his thumb slid across to trace my bottom lip soothingly, seductively. I gasped as I felt his tail gently press up against mine, and then wrap around it, the slither of his scales against mine sending a rush of pleasure up my body so intense I bit back a moan.

"How?" I asked simply.

"Your father was like me."

"Horny?" I replied, my snark returning.

He laughed, the twinkle in his eye brightening. "No. Well, actually—yes. But I meant he also had a tail."

I was astonished, but what was that information compared to discovering I was a freaking mermaid. "And here I thought my father was just a deadbeat dad, who left his family when he should have stayed."

"He *should* have been a more responsible parent. But he didn't leave because he wanted to—that I do know. He was Called back to the ocean and didn't know how to find you when he returned and discovered you and your mom moved. He never told your mom what he was."

"By 'Called' do you mean he could not stay away from the water any longer?"

"Yes. There is a pull—you will feel it now—not unlike the ebb and flow of a tide. As a half-breed, you had to wait until you felt The Call of the ocean—or met your Mate—before your tail first appeared. But once Awoken to the water, Merepeople can only be on land for a short period, and then the change is forced upon us—no matter where we are standing at the time." He paused as if considering his next words carefully. "The reason your father was a bad dad was because he should not have fallen for your mother—a full-blooded human—in the first place. He *knew* he would have to return to the ocean, eventually."

"Wait—back up, Casanova. Are you saying I was Called to the ocean? Or that you are…. I mean, that it's possible that I am—"

"My Mate. Yes." The certainty in his voice rang of truth.

The shock turned the water icy around me. "So that is why this—" I gestured down toward my tail "—happened now?"

He simply nodded, as if knowing too many words right now might send me over the edge.

"But, we *can't* be Mates!" I spluttered. "We haven't even had a proper first date!"

A ghost of a smile now played on his more seriously-composed face. "You now know how we communicate under water…"

Via telepathy, I thought into his mind.

His smile brightened. *Impressive. You are a quick learner.* "Yes. However, between Mates there is an extra special bond that forms—an invisible telepathic link that is only severed through death."

As if to illustrate his point, he let go of my waist and pulled back a little. I felt some kind of pull, instinctively maneuvered to come up flush with his chest again, relieved and pissed in equal measure when his arms slid around me to resume their former position.

I blushed, telling myself I was just clinging to him because of my nerves. "This is *not* the dark ages," I bit out, trying to calm myself. "I should have a choice in who I want to be with."

He nodded again, more gravely. "This is true." He tilted his head, considering me. "But you should not look at it as being forced to be with someone you did not choose. But, rather, that your unique body has the uncanny ability to innately know who its one true Mate is and choose it on a subconscious level."

"Intellectually, I can understand what you are saying. But it still does not *feel* like I have a choice, if you are telling me my choice only includes one option. You."

"You can choose not to answer the Call of the heart," he told her quietly, for the first time looking down, away.

I didn't have to ask him how much it cost him to make that statement, to give me an out; I could *feel* it. Proof we were already connected on at least some primal level.

Fuck.

I focused on a breathing exercise to calm down, eventually realizing his hand was rubbing the small of my back soothingly in circles as I took stock of my situation. "What does this, ah…connection mean if I'm a half-breed," I asked him. "I mean, I am not expecting us to…you know. Or to have a child. That is…" *Oh, shit. Edith Natalia Rennie, get a grip.* "But if we're together, how do we…"

He laughed softly, feeling my curiosity. "Are you willing to let me show you?" he asked, a hunger returning to his voice. A need.

Unable to trust myself not to put my foot (or tail?) in my mouth again, I nod an affirmative.

He didn't need any more invitation. He swooped in to kiss me, and I did not know what was more distracting, his lips pressed against mine or the sinuous way his rust-colored tail rubbed against my turquoise one.

His tongue darted out to lick the seam of my lips, encouraging me to part them, and I did upon a sigh. He surged in, and the kiss intensified as I gripped onto his arms and was lost in a maelstrom of feeling. Breathless, we sank under the water, our tails intertwining, and I realized I was still getting oxygen.

I no longer needed to breathe underwater!

I could hear a chuckle in his mind as his hand slid down my face, to caress the nape of my neck and grip in my hair as our kiss managed to get more frenetic—more impassioned.

The situation your parents were in doesn't apply to us, Edie, he informed me, when he eventually, reluctantly, pulled away.

It doesn't? I was dazed—not thinking straight. Bloody hell, he looked amazing, floating under the water like some kind of Sea God. Was this really happening?

Yes, it is, he responded gently into my mind. *What happened to your parents won't happen to us, because whenever we return to the water, we'll return together.*

Together, I repeated, mulling over what his words *didn't* say. *You mean, you will come onto land, with me, too?*

Of course. Merepeople mate for life. And I don't expect you to leave your mom or friends—your life on land—completely. His hand let go of the back of my head and floated up to brush my red hair back from my face. *It just means that you'll need to tell your human friends you intend to take regular, extended vacations to exotic locations with your boyfriend.*

I waited until his words sunk in. I have a boyfriend…who is a merman.

An even cooler realization: *I am a freaking mermaid!*

He chuckled anew as he tugged me deeper into the water, to show me depths of myself I had never known.

For who says dreams can't come true? I am four feet (fins?) and eleven inches tall, with a green tail—well, somewhere between aqua and teal, really, but who sweats the small details?—and red hair. I am now a literal cliché; The Little Mermaid, in reverse.

While Disney's Ariel had craved legs, and life on land, I had always wanted to be part of the sea. I had always felt my heart had belonged there. Now I know I was right—with Koral.

It was time for me to make the leap, to let myself believe in a happily ever after.

Copyright © 2018 by Petronella Glover.

Find Gracie Wilson in the trees enjoying nature's wonders, traveling to see the latest animal conservations, or at aquariums all around the world. This girl loves nature and all animals. She has many pets and is always adding new additions. The more the merrier in her mind. Sitting under the shade reading a book, letting the world around her pass by, while she is safe in her bubble of imagination. Well that is where she'd love to stay. She is a #1 Amazon Bestselling Author from Ontario, Canada. She is a first generation Canadian living in Ontario. Her family is from Scotland, so finding her in the hot sun for very long is unlikely, but give her rain and thunderstorms and she's golden.

BIG TROUBLE

by Gracie Wilson

The check-in desk is empty, thank goodness, so I approach the waiting clerk. "Hello, I called last night." The woman looks up at me with annoyance but I continue. "I was told I'd be able to check in when I arrived."

"You can't check in till four," she says with a snide tone and I sink back slightly.

I contemplate just checking my bag with the baggage holders and walking around but I'm absolutely exhausted.

"Listen, I'm sure you hear this all the time but, really, I was told that I could check in. I already paid for last night, so technically the room is mine now."

The hotel clerk looks up, asking me my name and I give it to her. With a few clicks she looks back up at me again, causing my stomach to sink. Oh no.

"Your room was given away as you did not check in," she states before looking back down at her computer, dismissing me.

"No, I paid for it. It's mine," I can't help the whimper that escapes me. "I need to sleep! I was put on the wrong plane and almost ended up in Los Angeles. Then I had to pay for *another* hotel, which then got hit with a storm and narrowly missed a being hit by a tornado, because of which I was woken up by the clerk wearing only this top and undies, because my luggage was already on a plane out here. Then my replacement flight this morning was also delayed, I didn't know if my luggage made it, I've worn these clothes for two days and I just want my bed." I say lowering my head.

"Sounds like one hell of a night," a male voice says from behind me.

The clerk perks up, looking through me to the man I know is just inches behind me. I want to turn to look but I freeze. The look on the woman before me says it all. She looks like she's just seen god's gift to woman and that's enough for me to know turning around would only play with my constantly blushing face.

"I'm sure there is something you can do for her," he says smoothly, encouragingly, and the girl clicks her fingernails against the desk.

"I'm sorry," she says to him, not even acknowledging me this time.

"Then give her a key to mine. I don't mind sharing."

Her mouth drops open which mirrors my own reaction to his declaration. His voice is alluring but the inherent sexiness in his tones is also a warning. Nope, don't need anymore men issues; I got to Vegas in one piece and I'm not risking anything. Kalee will get here and everything will be amazing.

"Oh, it's fine. No need to do that." I say to the woman, but she doesn't even register that I've spoken.

"Oh, well I could put you in the other tower, if that works." She also clearly didn't want me to be in the same room with Mr. Sexy Voice, so suddenly a room was now available. "You'd be on the fourteenth floor," she says, finally looking up at me. All I can do is nod as she opens the drawer pulling out a keycard. "Is that suitable?"

"Very. Just a few floors above me," the man drawled behind me, his words daring me to turn around. I keep my face facing forward.

The woman huffs, handing me my key and I grab it without hesitation or a thank you to her.

"Nice meeting you," he calls out with a chuckle and my cheeks burn.

"Gosh darn it. Get it together, Tatum," I say, trying to give myself a pep talk. I turn toward the elevator, without glancing behind me to see if Mr. Sexy Voice was matched in appearance.

"You forgot this." His voice alarms me, having thought I was now alone.

When I turn, there is the man I tried everything to avoid laying eyes on—and for a good reason. He's a girl's dream, which makes him my nightmare. His hair is dark but covered by his black Stetson. His eyes are crystal blue and penetrate me to my core.

"I'm Tyler," he says with a nod of his hat.

My mind is telling me to say who I am, but it's stuck in overdrive. From the perfectly fitting jeans to the amazing rodeo belt buckle with his plaid shirt, right down to his boots that I can tell aren't just for show by the wear of them—he was a feast for the eyes. A delicious one.

When he figures that I'm not going to introduce myself, he just watches me.

"Tatum! Finally!" Suzy makes her way back into the casino with a badge in her hand, holding it out to me. "I need to give you this. You're late, but I will catch you up…" She turns, seeing the man before me, and she smiles.

"Figures you two would meet right away. Tatum, this is Tyler Dawson. He's a country singer here for the convention. Tatum, here is our homegrown sweetheart. Treat her nicely," she scolds him playfully. "Don't let him bully you, he's all talk. He just likes to act like an alpha male."

Her words seem sincere, and everything in me is telling me that the man in front of me is dominant, all right. Suzy laughs and takes off back in the direction she'd just come from, leaving me there. Before he can say anything, my blush creeps down to my chest. Embarrassed, I grip onto my luggage and turn.

"Nice boobs," I think I hear him say, causing me to turn around with my mouth wide open.

"Pardon me?"

He blinks at my reaction. "What? Those *are* some nice boots. Real ones too, not like what you see girls wearing these days."

Ah, boots. He said boots. "Thank you."

"You should be more careful with your stuff. Don't want you to lose it," he says with a sly smirk, holding out the wallet I had obviously left on the reception desk. The reason he had halted me in the first place

Geez, this guy was doing a number on my concentration levels. I reach out to take it back and our fingers brush, his touch tantalizing. Something playful in me stirs. "I don't listen to strangers," I tell him. Then me and my newfound sass turn away, walking in the direction of my room.

"Tatum," he says, and I turn looking back at him from ten feet away. "Kick them up," and he nods to my boots.

Without a thought, my foot lifts and kicks up, showing him the bottom of my boot.

"Nice, worn in too. Not just for show or a gimmick." A sexy smile sweeps over his face, lighting it up with promise. "I thought you didn't listen to strangers."

My blush threatens to go nuclear. It's go time.

Without another thought I rush off.

When the elevator closes, I'm alone, and I feel like I can relax. My body was so uptight around him, like a constant hum was coming off of him, causing every cell of my body to resonate with things I've never experienced before.

"I'm in big, big trouble." The door opens, and I shake my head, trying to clear him from my mind, but all I can think about is when I might run into him again.

"Yup, big trouble."

Copyright © 2018 by Gracie Wilson.

Meghan Ewald was born and raised in northern California. She now makes her home in Texas with her husband, their two children and one very happy rescue dog. Meghan writes fiction in the wee hours of the morning before going to her full time job playing with NASA space suits. She loves good coffee, reading, working out and writing. When not writing fiction, Meghan blogs over at http://gettingthewordswrong.com/. She loves to hear from readers. You can reach her at gettingthewordswrong@gmail.com.

OLD SCARS

by Meghan Ewald

Judah Herman stepped out of the hover cab, gravel crunching under his boots. He took one look at the flashing neon sign of the whorehouse, the words The Coney Ranch lighting up the night, and he immediately wanted to get back inside the cab. His cousin, Seth Bailey, pushed him a step forward so he could follow him out of the cab.

"Move it, Hero," Seth said. "Your fat ass is blocking me in."

At six feet four inches and two hundred thirty pounds, Judah was anything but fat. But he'd always been bigger than Seth's five feet ten inches and no more than one hundred fifty pounds sopping wet, so Judah said nothing. Only slid to one side and let Seth out of the cab.

"I don't know about this," Judah said.

"Aw man, what do you mean you don't know? This is gonna be great! We've talked about coming to this planet since we were kids!"

Judah remembered a few conversations as hormone-driven teenagers about visiting the planet Skerth. Seth talked of a place where everything was legal if you had enough money. Women, gambling, aliens, even high stakes hunting expeditions where someone rich enough could shoot illegal immigrants from 'thopters. It all sounded too farfetched to Judah, and he'd never taken the conversations seriously. Seth obviously had.

Judah looked up at the low red one-story structure. It was seedier than he'd imagined, with a chain link fence running the perimeter.

Of course, it's seedy, stupid, Judah thought. *It's a whorehouse.*

Judah rubbed his robotic leg, felt where the prosthetic met his own. "Seth maybe we should—"

"Oh no. Hell no. Jude, we've been talking about this forever. You can't puss out on me now. Besides, what girl in there isn't going to want a piece of an interplanetary hero?"

Judah grimaced. "I hate when you call me that."

Seth grinned and slapped Judah on the shoulder. "I know you do." Seth's expression turned serious, and he put both his hands-on Judah's shoulders and looked him in the eye. Seth had to look up to do it, Judah being much taller and broader than him. "Seriously, man, you need to get laid. Need it bad. Besides, they're going to get one whiff of that Earthy southern boy charm and eat you up." He wiggled his eyebrows. "Maybe literally."

"You're an asshole."

"Probably." Seth dropped his hands and turned to face the building. "But I'm an asshole that's about to get laid." He started walking up the drive. Over his shoulder he said, "Come on, war hero. We can't stay out here all day."

Judah jogged a few steps to catch up. He snagged Seth's arm, and they both stopped walking. "Would you quit calling me that?"

"What?"

"*Hero,*" Judah said through gritted teeth. "They don't know who I am." He nodded to curtained windows of the building.

"Maybe not yet. But one look at that block head of yours and they will. Every girl in the joint is going to see the guy from TV and throw her panties at you. Your face is everywhere man. You can't hide."

Judah swore under his breath.

"Come on. Your dick didn't get blown off, just your leg. Don't be a pussy."

Judah's face flushed hot with anger. "Well, at least I was in the fight. Not all of us rode a desk through the war."

Seth's face tightened. "You know I didn't get a choice. They didn't want me out there in the fight. Not exactly my fault, remember?" He tapped an old scar that ran along his hairline, an old reminder of the time as kids Judah had played too rough, and he had ended the day with screws holding his cracked skull together.

Judah sighed. He looked away from the scar. "Yeah, I know."

"Look," Seth said. He pulled his communicator tablet out of a pocket in his pants and checked the time. "Let's have a good time. We're going to find you the hottest whore in the solar system."

Judah glanced behind him, but the cab had already pulled away to pick up the next customer. When he turned back, Seth was already at the door ringing the bell. He sighed again and trudged up the walk, his false leg growing heavier with each step.

Inside the lobby twenty employees lined up. Judah saw a good number of human women, but the house catered to everyone. A few very pretty men were in the lineup as well as the more exotic Skerth locals, with their blue skin and two long head tentacles draped across their shoulders. Judah watched, unconsciously rubbing his prosthetic leg.

There was every shape of being available. A buffet of flesh that made a part of Judah wake up, a hunger to touch each of them; a curiosity to explore mixed with an oily shame. The combination made his stomach turn. It had been a long time since he'd been with a woman. He thought back. Since before he'd lost his leg. His damn leg.

"This was a mistake," Judah muttered to Seth when the girls had assembled.

"Shut up and pick one," Seth muttered. "Hell, I might have two." His eyes eagerly feasted on the flesh in front of him.

Judah sighed and looked at the girls again.

The proprietor—a loud, boisterous Skerthian man with a paunch—approached. The blue skin on his bald head stretched back into two tentacles that tapered from the thick top to the base. He held them back with a thin strip of tied leather.

"Gentlemen! Welcome to The Coney Ranch. As you can see, we have something for everyone." He waved a hand at the lineup of girls.

And indeed they did. Judah saw every kind of girl and not all of them were human. Tall girls, some as tall as himself, and petite girls. Honey colored hair, dark hair, hair that seemed red with fire. Large breasts, small breasts, rounded hips and thin. Women with knowing half-smiles beckoned to him with blue eyes or brown eyes or hazel or—Judah did a double take which earned him an inviting smile and a hip wiggle from a dark-skinned Ounavi girl with white hair and purple eyes. The smile included a sharp looking row of filed-to-points Ounavi teeth. Judah blushed and looked away.

Judah saw one thing in common with all of them. A mixture of wanting to be selected and a boredom with the process. All except one.

She was hiding behind a tall, dark-haired woman in a leather corset and a long lacy skirt over leather boots. The dark-haired woman winked at him, but Judah barely noticed. He moved to see around the taller woman to see the girl.

The girl was petite, delicate. Her fair hair fell simply to her shoulders, framing a heart-shaped face. Her eyes were downcast, soot-colored lashes feathering the pale skin beneath her eyes. She wore a loose white nightgown that showed off muscular legs and bare feet. Only after he noticed her bare feet did Judah realize she probably wasn't short. She only appeared that way next to all the others in their high heels.

The girl wasn't looking at him, wasn't acting like the others. Judah saw no attempt to appear attractive—or what she assumed his version of 'attractive' might be. She looked like she wanted to be invisible. A feeling Judah shared.

Judah would have been surprised if she was even of legal age. Though she must be, he thought, if they'd hired her. This was a legitimate establishment, so they weren't allowed to hire anyone below the age of twenty-one. This girl must be about a minute over twenty-one.

Judah caught himself studying her bare feet. Her toenails were decorated with only a delicate coat of pink polish. He wondered what she'd think of his leg and almost bolted for the door.

Seth wandered over, his communicator in his hand, the glowing light of a message filled the small screen. Seth saw Judah glance at the glowing screen. He pushed a button and shoved the communicator into his pants pocket. "Is that the one?" He looked the girl up and down disinterestedly. "A bit predictable, don't you think?"

Judah said nothing, only looked at the girl. The girl did not look up at Seth, but a flush crept up her neck. Judah saw her embarrassment and suppressed a flash of anger.

Instead of calling his cousin an asshole, he said, "Yes," he said, turning to Seth. "I want that one."

Once the words were out Judah felt wrong acting like this woman was a pastry on a bakery shelf, but beneath that he was surprised to find that he did want her. He wanted to touch her hair. To feel her in his arms. To examine her pretty toes. He wanted to hear her laugh.

What he didn't want was anyone else, Seth included, looking at her.

The proprietor came up behind Seth and Judah. He clapped Judah on the shoulder. "This one? This is Honey. Come here, Honey." He crooked a finger at the girl.

Honey hesitated, eyes still downcast, then stepped out of the line and stood before Judah. She glanced up at him through her lashes. He saw a flash of pale blue before she looked down again and his heart beat a little harder.

The proprietor said, "Honey's my new one. First night. Not much experience but she makes up for that with enthusiasm. Don't you, Honey?"

The girl nodded silently. She didn't look enthusiastic. Judah thought she looked frightened. Judah wanted to carry her away from that place. Never let anyone else see her again. And here he was, not a protector. No, Judah was the asshole picking her out of a lineup.

"What's your name?" Judah asked her.

"Didn't you hear me? She goes by—", the proprietor said.

"I asked *her*," Judah said flatly, and whether it was his size or his tone, the proprietor shut up.

"My name is Honey," she said softly, still not looking at him.

"You sure you don't want someone with a little more experience?" Seth said. "Like," he stepped closer to the dark-haired woman the girl had been hiding behind, "how about her?"

The taller woman grinned and wiggled her hips.

Seth grinned back wolfishly then turned to Judah. "She could be fun—"

"No," Judah said sharply, then softened his tone as he looked at Honey. "I want this one."

The proprietor clapped his hands. "Sold! Let's get you a room!"

Seth opened his mouth as if to argue, then shut it again. He shrugged as though to say there was no accounting for taste. "Have fun," he said.

The proprietor handed the girl a key with a number imprinted on the tag. "This way, please," she said and started up the steps to the second floor. All the triumph Judah had felt a moment ago fled. He followed the girl up the stairs wishing like hell he'd never gotten out of the cab.

As soon as Judah was out of sight, Seth pulled out his communicator again. His frantic text messages hadn't been answered. He pressed a button, and the communicator rang a few times before a face filled the screen.

"Where are you? We're here, but I don't see a camera crew."

"Hold your water, kid. We'll be there soon."

"You better. It's been years since he's touched a girl. This isn't going to take long."

Honey escorted Judah to a sparsely furnished room. In it was a single chair and a bed. The one window overlooked the parking lot. The glowing neon sign out front threw a cheap orange light into the room. She shut the door behind him and turned on the single bedside lamp.

Now that he was alone with the girl Judah felt useless again. He didn't know what he'd envisioned happening when he got her alone. He hadn't thought that far ahead. He'd been caught up in the moment, only wanting to get her away from the vultures downstairs.

You're one of the vultures, a small voice said inside Judah's head. A hot burst of guilt accompanied the thought.

"Are you hot? Your cheeks are flushed. Please, take your jacket off."

Honey reached for the front of his coat. Judah watched the top of her head dumbly as her fingers worked at the top button. Her hands trembled, and she fumbled. Finally, he put his large hands over hers and said quietly, "I can do that."

Judah removed his coat and placed it neatly over the back of a chair. Buying a few extra seconds of busy-ness, Judah took his house keys and communicator tablet out of pants pocket and set them on the seat of the chair. Then they just stood before each other; her head bowed looking at her feet, Judah wondering what to do with his hands.

He cleared his throat searching for something to talk about. "What's your real name? I don't want to call you Honey."

"I'm not supposed to," she said.

"Come on," he teased gently. "I won't tell."

She was silent so long Judah didn't think she was going to answer. And then, very softly, she said, "Adelaide."

He put a finger under her chin and raised her head. He looked fully into her blue eyes for the first time and felt a shock down to his toes.

"Hello, Adelaide. I'm Judah."

"I know who you are. I've seen you on television."

"Oh," Judah said, deeply disappointed. Seth was right. Even here he couldn't be invisible.

She turned away and wrapped her arms around her waist as though she were cold. The white material of her nightgown pulled in, and he could see her curves beneath the material.

"Hey, listen," he said. "We don't have to do anything. I'm just here for my cousin. Whores are his thing, not mine."

As soon as he said it, he regretted it. Her shoulders hunched in and red splotches appeared on the back of her neck.

"Shit," Judah muttered. "Look, I'm sorry. I never was any good with words. That's Seth's job. He's the talker. Please sit down. I won't touch you if you don't want me to."

He sat in the chair away from the bed. Part of him was relieved this wasn't going well. The chances of him removing his pants and her seeing his prosthetic leg were diminishing with every stupid thing he said.

Besides, he thought, *my leg will only frighten her more. Her first trick with a cripple.* At least, he assumed it was her first trick. It seemed to be what the proprietor was implying. *Good job Judah. You fucked up someone else's day too.*

Adelaide sat on the edge of the bed, cautiously studying him. "Why do you keep rubbing your leg?" she asked. "Does it hurt you?"

Judah dropped his hand, made it be still. He hadn't realized he was doing it.

"Not anymore." Changing the subject, Judah said, "Tell me about you."

Adelaide took a deep breath. She seemed about to say something and then changed her mind. She moved on the bed, crossing her ankles primly, her hands wringing in her lap. "Please," she said. "It's my first night here. We should do," she hesitated, "something. I don't want to get fired."

Tears traced twin tracks down her cheeks.

"Hey, hey, hey," Judah said going to her on the bed. He sat beside her. "We don't have to do anything. I swear it. I'll pay anyway."

She took a deep breath and scrubbed angrily at her eyes. Only then did he realize she wasn't wearing cosmetics. Those dark lashes were natural. There was a stirring in his pants, and he willed it away. *Not now,* he thought gritting his teeth. *I just told her I didn't care.*

"I think I have something in my eye," Adelaide said. Judah let her lie while she pulled herself together.

Uncomfortable with the silence, Judah asked, "How did you come to work here?" He felt stupid asking, but he didn't know what else to say. He was never very good at making conversation. He was much better with a television prompter and a written script.

"You don't want to hear that story," Adelaide said.

"Sure I do. You know my story already." Judah laughed awkwardly. "You kind of have the advantage right now."

Adelaide gave him a small smile and Judah enjoyed the little victory.

"My sister needed an operation. I gave her a kidney." Adelaide a long scar down an otherwise perfect torso. She laughed sharply, without humor. "It's funny. I wanted to be a doctor. Instead, I had the operation and became an escort."

Judah noticed she avoided the word whore.

He swallowed hard. With no small amount of willpower, he pulled his eyes back up to hers. Adelaide dropped the hem of her nightgown and went on, as if suddenly realizing her action had exposed her underwear to him; her pussy, her thighs—everything he suddenly wanted and had paid to have but wouldn't.

"My sister died anyway. My parents are gone. They died, working in the ice mines. So the medical bills fell to the next family member."

"You," Judah said.

"Me," Adelaide nodded. "The law here says if I don't pay I work off my debt in the ice mines." She crossed her arms and cupped both elbows as though she were cold. "I lost my parents to those mines. I know what those conditions look like. I'm better off here."

Judah asked, "What about being a doctor?"

She shrugged. "I have some medic training, but no formal education. Out here on this world, school is for the rich kids. The owner hired me because I can sew the others up when a client gets too heavy-handed." She shrugged one shoulder.

"Why not join the military?" But even as he asked he suspected he knew the answer. "They would have paid for medical school."

Adelaide confirmed. "Not with one kidney."

He fell silent.

"So here I am," she said. "Here *we* are. And I have to do this." She took a deep breath, let it out and looked directly into Judah's eyes. "I'd rather my first be with someone kind though. You can touch me. I don't mind. I want you to. When I have to do this again, I want to remember a kind touch."

Judah pushed off the bed and walked to the window, turning his back to her. The red light streamed in from the glowing sign across the street. His stump throbbed in its robotic cradle. "I said you didn't have to," his voice came out harsher than he intended. "I'll just tell them downstairs—"

Adelaide pressed herself against him from behind, wrapping her arms around his waist. He never even heard her leave the bed, but now he felt her breasts press into his back. "Please," she said. "I can see you want me, but you're as scared as I am."

Adelaide dropped one hand, and she surprised him again. Instead of reaching for the obvious swelling in the front of Judah's pants she rested her hand on his damaged leg. Her palm lay half-way up his thigh, above the prosthetic leg transecting the invisible line only Judah knew about. The line between feeling and non-feeling where his nerves had been cut when his leg was removed.

His erection diminished almost immediately.

"I see you rubbing it," Adelaide murmured. "I see you don't want to show anyone. I'm scared, too, but not of this."

He stood frozen while her fingers explored. A trickle of sweat ran down his back as her hand traveled between his stump and the robotic leg.

She hesitated, then asked, "Can I see it?"

It was his turn to hesitate, then he shrugged more casually than he felt. He unbuckled his belt and let his pants drop unceremoniously to the floor. Judah's thigh ran out of his briefs; his muscles were kept strong by specific exercises. Midway down his thigh was a band that held the robotic leg in place. Below the band, the leg itself, clear and unhuman, the internal circuitry emitting a bluish light in the dim room.

As he stood there in his briefs, Judah closed his eyes and imagined Adelaide's questing fingers belonged to one of the many doctors who'd poked and prodded him before they finally declared it safe for him to leave the military hospital.

"Do you keep the leg on all the time?"

He shook his head.

Judah walked to the bed and sat down. With numb fingers, he unfastened the strap at the top of his leg and pulled it away from his stump. He left the leg standing on the floor beside the bed. The leg went dark, no longer powered by his body heat.

Judah sat on the bed looking down at empty space where his leg was not. He did not look at Adelaide. He felt naked and exposed, even while wearing clothes.

Adelaide asked softly, "Have you ever shown anyone?"

Judah shook his head. He couldn't speak.

She knelt in front of him, and he bolstered up the courage to meet her gaze. He expected her to be frightened or repulsed or both. She was neither. She seemed merely curious.

"May I?"

Judah nodded. He could not speak. The knots in his stomach were making him nauseous.

She traced the length of a scar down his thigh and cupped the stump with her hand. He could sense the heat of her palm but couldn't really feel the touch.

"Does it hurt you?"

"Not anymore."

"Did you ever have, you know, phantom pain?"

"Some, at first. My big toe would itch. Except there was no big toe. The more I touched the stump though and let other things touch it, like clothing or the leg saddle, I got used to it. Now it's just numb from all the nerves being cut."

Then Judah asked what he'd feared to ask. "It doesn't frighten you?"

Adelaide looked up from her exploration of his stump in surprise. "No. It doesn't frighten me. Your doctors did a good job on you. I've seen a lot worse."

"I thought I was the first," Judah said, feeling strangely possessive even though he knew he had no right to be.

"You are," Adelaide said, either not noticing his proprietary tone or not acknowledging it. "Some of the girls here—they've been through a lot."

Judah swallowed a lump in his throat and said, "You're the first person to see it who wasn't a doctor." He forced himself to finish the thought. "The first woman."

"Oh," she said softly and sat back on her knees. "But everything else…works?"

Judah laughed and felt his face blush to the roots of his hair. "Yeah. I got lucky. That part works."

"Yes, you got lucky," Adelaide said. She looked down at his stump. "And yet—no, you didn't."

"I don't want your pity." He felt his face turn even redder, his laughter gone.

"It's not pity," Adelaide said. "I'm only sorry for what you must have gone through. You weren't the first. You won't be the last. You might be the most famous though."

"I'm sorry," Judah said, trying to wrestle down his anger at the scrutiny. The anger didn't want to go. "I…I get angry sometimes."

"Of course you do."

"You my head doctor?" Judah smiled to take the sting out of the words, trying to joke to two-step away from the intense moment.

"I'm not," Adelaide said, ignoring his attempt to lighten the mood. "We all go through stuff. Some

worse than others. I wanted to be a doctor. Instead, my sister is dead, and I'm working off a family debt in this place. Life happens and when it doesn't happen the way we expect it to we get angry."

Judah had never had anyone speak so frankly to him of tragedy. Most people grew uncomfortable when he dared show anger instead of the two television-acceptable emotions: grief for his loss or positive exuberance at being still alive. No one ever expected the anger…the bitterness.

They stared at each other in tense yet somewhat companionable silence.

Judah said, "I'm sorry," just as Adelaide said the same. They burst out laughing. It was a comfortable sound.

"Old scars," Adelaide said.

Judah nodded. "Yep. Old scars." He looked into her blue eyes for a moment then said, "I should go downstairs. I'll pay the full rate—"

She leaned forward and pressed her lips to his. Judah stiffened in surprise, but she didn't pull away. After a moment he kissed her back. Tentatively at first, then with vigor.

The kiss was broken when he laughed. She gave him a puzzled look. "I don't know where to put my hands," he said.

Adelaide smiled back, crinkling the corners of her eyes. Judah had never seen a smile so beautiful. "I'll show you," she said.

The camera crew showed up, and Seth rushed outside. The crew's truck had KRTV on the side, the station known for gossip and celebrity dirt scandals. Seth heard people complain about the content, but the magazines flew off the shelves, and the station's ratings went up every year.

"You're late," Seth said. "Hurry up. I want the first shot of him coming down the stairs with the girl. Then you can hit him with the questions."

Judah and Adelaide lay in the tangled sheets, his arms looped loosely around her. His robotic leg still stood beside the bed; the sheet covered his stump. He wondered if he should put the leg back on and was surprised to discover he didn't feel the need to.

"I don't ever want to leave this room," Adelaide said.

"So don't," Judah said.

"You know I have to." Judah felt her face heat and knew she was blushing. "The boss will be looking for me soon. You only paid for two hours."

"I'll pay for more if I have to." Unconsciously, he tightened his arms around her. "I don't want you to go with anyone else."

"Judah, I have to. It's my job. I have a debt to pay."

"I have money," he pointed out. "Being an interplanetary war hero has its perks. The government pays me well to do their commercial spots for them. As long as I smile and play the good boy, it's fine."

Adelaide propped herself up on one elbow and looked down at him. "Rolling in it or not, I can't take your money. We met an hour ago. In a week or a month or a year, you'll slow down long enough to think I'm using you. And you wouldn't be wrong. I would hate myself for that."

"Look, we both want the same things, right?" Judah reached over and grabbed his communicator tablet from the chair where he'd left it. "We both want a life outside this place. I want to live a normal life after—" he gestured with the tablet toward his stump beneath the sheet, "—and you want a normal life after your sister. This isn't the way to get that life. I am."

Adelaide bit her lip and looked around the room.

"You know I'm right," Judah said. "Maybe it won't work, but maybe it will. All I know is I want to try. You are the first person I have had a genuine connection with since…you know. Actually, since *before* then."

Adelaide was silent a moment before saying, "I think there's something else you haven't considered."

"What's that?"

"You depend on that government sponsorship. What happens when word gets out that the golden boy of the propaganda machine falls in love with a whore? How do you think they'll react to that? What will you do for a living?"

"How will they ever know? The only person I ever told was I was coming here was my cousin, Seth, and he's not telling. It was his idea."

"How much do you trust your cousin, Judah? Is he a good person? A good friend?"

"He's family," he replied flatly. "I've known him my entire life."

She was silent, and he got the sense he hadn't answered her question.

"He's a good person. He's just rough around the edges."

"The way he talks to you though."

"He thinks it's good for me. And, sometimes it is. He's the only one who treated me exactly as he did before that landmine took my leg off. He didn't pity me. Didn't coddle me. I don't know how to repay that."

"I see," Adelaide said reluctantly.

"So you'll come away with me?"

"Are you sure?"

"I'll show you how sure I am." Judah tapped a few buttons on the tablet to bring up the whorehouse selection app and started scrolling through the members. "Is this you?" He showed her the screen to confirm he had pulled up her profile and she nodded. He tapped a few more buttons to bring up the Lifetime Purchase amount, not hesitating at the many zeros scrolling the screen, and pressed the confirmation button, then accepted the conditions, then watched the transfer be completed. "There. It's done. You're free."

"Judah…"

He pulled her face down to his. "Adelaide, in the last year I haven't looked ahead any further than the next commercial spot. Every time I'd think one month ahead, or of next year, I choke. I thought of killing myself more than once because I couldn't find a point to living. I don't feel like that with you. I want to know what comes next. Maybe it won't work. Maybe it will. I can't promise perfect, but I can promise better than this."

Adelaide blue eyes searched his for a long time. Finally she said, "Judah?"

"Yes?"

"Let's get the hell out of here."

He kissed her and whooped with joy.

Judah and Adelaide walked hand in hand down the stairs.

The proprietor said, "I see you had a good time. Maybe I should have charged more for the two hours."

Adelaide dropped Judah's hand and hung her head. Judah's face turned red, but it wasn't for embarrassment. He took her hand again. The owner smirked.

Judah said, "Adelaide will be quitting tonight."

The proprietor's expression turned dour. "She can't quit. She's got obligations." The last word was said in sing-song mockery.

Judah said, "I've taken care of that. I'm sure you'll be happy with your end-of-day takings."

If the proprietor was surprised, he didn't show it. He merely snorted. "And when John Q public finds out their golden boy frequented my establishment? Hm? People don't like their heroes any way but squeaky clean."

Judah asked, "How will they ever know?"

"Oh, they'll know, cousin." Seth stepped into the foyer. The camera crew followed. The equipment and extra bodies made the lobby appear smaller. "Oh, don't look so surprised. Everyone loves seeing a cripple find love. Especially in a story as sappy as yours. It's kind of pathetic, really." Seth clapped his hands in front of his chest and fluttered his eyelashes. "Judah the war hero, the guy without a leg but a heart of gold finds love at a whorehouse." He dropped his hands. "See? Pathetic."

Judah was too shocked to be angry. "You planned this? Why?"

Seth said, "Because I hate you. I've always hated you. I've been waiting to knock you off your high horse since we were kids. You shattered my head, and you still got everything you ever wanted. Even after you lost your leg, people still catered to you even though you were just a freak."

Judah said, "That's ridiculous. Why would anyone be jealous of me? I saw combat. I saw friends die. I lost my *leg*. Who in their right mind would be jealous of that?"

Seth's face turned a putrid shade of red. "It served you right! Your stupid leg. How hard could it have been? You didn't feel it when they cut it off. You never had to work hard at anything. I had to work twice as hard at everything just to keep up. But you—you were golden. Well, now your cushy little golden boy job is over. Welcome to the real world, Judah."

The employees of the whorehouse poked their heads out of doors and lingered in hallways to see what the commotion was all about. The lobby was silent with shock. And the camera crew kept rolling.

Adelaide stepped forward and slapped Seth. "How dare you. You should be ashamed of yourself."

Seth rubbed his face where she'd struck him. A red welt in the shape of her hand rose to his cheek. "Oh, look the little do-gooding whore. I hope he fucked you good, little whore because this place will be famous for the scandal. You'll get it from everyone now. Really, you should be thanking me. I just made you a pile of money, and all you have to do is lie on your back."

Judah lunged forward. He grabbed Seth by the front of his shirt and slammed his back against a wall. It was no contest. After the accident as children, Judah had always been careful with Seth. That restriction was gone now.

Over Judah's shoulder, Seth growled at Adelaide, still baiting her. "How was it fucking this scarred up freak anyway? Can he even get it up? Does his dick even work? Did you see his leg? You must be pretty desperate to fuck that."

Adelaide said quietly, "Everyone has scars."

Judah turned. Seth tried to wiggle away, but he pushed him into the wall again. Over his shoulder, he said, "Adelaide, no. The cameras."

Adelaide pulled her nightgown up, the scar on her torso clearly visible against her pale skin.

Seth laughed. "Get into a knife fight sweetheart?"

Adelaide studied him calmly. "No. I gave a kidney to my sister. Everyone has scars. Everyone has been through something that changed them. Even you."

Seth said, "I don't look anything like you freaks."

"Who are you calling a freak?" The tall woman in the slinky black dress, the one Seth had been eyeing earlier took her shirt off, too. Her perfect breasts turned out to be only one perfect breast. The other was missing a nipple. A six-inch scar transected the middle. Another woman lifted her hair to show a scar running down the side of her neck.

A man, the pretty one, took his shirt off displaying an elaborate tattoo along his ribcage. It read: Gay and proud of it. "I *was* in a knife fight. My father tried to kill me when I came out. I covered the scar with this tattoo."

Seth looked around the room, sneering. "You're all a bunch of freaks. Who has a whorehouse with a bunch of scarred up freaks?"

"I do," the proprietor said. He bent forward and pulled up his pant leg. His leg was a mass of melted tissue that crawled up out of sight. "I was in a house fire when I was a kid."

Seth looked around the room at all the half-naked men and women and the scars on prominent display.

"This is great stuff," the cameraman whispered to the reporter. "We'll air this tonight. The ratings are going to go through the roof."

The reporter gave him a disgusted look and reached over to flick a switch, turning the camera off. The reporter undid his tie, then the top of his shirt, and Judah saw a thick white scar that ran across his neck and down into his shirt. "I'm not airing this," he said. "I'm no different than they are." He reached over again, pushed a button, and a small disc popped out the side of the camera. The cameraman gasped and lunged for the disc, but the reporter was faster. He dropped the disc and stepped on it, it crunching beneath his polished shoe. The cameraman fell to his knees trying to scrape together the pieces.

"Get out, Seth," Judah said. He released his hold on Seth and stepped back. "Get out before I do something I will never regret. I never want to see you again."

"I'll tell everyone," Seth said. "I'll go on air and tell them all—"

Judah hit him, the power of his arm driving Seth to the ground.

"Get out," Judah said again. "And if you tell anyone…" Judah grinned. The grin was cold. "I told you, I didn't drive a desk in the war, Seth. You wouldn't stand a chance against anything I throw at you."

Seth looked into Judah's eyes for a moment, then scrambled toward the door. Judah let him go.

The lobby was silent with remaining tension. Cautious glances were thrown, and drinks were poured as the tension leaked out of the room.

Adelaide approached Judah and laid a hand on his arm. "Are you all right?"

"I don't know," Judah said, still looking out the door Seth had fled through. "I wanted to hurt him. Maybe even kill him."

"But you didn't. You proved you can control your anger. You can heal."

Adelaide wrapped her arms around his waist. Judah put one arm around hers and held her close.

She asked, "Where do we go from here?"

"Forward," Judah said. "We go forward."

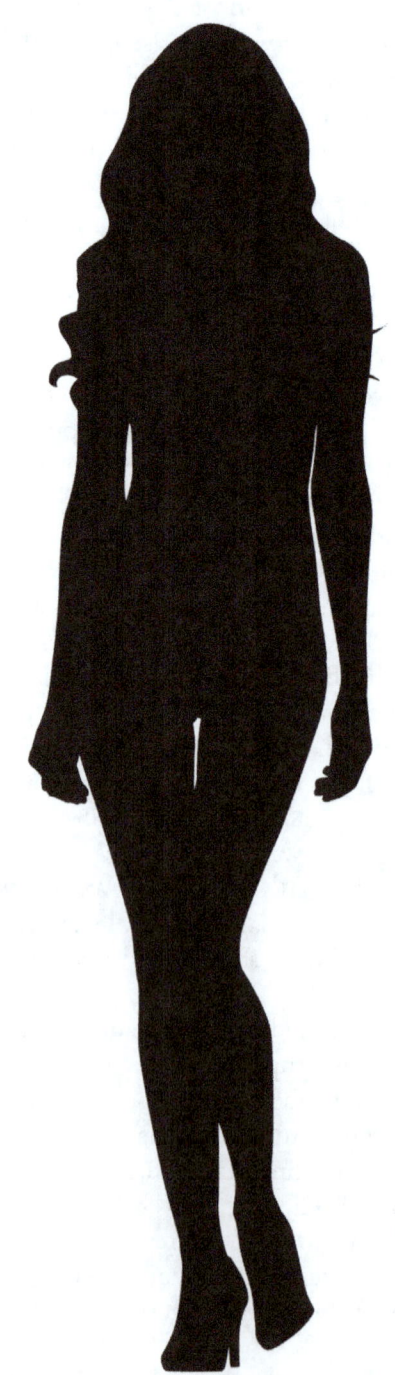

Rei Rosenquist is a queer agender (they/them) speculative and contemporary fiction writer who depicts a wide variety of identities struggling to find a place in a wide variety of worlds. They are also a lifelong barista, baker, and nomad. Over the years, they have traveled to many countries, engaged many peoples, picked up new habits, and learned new languages. But, some things never change. For them, the constants of life are made up of love stories, great coffee, delicious food, and traveling. Rei's work can be found in Enter the Aftermath *by* TANSTAAFL Press, Beauty & Wickedness *by Blackbird Publishing, and* Midwinter Fae *by Blackbird Publishing. You can also find more of Rei's work by visiting their website reirosenquist.com. Stay in touch by connecting via Facebook (Rei Rosenquist), Instagram (@rylrosenquist) and Twitter (@rylrosenquist).*

RUNNING FROM LOVE, ALREADY LOST

by Rei Rosenquist

The sky was moonless, speckled with stars. The air was still and warm, smelling of tall wavering grass that lined the dirt road on both sides. In the distance, tall pine trees stood tall on undulating hills, their arms reaching toward the black sky in silent reverie. The only sound in the air was the crickets and cicadas buzzing and chirping, loudly belting out their unnerving song for the roaming wild dogs and snoozing cattle to hear.

A perfect night for a post-funeral run through the darkened roads lined with the quietly watching houses of Kora's childhood.

Already midnight, Kora noted from the lens display of the rented jogging goggles. An app monitored the rate at which the cream cheese frosting she'd eaten was burning off. *Slowly,* Kora pouted drunkenly and pushed on up the steep gravel grade. Stupid, having that second dessert. And that fifth glass of wine.

Dark night. Bad day. Mistakes happen.

Which was exactly why Kora was out here running. To blow off the mistakes of this tiny town. And it was tiny. The one-stop post office. The general store that was just stuff bought at a big box store in the city and resold. The dirt paths clogged with fading tracks of tractors long since rusted out. The neighbors who knew your whole life story.

Like Mac, Kora thought. *Like trying to kiss Mac.*

Kora ran harder.

She swallowed, the syrah's bitter tannins refusing to fade. Sweat stung her eyes. Why was it so hot? Missouri in October should be cool, shouldn't it? But Leila, both travel agent, and friend, had said it was the hottest year on record. Big surprise. Yet another hit of bad luck to add to life's roster.

One piece that wasn't bad luck? Leila actually finding a hotel in this hiccup of a town. Not easy. Kora had always stayed with family or friends. Only this year, that wasn't an option. For a lot of reasons—all of them complicated. All of them were other people's problems now, though, and more than anything, Kora wanted to avoid everyone and everything about this place. So, Kora had enlisted the help of the unstoppable force that was Leila. She managed to get Kora booked in the only room in the only "hotel" within fifty miles.

It should have been nothing more than a room in a stranger's house. Only, that stranger turned out to be Mac's cousin, twice removed, who ran development in the next town over and rented rooms to make some extra bucks. Kora only knew that because said cousin left Mac with the responsibilities of check-in and check-out.

Small town, Missouri. Who's surprised?

Only Kora *had* been surprised, ridiculous as that was.

Check-in hadn't been awkward *at all.* Not even one bit. Ha. The two of them kept trying not to make eye contact; Mac fumbling with the keys while muttering something in a thick Missouri twang that Kora had a hard time understanding these days; Kora fussing with a bright teal over-sized bag, pretending like it was cumbersome even though it only had a small blanket and pillow stuffed inside. Then, Mac had opened the door and said those deadly words.

"Get you a drink after the funeral? For old times' sake."

Of course Kora had said yes, like a fool. They drank, and the past came bubbling back up like fizz in a bottle of champagne, and then Kora did what Kora did best. Darted. Out of the bar, back to Mac's cousin's place, grabbed a few items, and headed out for this run. She was trying to shake off the weight of the past. But even that wasn't working because here was Kora thinking about all of it.

Mom. The hitting and the screaming, the drinking and the throwing things. And Kora running. Always the running. To Mac's place. To Barb's yard. To the stables of unused barns.

Anywhere but home.

A cool breeze rattled the dry grass edging the running path, carrying with it a strange concoction of magnolias and dead fish. The magnolias reminded Kora of late summers in California. That yearly escape from Missouri. A week on Pappy's avocado farm in Southern California. Those had been happy, golden-tinged days.

Against the sweet floral air, the rotting flesh was a sharp reminder. Nothing good lasts.

Kora pressed on. The blocky press-board barn lay just ahead. It was cheaply slapped together, just like the rest of this town. But then, it wasn't so much a destination as it was an excuse. A place to escape to. Just like before. The blocky shape on the horizon itself was a comfort. Kora pushed harder, huffing and sweating, aching to reach those ugly barn doors.

As Kora approached and pulled off the jogging goggles, the barn came into full color. A bold rust red reminder of how cheap the structure was. Lilting to the left, those walls were. All four about to crumble—like everything in this town. Worn down, busted up, left broken until someone happened to remember. Then, poorly cobbled back together. Duct tape, super glue, ice packs and ace bandages. Y'know, whatever you could find in the kitchen junk drawer.

Kora spat out a sardonic laugh at the hanging barn door. Not because anything was funny. But out of defense. As if to say: *You're dead. You can't scare me anymore.*

In response, the voices of past lovers bubbled up out of the gaping black arch of a mouth.

Stan-the-runner saying, "You need help." Darlene-the-accountant saying: "Broken beyond repair." Corry-the-bartender adding, "You're a real mess," in that clipped tone that meant more than the words. Meant you were a disappointment just for existing. And finally Leila, the beautiful openly trans travel agent, confirming Corry's words with, "It'd just... never work out."

And Mac? What about Mac? something gentle somewhere in Kora's mind asked in a reminding voice.

Well, yes. Mac would bring a bottle of wine inside regardless of the state of things. Try to make Kora feel...not better but just less bad. If only for a while.

Good old Mac. Some things never change.

Kora pushed open the rusted gate. It complained at having to do its goddamn job.

"Hey," came a voice, when Kora was hoping for nothing but a roosting murder of crows.

Kora started. "Oh, um. I'm sorry. I didn't think anyone was here, and I—"

"Don't mind. Come on in."

The voice sounded like a high tenor, dark and broody. As if Kora and this stranger had the exact same reason for coming out here. Might as well see who it was. Kora shut down the jogging app, noting how few calories had burned, and toed into the barn.

"I'm chillaxin' in the loft. Come on up."

Kora, used to taking instruction, good at following direction, found the ladder and climbed up. There, lo and behold, leaning against a tousled bale of hay was the very person Kora had been trying to avoid. Hair a silver-blue slab of too-much hair product, eyes a smoky moody 1990's emo-punk-band raccoon mask. Silver and neon green pump-up Nike trainers with hot pink twizzle laces, like this scene was stuck in the 90's. Plump legs stuck out straight from the soft, pear-shaped body. "Barb."

And in the first flash of those brown eyes, every brutal childhood memory hit. A twenty-foot wave, rising up, and there was Kora standing unsuspecting on the beach, blank face to the ocean. It came crashing down, white froth of endless heavy nights. Two bodies pressed together. Aching, bruised and beaten in. Crumpled up, that's how life had been back then. A dirty cardboard egg crate Mama used to crinkle up with one hand and throw with a frown on the backyard bonfire made of trash.

"Kora," Barb said with one of those not-quite smiles.

Kora stopped short on the ladder in a sudden sweat, desperate to slink away. Hide. Escape. Kora had one wish coming back to this shit hole town. Avoiding Barb. That'd been it.

"Imagine finding you here." A cheesy cheese-face grin on Barb's face beamed back. Too late.

"For the record, I found you here," Kora huffed.

Barb waved a wrist layered in tarnished bangles. "Does it matter?"

Kora frowned. "I think it does."

"You think everything matters when it doesn't."

"Bacon bits of wisdom."

"Come on, have a smoke with me."

"Oh, what the hell. I'm already this far up," Kora said with blunt resolve.

"Yeah, you are," Barb said and winked, seeing through the deflection.

Kora clamored up onto the loft's hay-padded landing and with a sobering sigh, leaned back against the rough splintering wood beside Barb. It felt like leaning into a handful of acupuncture needles all at once. No good came of it, but the pain was only mildly irritating.

"Your voice's changed," Kora said, looking at Barb's new elaborately loud hair-do and outfit. Still screaming for attention that wouldn't come from anyone around these parts.

"So it has," Barb leaned forward, a hand extending a cigarette.

"So. What do we talk about now?" Kora took it, took a short puff, coughed, and handed it back. Feeling drunk was bad enough. Adding tobacco jitters didn't feel like any fun.

Barb accepted and dragged on it, hard and long. "I'm wondering why you're in jogging clothes with a heart-tracker on and you can't handle a little teeny bit of smoke. You got some kind of health problem now?"

"As a matter of fact, I do." Kora lied, hoping Barb wouldn't dig in.

It wasn't really a health "issue" as much as an image problem. But the people here in backcountry didn't need to know that. That Kora didn't have it together yet.

Barb did what Barb always used to do as kids, flicked the cigarette butt off the edge of the loft, rolled those big brown eyes, and laughed, full-belly.

"Sure," Barb laughed some more, holding the pack of cigarettes up. "Everyone around here has one addiction or another."

"It's not an addiction," Kora huffed a little too drunkenly. "Why can you never take anything I do seriously?"

Even in the dim light, Kora could feel Barb's eyes roll. "I'm trying to help you feel better."

"It's not working. That call-shit-out attitude never worked on me," Kora pouted, secretly just wanting Barb to drop the subject.

Barb shrugged. "What can I say? We were kids. That was ages ago."

"Twenty-two years, six months, two days, and thirteen hours."

Barb's shocked silence was a kind of prize in and of itself. "You've got to be joking."

"I am," Kora admitted, laughing.

Barb laughed again, only now it was genuine. The soft curves of Barb's body rolled like thunder from a sky pent up too long with too many electrons. Or is it neutrons? Whatever causes lightning to strike. It struck Kora now in a new light. Something about Barb had indeed changed. Lightened from the bitter kid into someone genuine and real. Maybe it was just age, time inevitably passing—but the softening had made Barb gentle and more…beautiful. Yes, that was it. And the sound of that laugh—spiked and shrill—was a downpour in a drought of tension and fear.

It was infectious. Like a yawn or a sneeze from someone who's caught this year's iteration of the bird flu. From sheer proximity, Kora couldn't help but catch it. Take all the bitter pills you want—no good. Nothing against this rumbling mirth. It was cracking the both of them up.

Time passed without notice. The storm of giddiness seemed to pass, then a giggle would set them back off. Or a look. Or a snort. The stars shifted, and two old friends laughed and laughed into the darkness. Eventually, exhausted, they leaned together as the soft blue glow of coming dawn spread like butter across the distant grasses outside.

"You know, Kor," Barb finally managed to gasp in between dying laughs. "Your crazy mama was—"

Kora snapped up and slapped sweaty palms to-gether. A different kind of thunder. "Oh Barb. Don't start that now."

"Oh." Barb stared wide-eyed in shock, mouth a gaping hole.

Kora rubbed stinging hands together and looked away sheepishly. "Too firm?"

Barb's head shook, and a chunk of silver-blue gel-caked hair fell like a slab across Barb's brow. "I'm just surprised to see you all grown up and taking charge. Not the Kora I recall."

"The Kora you recall is six years old forever."

Barb's smile faded to that old scarred-up frown. "That's because things felt stuck back then. But I guess we've both changed, haven't we?"

"Inevitably. That was what, ten years ago?"

"Twelve, actually. But to be honest, I'm glad to see you."

Kora hesitated, unsure how to reply. "I've been trying to avoid you because I'm still afraid of our past," just didn't sound right.

Barb turned to face Kora, twisting onto the side of a robust thigh. That thigh, with its unique curvature and big dimple like a crater right below the full ass cheek still reminded Kora of their long secret nights, tucked beside one another, crying silently in this same barn. Both their houses, not a kilometer away, but another world. A place where parents claimed to love their kids and then beat them to blood. A place where lessons left black and blue sized lessons the shape of golf clubs and sores the shape of cigarette butts. A place where all the trauma drama of their tangled-up lives earned them the term "troubled youth."

Kora's mama was dead, buried, in the ground. At the funeral, everyone'd said, "Welp, now that's done," in a voice that wasn't really sad enough. Kora wanted to believe them, too, but something felt stuck.

Barb put a hand over Kora's. "You got me through those years. You know that, right?"

Kora nodded. "You too," came out hitched and thin.

The words hung.

Chances were, Barb already knew. Knew that Kora had never really moved on. Not from Barb. Not from home. Not from the "propensity to look for abusive relationships" as Kora's counselor would

say. Not just Dr. Harmon, either. One after another after the next. Kora kept giving up on counseling. Not because they were wrong. They were right, but it didn't seem to make any difference. No matter what, Kora just kept coming up with short-ended sticks.

Stan, the clinically diagnosed narcissist. Darlene, the bitter alcoholic who bluntly refused to quit. Corry, the overprotective meth addict who dragged Kora into a codependent relationship. And Leila who was just too put together to want anything to do with the likes of Kora.

"What about Mac. You run into each other yet?" Barb asked.

Kora blanched, wanting to lie. But there was no reason to lie, really. They'd run into one another the same as Kora and Barb. Completely by accident. And yet, Kora had gone out drinking with Mac, al-most kissed him, and now? Well, now Kora was con-fused. Was their post-funeral drinking going to turn into something? Or was this just a "funeral fling" like Kora had promised herself she could have. Just a warm body to help her get through the tough stuff. Like saying goodbye to the cancer-devoured body of a mother who'd never apologized for anything. Like seeing the house, the stable, the barn. Like running into Barb.

Besides, it'd never work. Mac was genuinely nice, which was exactly why it'd never last.

I don't know how to do nice.

"Why did you come back?" Barb's voice cut in when Kora didn't answer back.

"What? My mom died. I had to—"

"You know nobody would have held it against you, not coming. That monster beat the spit and snot out of you every day. We'd have understood."

"We," Kora scoffed. "Who? You mean the walls?"

Who else was left? The pastor from the church no-one had ever attended? The two ex-husbands who were both remarried? The step-kids who want-ed nothing to do with Kora or her mom or Fishtail, Missouri?

"I mean me," Barb said and looked away.

Kora coughed to cover the shock to the heart. "Ma had lung and breast cancer, Barb," Kora deflect-ed instead of saying, "Thank you."

"I say she got what she deserved," Barb spat.

Kora flinched. "She tried to do her best."

"Debatable."

It was as if Barb's head had been transformed. And there sat Dr. Harmon, and every other doctor Kora had seen over the years. All of them, with that exact same look on their face. The pursed lips and narrowed eyes, down-turned frowning eyebrows that said things like "it isn't your fault" and "you need to break away" and "debatable."

"I couldn't stay away forever," was Kora's typical excuse.

"You know," Barb stood, stooping there in the loft, hands on knees for support. "I never understood why you loved that demon of a mother but didn't love youself back. But now, I get it."

"What do you mean?"

Barb brushed past, walking in a duckish way for the ladder. Stopping briefly, one hand came up from knee to Kora's shoulder. It was warm and gentle as it'd always been. It grated the nerves.

"Go look in a mirror for a while."

"What's that supposed to mean?"

"Try it out. You'll see," Barb said and staggered down the ladder.

"Hey!" Kora called out, but Barb was already gone without another word.

Back in the center of town, Mac had turned up outside Kora's place, wanting to talk. When Kora pulled up, the first thing Mac did was hold out a bag from the general store.

"Let's go to my place," Mac had suggested.

Kora had leaned in and peaked inside the bag, feeling obliged to go with Mac without really knowing why. Most likely, the very expensive bottle of pinot noir. Spending more time with Mac was a good excuse as any to get drunk.

And yet, thirty minutes later, it still sat uncorked on Mac's kitchen counter. Meanwhile, Kora was staring into a frowning face reflected in the polished stainless-steel refrigerator door.

"Do I look busted up?" Kora said, already drunk.

"No, you look like you," Mac said from the center living room where there were ritz crackers with processed yellow cheese from the mini-mart down the street. "Come on, have some food."

"What? Are you saying I'm drunk?" Kora laughed lopsidedly.

"Not exactly," Mac answered diplomatically.

"Because I am. I had some Jack Daniels on the way here," Kora laughed and flumped into the overly worn periwinkle love seat. A big floor pillow was reclining against the chewed up leg of a box-store DIY coffee table that looked like it should be thrown out. Kora set both black fishnet covered feet on top of the pillow to avoid the carpet. Carpets are dirty, no matter what. No sense messing a good pair of stockings. "Now, Mac."

"Yes?" He picked up a cheese and cracker stack and offered it to Kora, who snubbed it like a rude friend in high school.

"You are single."

"Yes."

"Good," Kora leaned in, hand on Mac's knee.

Mac frowned. "And not looking."

"Tch," Kora laughed, but had the sense to remove the hand. "Everyone is 'looking for love.'"

"I guess maybe that's one way of looking at the world. But I think I'm happy with how things are."

"*How things are,*" Kora mocked. "As if loneliness is hip and cool these days. Oh sorry, I forgot. It is."

"What's that supposed to mean?" Mac picked up another stack and offered it to her again.

Again, Kora snubbed it. "In New York, at least. Everyone's into being lonely and feeling sorry for themselves and throwing pity parties. All the rave."

"That's not what I meant. I just...if I were looking for love, it probably wouldn't come."

"Tsk tsk. Pessimism is never attractive," Kora said and uncorked the wine. "Full glass or half?"

"Half, please."

"See what I mean?"

Mac's puppy dog brown eyes rolled. "I see what you did there."

"Can't an old high school friend tease?"

"You always teased, K. And see where it got us?" Mac said in a not entirely careful way. One, Kora thought, that was full of the past. Full of two lives that'd never aligned. Full of sadness and regret.

"Ha!" Kora pranced about, proud to have earned Mac's concern. It felt like a gold star on a report from your favorite teacher.

"What'd I say?" Mac stood in the center of the show, confused.

"I knew it. You want me. You want me bad!"

"I don't," came out hesitantly from Mac's suddenly unpleasant face.

Kora frowned. "But you *did*."

"Not like that. I just always wanted to see you happy."

"Happy," Kora muttered and mentally flipped through every page in the book of model relationships. All of them went like this: friends, fun, sex, compassion, love. But model relationships were like model houses. They looked good in their pre-made little block of the neighborhood, but you didn't live in them. They just sat there looking pretty until a storm came and tore them apart. Or, they got shoved on the back burner and fell apart all their own. Mac was a back-burner kind of love, Kora guessed.

Mac's eyes were looking at Kora's face, studying it, sad. "That never really happened, did it?"

"What? Happiness? Overrated. Besides, model-wise, you and I are doing great. We're already on fourth base."

"Wait, what?" Mac gaped, stumbled, tripped over the edge of the ridiculous shag rug, and nearly fell over. A shower of red wine cascaded from the toppling glass and went everywhere.

"You know…" Kora ran through the basics, then held up a full wine glass and downed a third of it. "And you have enough compassion for the both of us, so that puts us at fourth base. Home run, coming up."

Mac laughed, suddenly amused instead of humdrum, then grimaced when he saw the wine sink into the carpet. "Well, that's not how baseball works, and it's certainly not how I think of us."

Kora moved toward the kitchen for a wet towel, feeling the downsides of drinking. Fuzzy logic, bad balance, feeling bloated.

"Sorry for coming on to you. I must be off my head." Kora said, and mentally added: talking too much.

Mac came over and took the towel Kora was drenching under the faucet. Wringing it out, Mac edged around the bar and slipped back into the living room to pat off the big stain soaking into the light grey carpet. Kora came back in, sheepishly leaning against the far wall.

"But really. I am sorry," came out of Kora's lips softly. It splashed on the carpet. Another kind of stain soaking in: shame. Always more shame. Covering everything.

"It's alright," Mac patted the rug, spraying some cleaner on the spot, and standing up.

"I always make a mess of things, I guess."

"It's not that." Mac came a little too close. Kora could smell the wine soaking into both their breaths.

"You were always so understanding."

"I've always cared about you Kora," Mac said in that voice that negates lust. It's so earnest Kora nearly chokes.

Mac's face scrunched up. "Did I say something wrong?"

Kora shrugged stiffly. "Not exactly."

"Then, what is it?"

Mac's face was a perfect example of what the issue was. Eyes carefully focused. Body poised, not too close as to be pushy but not too far away as to be distant. Lips in one of those careful not-smiling but not-frowning "open" expressions. Hands held palms out. Everything about Mac said: peace. Kindness. Nice.

"You're too good for me," Kora said and turned for the door. "I should never have come."

"Kora," Mac called, just as Kora's hand hit the doorknob. "Wait."

"Why?" Kora's voice was hot and sharp. "You're right. I don't deserve someone like you. I'm too much of a fuck up. I deserve Barb."

"You don't mean that."

"I don't know what I mean," Kora sobbed, bitter, ugly tears dripping from tightly closed eyes.

You can't even do a fling right.

"Wait, please," came softly from over Kora's shoulder.

Words were supposed to come out, but instead it was a blubbering, slobbering embarrassing mess. Hiccups seized the chest next, and in an instant, Kora was slipping down the wall, and everything inside was busting at the seams.

"Why am I such a mess!" She sounded so shrill it practically broke the wine glasses.

"Oh, Kora, honey," Mac whispered more to the room than to Kora. "I'm so sorry."

"J-j-just don't make me go. P-p-please."

"Of course not. Come back and sit. Please. I'll leave you alone if that's what you need."

Kora reached up and grabbed Mac by the fore-arms so her knuckles went bright white. Red indents appeared where Kora gripped. Feet floundered drunkenly. Tunnel vision. Heart shuddering and sputtering—that damned leaky valve. Kora managed to make it to the couch before bursting into more sobs.

Mac sat there quiet the whole time. And each time Kora would look up, Mac had a glass of water. A bag to vomit in. A cool towel. A handful of crackers.

Mac did everything right. And in Kora's heart, it should have meant more than just a good friend, shouldn't it? And yet, all Kora could think is one thing.

"I've messed it all up with Barb."

"I doubt that," Mac would say, over and over again.

But Kora couldn't let it go. "Barb'll hate me forever."

"No—"

"Mac. Barb called me my Ma."

"I doubt that's what they meant," Mac's brow furrowed so deep it might as well have cracked.

"Told me to look in the mirror. Said I hadn't changed a scratch. And you know what?"

"N-no, what?" Mac stammered, wide-eyed.

Sweet Mac, who'd grown up as the innocent and sheltered neighbor kid who'd always been told to go home at just the right time. Mac who, when the truth finally got out, did the good-neighborly thing and became a stable hand. Not to get under the girls' skirts like everyone in the whole town joked. But to look out for them. To be a voice in the dark.

Well. Those days were gone and sweet model-house Mac was in for the big surprise of the night. Because Kora was tired of being that way. It was time to change. And not with jogging trackers and heart-rate counters and calorie restrictions. Getting a new face when the same old junk was hanging around. No. It was time to let it out.

"Barb's right; I looked. And you know who was there, looking at me from your fridge door? Ma. All the way."

"That's not what I see." Mac drew in now, hands on the couch not on Kora's leg. But close enough to feel their warmth. Always waiting, Mac was, for Kora to reach back. "I see someone who is struggling

to overcome the weight of the world. And doing a damn good job." He paused, a lopsided smile turning up the corner of his mouth. "Well, maybe not doing so good tonight, but…you get my point."

"You're too kind," tumbled out of Kora's parted lips. It wasn't bitter or sarcastic, snarky or snappy. It wasn't New York, that's for sure. It just was.

"No. You've changed, and I'm sure Barb sees it."

Kora reached for Mac's hands. "You think?"

"Why else would Barb say to look in the mirror?"

Kora held up the wine glass and downed another third of it. "Because I'm still a wreck."

"Barb is trying to help you. And I think it's time you were honest back."

Kora was about to play the old game. Ask: "what's that mean?" and pretend it wasn't obvious. That the only reason Kora was here at Mac's house fighting about Barb was because Barb's opinion was the one that mattered the most. More than Mac's or Ma's or anyone else's in all the world.

Above all, it was Barb.

"You think I could ask Barb to come to New York?"

"For good?" Mac's eyes narrowed. "Doubtful."

"Heh," Kora laughed. "Big dreams, Mac. No. Not yet anyway. Just for…y'know. A visit."

Mac shrugged. "What harm can it do?"

Kora slumped against the couch. Knowing the standard flavor of reality—bitter and too strong—the honest answer was: "A lot."

"I think it's worth a shot," Mac said more sincerely and patted Kora's arm.

"Maybe."

"Sleep on it. You need some rest. Come on."

Kora went to stand, then decided it wasn't worth it and slumped back onto the couch. "Mind if I just sleep here tonight?"

Mac chuckled sadly, already reaching for the familiar ruby red blanket that was worn to shreds all around the edges. "Just like old times."

Kora took it and wrapped it around the way-too-expensive fishnet stockings. Part of the high life Kora was trying to use to stuff the hurtful feelings down inside of her. *So big city of me. Foolish big city.*

At least I burned off the calories of the wine crying my guts out.

"Just like old times," Kora said as Mac flicked off the light.

"Sweet dreams," Mac paused outside of his bedroom's door jamb. "Sleep alright."

"I'll try."

Their mantra, their friendship, their trust in one another's good intentions—all unchanged.

Just like old times.

First thing that next morning, Kora got up and phoned Barb.

"Where are you?"

"Where else? Big Rooster Cafe."

"I'm coming," Kora said and hung up without explanation.

The Big Rooster Cafe was a divey greasy spoon that stayed open twenty-four hours at the gas station during their childhood. Nowadays, it was open for "All Day Breakfast" from noon to three in the afternoon. The smell of fried chicken, ancient canned coffee brewed through a dirty sock, and burnt margarine toast never left the air. Mare, the wait-staff, had silver hair and had worked there since Kora was born, eternally wiping down tables and taking orders on a grimy notepad with carbon paper that served absolutely no purpose.

Kora came in to the jingle of a broken bell, took one look around, and spotted Barb in the usual corner booth. Sliding on to the red vinyl bench, Kora flashed a toothy grin. "I found you."

Barb sucked light brown chocolate milkshake from a blue and white striped straw. "You always find me. But for the record, I found you way before now."

Kora leaned a cheek into a propped up hand, knowing just what Barb meant. It was just like Mac had said. "You did. My defender."

Barb slid the milkshake away, frowning, picking at a basket of greasy over-cooked fries. "But it was never enough."

Kora reached out, tentatively placing a hand over Barb's. "I think it is now."

"Now is the same as before you came."

"No. Mac and I talked. I get it."

"It's about time," Barb chuckled, trying to fill the booth with mirth. But it fell short. "But that doesn't change things."

"Are you saying you won't take my invitation to come back to New York with me, then?" Kora tried

to say it off-hand, playful. Like if it were brought up as half a joke, it wouldn't hurt so bad when the answer was no.

As expected, Barb didn't look up but kept picking at a single fry until it was a potatoey pulp. After a long pause, an uneven tenor voice managed to squeeze out between pursed lips and a tense jaw. "I'm saying I love you too much to come. Correct."

Kora pulled away, back straightening, face hard as a rock. Eyes flashed, suddenly angry, trying to hide her pain. "What's that supposed to mean?"

"It means I don't want to become another piece in the game you've been playing since we were kids. You always loved your suffering more than any person."

"How dare you!" Kora shouted and slapped the table.

Barb pulled back away as condensation from the milkshake glass dribbled off the edge of the table. "See what I mean?"

"I don't see anything!" Kora shouted louder.

Then froze.

The words sounded exactly like Ma. Tone and all. And for a brief moment, the whole world stood still. Every detail jumped out as important. The curves on the glass of Barb's drink. A smudge on the windowpane. The clouds, grey and heavy thunderheads passing outside their window. Kora's mouth hung open, hollow and empty. Every possible excuse, blasted away.

"We're too much the same," Barb said from a million light-years away.

"Y-you're not wrong," tumbled out of Kora's gaping lips. "But that's why I..."

Kora's words died. Barb's crumpled-up, frowning face already said it all. *That's why you what, Kora? Thought you'd swoop in from New York and fix everything and everyone in one dramatic loving swoon?*

Yes. That had been her plan at first. Come back, make a big show of how grown up, how fixed she already was. How much she'd changed simply by leaving this place behind. But, Barb had seen right through that act. And Mac's counsel had helped Kora see that, if she wanted to truly change, she had to do the work. And that would take time.

A silence spread between them.

Barb broke it first. Not Kora. Same as usual. That also had to change. "If I came to New York with you, we'd end up like your Mom and Jack. Or my dad and Sam."

Eyes, full of shame fell to Barb's mashed-up fry. Straight out of the freezer bag, that fry never even stood a chance to be good. Overcooked, served to the wrong person, and now—a pulp. It felt like a symbol for everything that was wrong in their lives.

Kora sagged. "You're right. But Barb. I'm ready to change."

Barb's big brown eyes were not cold or distant—but warm like the sun. "Good. Then go back to New York and change. But do it for you, not for me."

"I'm trying."

"I see that. And I'm so proud of you."

Kora looked deep into Barb's face. It was so full of resolve. And in that one look, all the begging and pleading planned back at Mac's apartment came crumbling down in a heap of useless dirt to the ground. Barb was saying "no."

Worse. Barb was saying "go."

And that single word was every truth that Kora had never wanted to hear. Every reality that Kora had been too afraid to admit. It was Barb's thighs pressed hard again Kora's body in the dark, long nights spent hiding from both their families in the barn loft. It was Barb's strong welder's arms curled around Kora's heaving middle. Barb's gentle but calloused hand pressing a dripping bag of gas station ice against yet another bruise. An alcohol swab carefully cleaning out another wound. And just like the disinfectant, that word stung.

Kora's eyes blurred with tears. "I can't do this alone."

"You are never alone. I'll be right where I always am. Right here in Fishtail, waiting. And when you need a friend, I'm just a video call, text, and snapchat away."

"Friend," Kora said with disdain.

"Yes," Barb said, reaching Kora's hand. "Friend. Someone who means everything to me."

Kora hesitated. "Then, why just friend?"

Barb's silver-blue head shook. "I never said 'just.'"

"Wait what? You're the one who said *friends*," Kora said with an emotional punch, brow a craggy ravine of bitterness. "Stop playing games with me, and maybe we'd make some progress."

"I am not playing games," Barb said carefully. "My friends are the ones I love the most."

And right then, lightning had struck between them and turned the sands of time into glass—Kora got it. She had to work on herself first…her problems. Mend her fractured, leaking heart, before she could properly offer it to another.

At the moment, she didn't know how to be in a healthy relationship with Barb. Anything they'd have now would be marred by the sharp edges of their shared past. Right now, this was the best they could do together. This part-way-there love. It didn't look like anything Kora recognized in other couples, but she knew it was there.

Barb's scarred up, callous hand, reached out. There was hope in that gesture. Promise.

Kora took it, swift and firm. It felt warm and safe and right.

Barb squeezed, their fingers lacing so easily together. Kora's thin pianist's hands and Barb's tough farmer ones. Their eyes met, glistening, in the cheap greasy diner light.

"Okay?" Barb's bushy silver-blue eyebrow went up. So characteristic.

Kora nodded, trying to mimic that same depth of resolve. "Okay."

Barb lips curled into a rare full smile.

And for the first time, Kora didn't feel alone but supported. Held up instead of pressed down.

The floodgates in Kora's chest burst open. Out poured pain and in poured love in the same amount. It felt just like beginning again; she would do the work needed. Barb was worth it. *They* were worth it.

"You know right where to find me," Barb said with that old resolve.

"I do," Kora hiccupped, coming apart. "I do."

Copyright © 2018 by Rei Rosenquist.

USA Today bestselling author and two-time RITA nominee Anthea's books have received starred reviews in Library Journal *and* Publisher's Weekly, *and she has been named "one of new stars of historical romance" by* Booklist. *Make sure to pick up her full-length spicy historical romances, available online at all digital retailers. Anthea lives with her husband and daughter in sunny Southern California. In addition to writing historical romance, she plays the Irish fiddle and pens award-winning YA Urban Fantasy as Anthea Sharp.*

THE PIANO TUTOR

by Anthea Lawson

"My lady." The butler tapped at Diana Waverly's half-open door. "The piano tutor is here." He hesitated, a furrow marring his usually placid brow.

"Well, it *is* Wednesday." Diana laid her last black dress in the trunk she had been filling, then carefully closed the lid. "Tell Samantha it's time for her lesson. I'll be down directly."

The butler remained in the doorway, shifting his weight from foot to foot. "Forgive me, my lady, but it…er, it is not the customary piano tutor. It is an altogether different gentleman."

She blinked. "But—Mr. Bent is Samantha's tutor. We have no other."

"I tried to tell him as much, but the gentleman insists."

Diana stood, frowning. "I'll see to him." They had few callers—the inevitable result of turning down a season's worth of invitations—and never unannounced visitors.

Tucking up a stray auburn curl, she started down the hallway toward the wide second floor landing. Mr. Bent had said nothing of this. He was quite reliable—if a bit dour to be tutoring a girl still recovering from the loss of her father.

At the top of the stairs she halted, pulled from her thoughts by the sound of music pouring from the parlor below. Someone very skilled was playing the piano.

She rested her hand on the mahogany banister and listened. Note after note tumbled through the entryway, reverberating between the high ceiling and marble floors. Sunlight streamed through the landing windows, making the dust motes swirl and glitter like gilded dancers.

Her stepdaughter, Samantha, joined her, her wiry twelve-year old body leaning over the railing. "I didn't know Mr. Bent could actually *play* the piano."

"It's not Mr. Bent." That much was clear, though who it might be and why he was in her parlor was a mystery Diana could not fathom.

She descended the stairs, the music growing fuller and more present with every step. She paused a moment at the parlor door, then, with a fortifying breath, went in. The instant she crossed the threshold, the music ceased. The magic that had been spilling into the house folded in upon itself and disappeared.

But its source remained—a broad-shouldered man with brown hair and intelligent grey eyes. He stood when he saw her and bowed with an easy grace.

"My lady."

She studied the stranger. Handsome, undeniably, with those compelling eyes and a smile that seemed genuine. He looked nothing like the stoop shouldered and outmoded Mr. Bent. For one thing, he was a good deal younger—he looked to be no more than a handful of years older than herself.

"Sir?" She hardly knew what to say. "Please explain yourself."

"Viscountess Merrowstone." The stranger's voice was rich and complex, the syllables of her title unexpectedly smooth to her ears. "Mr. Nicholas Jameson, at your service. I've come to substitute for Mr. Bent, who has been called away unexpectedly."

"This is most irregular. I was not informed there was to be a replacement." She faced him squarely, ready to send him on his way. That was what she intended to do, but the words came out all wrong. "You play quite well."

He tipped his head, a smile lifting the corners of his mouth. "That would be a requirement, wouldn't it?"

"One would assume so." Though his bearing made her think he would be more suited to leaping a stallion over hedgerows than giving piano lessons to a twelve-year old. "You're quite certain you're a piano tutor?"

"Let me assure you of my qualifications." He extended an envelope. "I've a letter of recommendation from Lady Pembroke. You're acquainted, I believe?"

Diana nodded. Indeed, Lucy was a good friend, possessed of a generous spirit—though she was more than a little scandalous.

Henry had not approved of their friendship. Diana's gaze slipped past Mr. Jameson to the portrait of her late husband, Lord Henry Waverly, Viscount Merrowstone. His stern, formal features watched impassively, a cultivated remoteness in his expression. Solid and predictable in the portrait, just as in life. Lucy had annoyed him to no end.

Swallowing a sigh, Diana turned her attention to her friend's curling script.

Dearest Diana— I commend Mr. Nicholas Jameson to you as a piano tutor. He has provided my own Charlotte with lessons and has proven quite satisfactory. May I also point out—in case you had not noticed—that he is extremely handsome. He strikes me as a perfect diversion now that you have finally come out of mourning. I encourage you to take him on—in whatever capacities suit your needs. Pianists have such skilled hands.

She felt her cheeks burn as she glanced up at the gentleman in question. No doubt it had amused Lucy to have Mr. Jameson deliver such an outrageous "reference" in person.

"I see that she recommends you highly, sir," Diana said, biting her lip to avoid an embarrassed giggle. "I suppose we might consider having you." Oh dear, that hadn't sounded quite proper. She cleared her throat. "I mean *hiring* you. It wouldn't do to neglect Samantha's lessons while Mr. Bent is away."

"Oh, please hire him," Samantha said, peeking out from behind the doorway. She came in and stood on tiptoe to whisper in Diana's ear. "He seems ever so much nicer than Mr. Bent."

It was quite outside the regular course of things, yet there was no mistaking the eager note in Samantha's voice. No mistaking that Mr. Jameson was, as Lucy had mentioned, a very handsome man.

Her stepdaughter turned to him. "I heard you playing. It was marvelous! How do you do the part with your left hand? Could you show me?"

"Of course." He gave her an encouraging smile. "It's simple once you get the trick of it. Have you played any Mozart?"

"Oh yes!"

"Then you'll be able to master it easily. That is…." He raised a questioning brow at Diana.

"Oh, very well," she said. "It appears you will be our replacement tutor until Mr. Bent returns." She ignored Samantha's muffled squeal. "Can you begin today?"

A spark leapt into his eyes. "Immediately."

Looking at him made heat creep into her cheeks. Despite herself, Lucy's advice rang in her head. As if she would consider something so scandalous as commencing an affair with the piano tutor. Really, her friend had no sense of propriety.

Samantha hurried to seat herself at the piano bench. "I'm ready!"

Diana was not sure whether she herself was ready, but events seemed to be carrying her along. She settled into the nearby wingback and straightened the rich indigo skirts of her new dress. It was odd to wear colors again. She had grown so accustomed to the solid black of mourning that she felt vulnerable without it. A part of her wanted to retreat back into its safety—but that was not fair to Samantha. Diana could not deny the hopeful light in the girl's eyes, the flash of her rare grin as she attempted to mimic Mr. Jameson's command of the keyboard.

As was customary during Samantha's lessons, Diana picked up her newest copy of *The Ladies' Monthly,* but the fashion plates held no interest for her. Her eyes kept wandering from the illustrations to steal quick glances at the new tutor—his long-fingered hands as he played a run of notes, the way his brown hair tumbled over his collar. More than once he seemed to sense her attention and she had to quickly drop her gaze back to the unseen pages.

The sound of his voice was so different from Mr. Bent's dry tones, and his praise and encouragement drew another flashing smile from Samantha. Something inside Diana uncoiled a notch, a deep tension she had not realized she had been carrying.

The shape of his muscular shoulders was barely concealed by the cut of his coat as he leaned forward to demonstrate some point. He radiated confidence and mastery. She imagined that everything he did would benefit from that focused energy.

From this angle he was in profile. His jaw was firm, his nose straight, his mouth strong, yet sensitive. She traced her own lips with a fingertip, then caught herself and hurriedly dropped her hand before he could notice.

Mr. Jameson turned to face her. "Will you?" he asked.

Diana's breath faltered as their gazes held a heartbeat too long. Clearly she had missed an important turn in the lesson while daydreaming.

"Sing for us," Samantha said, a touch of impatience in her voice. "Mr. Jameson has been showing me a marvelous pattern for accompanying songs, but I don't think I can sing and play at the same time."

Diana set aside her magazine. "Oh—I really couldn't. It's been so long." There didn't seem to be enough air in the room for her to breathe, let alone sing.

"Of course you can." Mr. Jameson's tone was assured. "Miss Samantha says you have a lovely singing voice." There was a challenge in his expression, as if he were curious to see what she would do.

"Please, Mama. Let's do *The Meeting of the Waters*."

"Very well. If it's part of the lesson." She stood and took her place beside the piano, oddly reluctant to disappoint Mr. Jameson. Still, it had been a very long while. What if she had lost the knack altogether? "Samantha, you and Mr. Jameson must help by singing with me."

The piano tutor counted the tempo then signaled Samantha to begin. Diana took a deep breath and sang the first words. Mr. Jameson's rich baritone joined her, while her stepdaughter concentrated on the keyboard.

At first her alto sounded husky to her ears, the notes unsure. Soon enough, though, her body took over and she remembered how to breathe, how to put herself into the song and carry each tone to fullness. Mr. Jameson was solid beside her, his singing voice even fuller than she had imagined. When her pitch wavered, he was there, and soon their voices began to blend in a most pleasing manner. Unbidden, her eyes met his, and the appreciation there nearly made her lose the words. She forced her concentration back to the final phrases of the song.

Samantha was giggling as she played a last flourish on the piano.

"Splendid!" Mr. Jameson said. "Miss Waverly, you have a deft touch on the keyboard. And Viscountess—your voice is lovely."

Diana smiled back at him. The parlor had not rung with such happy sounds for too long. It seemed that Mr. Jameson would be a splendid substitute.

The clock on the mantel struck the hour, and Samantha let out a protest. "So soon? But we've just begun!"

Indeed, the time had sped. "Thank you, Mr. Jameson. Shall we expect you next week?"

"I would be delighted." He took Diana's hand and, bowing, lifted it to his lips.

The warm press of his mouth on her skin sent a shock of sensation through her. It was very forward, yet she could not bring herself to reprove him, not with the heat of his kiss disordering her senses.

Still clasping her hand, he looked into her eyes—a look full of promise that made her heart race. "Until next Wednesday."

The tea shop on Bond Street was filled with the cheerful babble of conversation. Diana had requested a table in the nook—the safest place for a chat with Lucy, whose voice had a tendency to carry.

"Tell me, darling." Lucy arched an elegant eyebrow. "Is Mr. Jameson proving to be…satisfactory? I'd like to know if my recommendation was well-advised."

Mr. Jameson. Diana let out a slow breath.

She could not stop thinking of him—his grey eyes and handsome features, the confidence that accompanied his every movement. The past three Wednesdays had found her with a giddy lightness of spirit. She was attuned to each nuance of his expression, addicted to the heat that his slow smiles sent through her. At the conclusion of every session, he had kissed her hand. Last Wednesday, his lips had seemed to linger, the heat of his breath playing against her skin for a long moment. The memory of it sent a fluttery breathlessness winging through her even now.

"He…." Diana ran her fingertip back and forth across the rim of her cup. "He seems an excellent teacher—very patient with Samantha, and kind. She is enjoying music lessons far more than she ever has before. It's a pity he's only a *temporary* tutor. There's a certain quality about him…"

She took a hasty swallow of tea. Goodness, she shouldn't be prattling on. Whatever secret thoughts she had of the new piano tutor should stay exactly that—secret. Although, of anyone, Lucy would understand.

Her friend tilted her head, a speculative light in her eyes. "Why Diana. Are you developing an *interest* in Mr. Jameson? How marvelous. As I told you, I think he would prove an excellent diversion. You should commence an affair immediately."

Diana set her cup down so quickly that a bit of tea sloshed over the edge. "Lucy, you are shocking."

Even worse than Lucy's suggestions were the images that flooded Diana's mind. Heat bloomed in her cheeks. What if Mr. Jameson did not stop when he kissed her hand? What if he continued, his warm lips laying kisses up her arm, along her neck? What if he reached her mouth and covered it with his own?

Her friend gave her a shrewd look. "High time you began thinking of yourself. You're out of formal mourning now. And you've admitted that your marriage to Lord Waverly was never one of deep passion."

"A marriage does not need passion if it has respect and…" She searched for the proper word. "Goodwill."

Lucy waved her hand. "Goodwill is all very well, in its place. But now you have an opportunity—you should seize it! If you are careful and discreet, no-one will suspect. You are free to follow your heart, or your whims—or both."

Lucy made it sound so simple.

"I must admit…" Her chest tightened, excitement firing through her blood as she spoke aloud the words she had been holding inside for weeks. "I find Mr. Jameson quite attractive. And his manner very pleasing."

Lucy nodded approval. "Indeed."

"What does it mean," Diana continued, "when a man's presence makes one feel so very *awake?* I can scarcely sleep for thoughts of him, and when I do, my dreams are…." She lowered her voice. "Oh, my dreams are most wicked."

"That is excellent news." Lucy's eyes were bright. "Perhaps you should make them come true."

Diana dropped her gaze to the tablecloth. "I doubt I'm ready to embark on such a course." It was one thing to indulge in such imaginations, quite another to act upon them. She had never considered herself bold of spirit.

"Well." Lucy dabbed her lips with her napkin. "It is your choice—but regardless, it's high time you began going out in society again. Gracious, Diana, people will scarcely remember you if you keep yourself locked away."

"In due time, Lucy." Her friend was a master at maneuvering people when she thought she knew what was best for them. Which was most of the time. "There's Samantha to think of, and—well, I'm comfortable as I am." Though she was markedly less content since a certain piano tutor had come into her well-ordered life.

"Comfortable?" Lucy lifted her nose in disdain. "That's almost as bad as *goodwill.* You need more interesting words to fill your life. *Passion*, for one. And *delight.* And best of all," her eyes sparked with mischief, "best of all—*ravishment.*"

"Lucy!" Diana clapped a hand to her mouth to stifle her giggles. "You're outrageous!"

Her friend joined her laughter, oblivious to the disapproving looks of the nearby patrons. When their mirth finally subsided, Lucy assumed the commanding tones of Lady Pembroke.

"Call me what you please," she said. "I only speak the truth. Regardless of your obvious fascination with the new piano tutor, you *will* come to the musicale I'm hosting on Tuesday. It will be a small gathering—nothing too overwhelming. I'll expect you promptly at eight."

"I—"

"Pray, do not disappoint me. If you don't arrive promptly, I'll dispatch my burliest footmen to fetch you."

"Oh very well," Diana said. There was no arguing with Lucy. "As long as there is no more talk of affairs and…." She could not even say the word *ravishment* aloud, though it echoed through her thoughts. "I'll come to your musicale." She made no promises, however, as to how late she would stay.

Her friend gave a nod of satisfaction, then consulted her dainty silver pocket-watch, as if recalling something urgent. "Goodness, the time has flown!

I'm nearly late for the modiste. Delightful to see you, Diana. Til Tuesday." She brushed a kiss across Diana's cheek, then hurried off, leaving Diana alone with her unsettled thoughts.

Their chat had left an edgy restlessness humming through her. Her carriage awaited outside, the driver ready to take her wherever she pleased. If only she knew where that might be.

Diana gathered her reticule and pelisse and left the shop. The air outside was pleasantly warm, and she turned her face up to the pale May sun. It was too lovely a day to waste in simply going back to Waverly House and going over menus with the cook.

She lingered, looking in the shop windows. A glorious fan painted with swans—she could nearly imagine herself with it at some ball, laughing and dancing. Or that bracelet set with sapphires, clasped about her wrist. It was frivolous, the gems sparkling beautifully in their settings. Still, she turned away from the window. No purchase could soothe her restiveness.

She had just resolved to return home when she caught sight of a certain broad-shouldered, brown-haired gentleman striding toward her. Sparks raced through her entire body. Mr. Jameson! The loveliness of the day exploded into fiery brilliance.

He met her eyes, a smile spreading across his face as he made his way to her side.

"Viscountess." He doffed his top hat. "It's a fine day. Would you care to join me for a stroll in St. James's Park?"

"That would be"—ill-advised, besotted as she had become with him—"delightful."

He offered his arm and she tucked her hand through with no hesitation. She was keenly aware of the places their bodies touched, and it was difficult to resist the urge to lean too close.

They walked side-by-side down Bond Street to the park. The feel of his firmly muscled forearm was not disguised even through the layers of his coat and her glove, and she found it deliciously distracting. The rest of him seemed as toned and muscular as his arm. Diana shot him a sideways glance. His well-fitted breeches showed his thighs flexing taut with every step, and his stomach seemed perfectly flat beneath the blue silk of his waistcoat. Lucy's words echoed through her. *Passion. Delight.*

The green trees of St. James's closed over them as they entered the long promenade. A lazy pond curved to one side, insects buzzing beside the water. The day was fine, the scene peaceful, but Diana felt unbalanced and strangely giddy.

There were so many questions she dare not ask. They scalded her tongue. She wanted to know everything about him, yet was afraid the answers would spoil the perfection of the day. Where are you from? Have you a wife? A mistress? She swallowed them unspoken.

"Do you enjoy teaching the piano?" she finally asked.

He nodded, his twilight eyes regarding her. "I'm finding a great deal of satisfaction in it. Miss Samantha is a quick study, and a fine musician. As are you, my lady. Have you ever considered taking lessons on the piano?"

"Taking lessons myself?" She blinked up at him. "I have always simply sung, Mr. Jameson. That is enough for me."

"How do you know?" His hand covered hers. "You should try something new. You might find that you like it very well." His smile held more than a little wickedness. Goodness! Was he suggesting….

Diana dropped her gaze, hoping her blush was hidden by the fashionable plumes in her bonnet. It seemed to be an afternoon for improper conversations.

With a sudden daring, she asked, "If I were to become your pupil, when might these tutorials occur? Before or after Samantha's lessons?"

"Not on Wednesday." His voice was warm honey, drizzling over her senses. "My instruction would require sufficient uninterrupted time. Perhaps Thursdays."

"Surely your other pupils would object to the change of schedule."

The pressure of his hand over hers increased. "It's all a matter of priority."

They were passing a weeping willow, the leaves tender and newly green, swaying lightly in the breeze. Diana took a deep breath of the soft air to steady herself.

"I would be your priority on Thursdays?"

He stopped and gave her an intent look. "You would be my priority every day."

Oh, it was the purest flirtation, she knew it, but still her heartbeat stumbled in giddy joy.

"Really, Mr. Jameson—"

"Call me Nicholas." He drew her off the pathway, beneath the sheltering canopy of the willow tree.

"Nicholas." She half-whispered it, a bold exhilaration tingling through her. "Then you must call me Diana."

Suddenly they were not tutor and lady any longer, but only man and woman. The air between them was alive with possibility, the spaces where bodies were, and were not. And could be.

Had she had taken complete leave of her senses? She did not care. In one twist of an afternoon a gate had opened that she had thought closed forever. A pathway back to herself. Not the young widow. Not the capable stepmother, but *her*, Diana, who had once been full of passionate dreams.

Her senses were sharpened by an almost unbearable anticipation. Everything was magnified—the light breeze, the scent of his bergamot cologne, the sound of water quietly lapping the shore. There was something excruciatingly wonderful about knowing she was about to be kissed. He leaned forward, a smile dancing in his eyes, and she tilted her face up to him.

His mouth brushed hers, their lips meeting, parting, meeting again—like a musician sounding a note, over and over, until it was perfect. She slid her hands up to his shoulders, learning the shape of his mouth against hers.

He increased the pressure of his lips. The smooth slide of his tongue against her lower lip made sparks scatter through her, and she willingly opened her mouth to him. Nicholas dipped his tongue inside. He tasted of tea and desire, and something inside her gave way, melting like late frost before the sun.

This was no debutante's kiss. It carried the full knowledge of how a man and a woman fit together. The plunge of his tongue into her mouth, her yielding softness—all this was part of the dance, a promise of deeper intimacies. She pressed herself closer to him, yearning spiraling out from her center.

Nicholas Jameson was a wonderful kisser.

It was more than the way he fitted his lips so perfectly over hers, or the velvety warmth of his tongue. More than the feel of his hand curving around her

shoulder, the brush of his thumb over her bare collarbone. His kiss flared through her entire body.

She was aware of her toes, warm and content in her buttoned boots. Her legs, cased in silk stockings with ribbon garters above her knees. The soft cotton of her chemise where it lay against her skin. The fine silk of her drawers, heated at the juncture of her legs.

And she was aware of him. Wonderfully aware of the slight roughness of his jaw as he kissed her, the warm maleness of him as they leaned into one another, the smell of spring willows and fine wool, and arousal. His. Hers.

They kissed and kissed, and then it was over. Diana opened her eyes and smiled up at him, as though she had just woken from a perfect dream.

Diana set a smile across her face and nodded at the conversation flowing past. Oh, she should never have agreed to come to Lucy's musicale. She had no heart for it. It had been too long—she did not know any of the current *on dits* and was relegated to standing awkwardly at the edges of the company.

Besides, how could she possibly be a witty conversationalist when all she could think of was Nicholas's hands at her waist, drawing her into that intoxicating kiss?

With his talk of "piano lessons" had he truly been suggesting that they become lovers? Her pulse sped at the thought. Her sleep had been restless, her skin too sensitive ever since that kiss. Even now the slide of her petticoats against her legs sent a shiver through her. What if Nicholas touched her there—and everywhere? How would it feel to embrace without the constraints of coat and skirts, to lay together skin-to-skin? Her throat went dry with longing at the thought.

"Ladies and Gentlemen!" Lucy stood at the front of the room and clapped her hands together. "Please take your seats so the musicale may commence."

Diana sidled to the end of the back row. Perhaps, once they put out the lights, she could make her escape. She did not think she could bear more awkward conversation during the intermission.

The featured performer of the evening was introduced—a young harpist who was the newest musical sensation. The room darkened, and Diana let out a breath of relief. Now she could lose herself in thoughts of Nicholas. She closed her eyes as the harpist plucked the first chord.

Someone took the seat next to her, startling her from her reverie. Cloth rustled, and then the familiar scent of bergamot cologne tickled her nose. Her eyes flew open and she turned, surprise jolting through her as she glimpsed the white gleam of Nicholas's grin. It was as if her thoughts had summoned him here.

He leaned close. "Good evening, Diana." His breath was warm against her cheek.

"Nicholas—whatever are you doing here?"

His hand found hers in the dark, his clasp sure as he twined his naked fingers through her gloved ones. The intimacy of it made her gasp. Surely her heart was beating so loudly that everyone could hear.

"Come," he said.

A glissando of harp notes shivered through her. What were his plans for her? What if he had no plans?

She would never know unless she went with him into the wicked shadows. For a moment fear held her in her seat. She could not, she could not…. Then he tugged gently at her hand and desire rose up in a wave and lifted her to her feet.

Nicholas drew her out of the darkened drawing room. The lamps in the hallway shed a beckoning light, their flames echoing the excitement flickering through her. No-one was there to mark their illicit departure. He led her down the hall and up a short flight of stairs, the music growing fainter behind them. Without pause, he opened a door and ushered her through.

They were in the library. Lamplight glinted on gold-lettered spines and she breathed in the scent of books and leather. And Nicholas. He closed the door, shutting out the last lilting notes. When he turned back to her his expression was intent, his grey eyes lit with desire. For her.

Diana caught her breath, heat blossoming inside her.

Without a word, he strode forward and took her in his arms. Her breasts pressed against his silver-embroidered waistcoat—softness against hardness, woman against man. Her breath swept between her lips, flavored with passion. When he bent his head, she eagerly opened her mouth.

It was as delicious as she had remembered. His tongue played against hers, sweet and hot, and she felt her fears dissolve into acceptance. A low, insistent pulse began within her, as if she were an instrument responding to his touch.

She slid her hands to his shoulders, then dropped them in frustration to tug urgently at the fingertips of her gloves. She needed to feel his bare skin beneath her palms, the planes of his cheek and jaw, the softness of his dark hair tangled between her fingers.

He helped her strip the gloves off, as hungry as she. For a moment he held them dangling in his hand and gave her a penetrating look.

She stepped forward and kissed him. By heaven, she had made her choice, and she was going to embrace it with all the long-banked fire in her soul. She tasted his laughter, and then his arms came around her and the kiss deepened.

So sweet and fierce. Embers flickered to flame, scorched to need. His palms smoothed the emerald satin of her gown and she leaned into his touch. There was no doubt he found her desirable—his body proved it, the hardness of him pressing against her center. He bunched her skirts in his hands drew them up, cool air caressing her legs.

Wordlessly, she stepped back and let him pull her gown off. Her chemise tangled in her arms, and then it, too, was gone. She stood before him, naked but for her undergarments. It was outrageous, and wonderful.

"So beautiful," he said, his eyes alight with hunger.

He stroked his hands up her sides, then covered her breasts. She sucked in a sharp breath. Little fires quivered beneath his palms, and she could feel her nipples tauten under his touch. She arched into his hands, threw her head back, and sighed. What a picture she must make, wearing only her stockings and drawers, wanton and sensual under the hands of this darkly handsome gentleman.

But he was wearing too much clothing. Her hands went to his cravat, making quick work of the elegant knot. Next, the buttons of his waistcoat, his fine linen shirt. She tugged the fabric free of his breeches and, hands trembling, pushed his shirt open. His chest was firmly muscled, a light dusting of hair tickling her fingertips as she stroked his skin.

He made a sound of longing, then pulled her to him, his chest hot and hard against hers. It was as delicious as she had imagined. Another blazing kiss, and then he stepped back. She helped him pull off his coat and shirt, then he scraped his boots off and removed his breeches.

Diana peeked between her lashes, curious and eager, then caught her breath at the sight of him. He was erect and strong, and she felt suddenly powerful, to bring him to such a rampant state.

Henry had always insisted on taking his husbandly prerogatives with the lights off, the two of them securely between the sheets. He had never made her feel like this, had never openly admired her, or told her she was beautiful. It had been pleasant enough, their marital relations, but nothing like the fire that now seared through her.

And that fire was nothing compared to the sensation that engulfed her when Nicholas took her in his arms and dipped his hand between her legs. This tempest of want scorching her to her soul—this was new. This was *passion*.

"Ah!" she cried as his fingers stroked and played beneath her drawers. She gripped the strong sinews of his arms—she was going to fly to bits if she did not hold tightly to him.

Nicholas withdrew his hand and she moaned in protest. With a devilish smile, he stripped off her drawers, then maneuvered her backward until her legs bumped the settee. They tumbled down together onto the gold velvet cushions and he braced himself over her, setting his member where his fingers had been. Slowly, inexorably, he pressed forward, opening her. Their gazes locked as their bodies fitted together, imperfectly at first. Then easier as he slid back, and forward again.

"Yes," she breathed.

It was lovely and heated and, oh, she couldn't bear how deliberately Nicholas moved in her. She caught at his shoulders and tilted her hips up, urging him to stroke deeper, faster. His breath hitched as he quickened his pace, the pulse at the side of his neck beating urgently.

More. Yes, and *more*, until the pressure she felt coiling inside her finally released, exploded like an errant firework to spangle her senses with light and color.

He let out a muffled shout and pulled free, spilling himself on the fine linen of his shirt. Sweat gleamed on his arms, his chest.

She let out a sigh of pleasure, her body sated, her whole being utterly, perfectly content. She brushed her fingers through his silky hair. Nicholas Jameson—masterful and tender, patient and passionate. The door to her heart swung open.

A smile illuminated his face and he brought one hand up to cup her cheek. "Now that, my Diana, was splendid indeed."

It was Wednesday.

Diana sat in the music room, waiting for the sound of the knocker to reverberate through the entry. Nicholas would be here at any moment. Anticipation fluttered all the way down to her toes.

Samantha played another run of notes, then glanced at the clock. "Perhaps Mr. Jameson has forgotten," she said. "He has not developed the habit of coming to Waverly House."

"Nonsense. He's been our piano tutor for weeks now." Diana infused her voice with certainty. "He has only been delayed twenty minutes. There could be any number of reasons for it."

"Perhaps he has been crushed by a carriage, or—"

"Samantha, enough! I'm certain Mr. Jameson will be here momentarily."

After the lesson, she would ask him to stay for tea. She would ask him everything and have no fear of the answers.

He had brought music and light into Waverly House. He had coaxed her from behind her comfortable boundaries and shown her what true passion was. Every day from now on would be richer because of it. She would be richer. The memory of his touches, his words, flared through her. She had never felt so beautiful.

"It's half past the hour." Samantha sounded glum. "He's not coming."

Diana bit her lip. Where was he? Anticipation curdled into apprehension. "Practice a bit more, dear. I'll go check with the butler." Though of course he would have shown Mr. Jameson straight in.

The heels of her boots clicked across the marble floor of the entryway. When she pulled the heavy front door open, the butler raised his eyebrows, but said nothing.

The street outside was quiet. No handsome grey-eyed man striding up to her door, no cabs to be seen the entire length of the block. She stood on the threshold for several minutes, the distant clamor of London washing past her, but the street remained empty.

The butler cleared his throat, and she slowly shut the door. Head high, she re-entered the parlor.

Samantha's expression lit. "Is he…?"

"No. Not yet." She couldn't help but glance at the clock. The entire hour had run. Did she mean nothing to him? An ugly sob rose in her throat.

"Mama?" Samantha sent her a concerned glance.

Diana swallowed. "I suppose something important has detained him. You may go." She blinked rapidly against the sting of tears.

Samantha gave her a hug, then slipped out of the room. Diana bowed her head. Had she been such a fool to listen to Lucy? It had not felt that way at the time. But it seemed she had made a dreadful mistake.

She had practically seduced him. The piano tutor. He must be too embarrassed to face her, here with her stepdaughter, after what had been between them. He must despise her, think her a woman of exceedingly loose morals, to take such base liberties with her employee.

Yet he was far more to her than that. Her heart ached with lost possibilities.

They had, neither of them, promised more than a single hour of unbridled desire. Their banter about tutoring had hardly been talk of courtship, of love. If her actions had been spurred by deeper feelings, as she must now admit, what had she been to him? Only a willing female—one whom he evidently had no more use for.

She knew nothing about him. Nothing except that he made her feel more alive, more daring, than anyone she had ever met. And now it was ended.

She could not bear the thought.

The servants at Lucy's mansion knew Diana well enough to admit her without hesitation.

"Is Lady Pembroke in?" she asked.

"She is, madam," Lucy's butler said. "She is taking the air in the garden. Shall I escort you?"

"That won't be necessary." If, as she feared, she was going to burst into tears the moment she saw her friend, she would prefer to do so unobserved.

"As you wish." The butler bowed her toward the French doors overlooking Lucy's grounds.

Diana stepped out and took a deep breath of the late-spring air. Lucy would know what to do. A woman of her experience surely knew all about broken hearts.

Rounding the yew hedge, Diana heard voices. Lucy's. And a man's, painfully familiar. Sudden fear knifing through her, she crept forward.

"Damn it Lucy, I have to tell her." Nicholas's voice was strained. "It's gone too far. She deserves to know the truth."

"She's not ready." Lucy sounded resolute. "Think up some excuse—tell her you were unavoidably detained. But don't tell her what you and I have been up to."

Ice swept over Diana, comprehension settling cold and dreadful against her bones. Lucy's talk of handsome piano tutors. Nicholas, here in her garden, using Lucy's given name so intimately. His presence at the musicale last night, his familiarity with Lucy's house….

Anger flared through her. The scoundrel! To use her so, when all along he had been Lucy's lover. What a contemptible rake, to seduce Diana—here of all places.

She swept out from behind the hedge. "Unavoidably detained?" She raked her gaze over Nicholas. His eyes widened, and he took a step toward her.

Lucy grabbed at his arm. "Diana. We were just speaking of you—"

"Yes," she said. The word was coated in frost. "And what exactly were the two of you doing while my *employee* was supposed to be giving a piano lesson?"

Nicholas shook himself free of Lucy's grasp. "Let me explain—"

"You should have explained before the musicale." Her voice caught, snagged on memory. "But it seemed you had *other* priorities. Perhaps you had forgotten you had a music lesson to teach while you were 'unavoidably detained.' You've behaved most unprofessionally, sir."

She fought to speak against the tightness in her throat. Nicholas reached for her and she pulled away.

"I no longer need your services, Mr. Jameson. You are *fired*."

Hot tears blurring her vision, she turned and ran. Dimly she heard Nicholas calling after her, Lucy remonstrating, but she did not pause. She rushed back to her carriage and flung herself inside, slamming the door before the footman could even approach.

It was far worse than she had suspected. And still a part of her had wanted to stay, to listen to his pleas. She was so unbearably weak. As the wheels rattled over the cobblestones, she dropped her head into her hands and abandoned herself to grief.

"Mama?" Samantha pushed open the parlor door. "Are you ill? I had cook make you some chocolate."

She entered the room, carefully balancing a tray holding the silver chocolate pot and two cups. Diana mustered a smile for her stepdaughter and hoped her eyes were not too red from weeping.

"Thank you, dear. I am not unwell, just a bit tired." Did heartsickness count as an illness? She did not think so. "Come, sit by me." She patted the settee.

Samantha set the tray down and curled up close. Diana put her arm around the girl's shoulders and gave them a squeeze—the reassurance as much for herself as for her stepdaughter.

"I have some unhappy news for you." She heaved a breath. "Mr. Jameson will not be returning as your piano tutor."

"Oh." The girl's shoulders slumped. "That is too bad. He was ever so charming—and smelled much better than Mr. Bent."

Diana smiled—it was the only way to keep the tears from welling up again. "That he did." She leaned over and rested her head against Samantha's. All brightness was not gone from her life, no matter how dreary the day might feel.

"My lady." The butler bowed at the parlor door. "Forgive me for interrupting. You have a caller. Are you at home?"

She straightened. Nicholas wouldn't dare—not if he had a shred of sense. It had to be Lucy. One way or another, she would have to face her friend.

"Yes, I am receiving."

"Very good." He extended the silver salver, a vellum card centered on it. "Shall I show him in?"

"Him?" Her lips pressed tightly together she took the card. If it were Mr. Jameson…. "The Marquess of Somerton?" She stared at the unfamiliar name. "I don't believe I know any such person. Please tell the gentleman I am not taking visitors today." Particularly uninvited ones. She could not face another stranger in her house.

"Very good." The butler departed.

"Thank you for the chocolate, Samantha." Diana gave her stepdaughter another quick embrace. Really, she ought to bestir herself. There was no use sitting in the parlor when it held such memories of Nicholas.

"I'm glad it helped. Chocolate often does." The girl jumped up and gathered the cups and tray, then paused and kissed Diana's cheek before bustling out the door.

Voices filtered from the hallway, and then the butler was back.

"I am sorry, my lady, but the marquess insists he will see you. He vowed to toss me into the street if I stood in his way."

Diana rose, then nearly folded back down on the settee when she saw who had followed the butler in.

Nicholas. The breath squeezed from her lungs while a wild, giddy clamor started up in her blood.

"Please go," she breathed. No matter how much she wanted to remain unmoved, the expression in his familiar grey eyes nearly undid her.

He was carrying an exuberant bouquet of roses, which he handed to the butler. "See to these."

Clever man—if he had given her the flowers, she would have flung them back in his face. As soon as the butler departed, she turned on Nicholas. Piano tutor, marquess—whomever he claimed to be today.

"How dare you?" Her ribs felt as though a band of silk were wrapped around them, pulled too tight. "To think, what we did under Lucy's very roof! And then you come here, bullying my servants, and—"

"Diana." He closed the distance between them and took her by the shoulders. Fool that she was, she could not move away from his touch. "I don't think my cousin begrudges the use of her library. She has done far worse in my best carriage, with never a word of apology."

"Your…your cousin?" She blinked up at him, her heart catching with a wild, irrational hope. "Lady Pembroke is your cousin?"

"Yes." A mischievous light sparked in his eyes. "Lucy. My meddling plague of a cousin. The one who bribed Mr. Bent to take an extended holiday, then suggested I pose as a piano tutor and tempt you out of hiding." He shook his head. "But it didn't work."

"No?" She had been tempted, all too easily. Even now she felt breathless.

He smiled at her—rueful and amused all at once. "My plan was to slowly draw you out. To, as Lucy put it, 'help ease you from your widowhood.' But falling in love with you made things bloody awkward."

Falling in love? Happy tears tingled at the back of her eyes. The Marquess of Somerton? "But…you make an excellent piano tutor."

His hands tightened on her shoulders and he drew her forward. "I assure you, I make a far better suitor."

She went willingly, lifting her face to his kiss. A kiss that swirled her senses, even as it anchored her fully to herself. A kiss full of passion. Delight. Life.

Alice Faris grew up in a small community in Northern California that proudly boasts of having more cows than people. She raised guide dogs for the blind, is dyslexic, and can shoot a gun or bow and miraculously never hit the target (which at some point becomes a statistical improbability). Alice worked as a school psychologist and counselor for local schools. Alice also writes paranormal romance as Tina Gower. She won the Writers of the Future, the Daphne du Maurier Award for Mystery and Suspense (paranormal category), and was nominated for the Romance Writers of America® Golden Heart®. She has professionally published several short stories in a variety of magazines.

PREGNANT GIRL'S GUIDE TO FALLING IN LOVE

by Alice Faris

CHAPTER ONE

There it was. That tingle up Zoey's spine, an alert that something no-good was about to blow into her life…again. As a colossal, perpetual fuck up, she got that zing of *trouble's coming* a lot. It excited her. Invigorated her. Made her stomach flip flop like a trapeze artist fifteen feet off the ground with no net. But she couldn't afford trouble. Not now. Not while she was pregnant with someone else's child.

The fetus was her meal ticket. She patted her eight-month belly to calm Baby down. She apparently felt that live wire jolt and the promise of excitement—the bad kind—too.

"Of all the things to inherit from your surrogate mama," Zoey murmured to the bulge that could have been a leg or an arm pressing against her belly button.

She sighed and paced the room. Maybe she should call in sick to the restaurant? No. Jason would skin her. Especially after he'd done Zoey's cousin a favor by hiring her. This is why Zoey never let family do things for her. She didn't like eventually disappointing them.

Unable to hold down a job or find a decent place to stay, Zoey moved in with her cousin East. The dependable one. The organized one. The one who had her life in order—until a few weeks ago. East had lost her steady school psychologist job and went on a cross-country road trip, falling in love with the trucker she hitch-hiked with.

Zoey smiled at the rare moment of the tables turning. It had felt good to be the one with her shit in order for once. Being a surrogate, she'd lined herself up with a steady paycheck for at least nine months. Well, until a week ago. Like clockwork, East's life was back in order and so the natural order of the universe meant that Zoey's plans would plummet. Her bank had called and said her latest payment never arrived.

It meant she couldn't pay her doctor for Baby's check-up. When she called the family she was a surrogate for, they wouldn't pick up the phone.

As if on cue, her phone chimed, alerting her to an incoming text message: *Zoey, I'm looking at the clock and staring at the door. Where's my new waitress?*

From her friend and boss, Jason.

She frowned at her own clock. *I still have ten minutes 'till my shift.*

It will take you ten minutes to get here, he reminded her. Again.

They'd had several talks about allowing for travel time, so she'd start on time. Seriously? What was five minutes in the scheme of things? Just pay her for five minutes less. Or she'd stay after for five. He'd batted his eyes as if she'd said the most outrageous things and said "It's the principle of the thing."

How many times had she heard that as a kid? "I'm the grown up, that's why" or " 'Cause I say so" or "It's the way the world works, deal with it." Jason was just another beat in the dulldrum of life, telling her she had to follow. Zoey wanted to make her own rules.

But she knew. She needed to be an adult now. She promised herself to improve and that started with adulating to the full level, which meant being on time.

Even though Jason was more her friend, and somewhat family now that East was dating Ansel, that didn't mean she could take advantage of him.

She tossed her phone into her purse along with her empty wallet. The waitress job had been a safety net (according to East). And now it had become her emergency back-up. She couldn't fuck this up. East couldn't afford to pay both their halves of the mortgage. True they lived in the less expensive part of Northern California, but for a tiny two bedroom, two bath house the price still made her calculate how many luxuries she'd need to sacrifice. So would it be water or power? She'd already sold the car. Her life wasn't improving to the level she hoped. Baby kicked as if in agreement.

The deep, throaty rumble of a truck pulling into her driveway gave her a sigh of relief. Crypt, her best buddy from the garage coming through for her again. He knew her work schedule better than her and he'd saved her ass more than he should have to. She'd have to bake him some cookies or something. She pulled her apron from the hook by the front door and tied it around her and avoided the mirror. These things made her look like a smock-wearing puritan.

Crypt's shadow seeped through her open door. Something about the composition was way off. As if Crypt had worked out, gotten taller and broader and more muscular. Play of the light, surely.

"Doesn't this smock make me look pregnant?" she called out through the door, laughing at herself.

He didn't answer. Not like Crypt. He'd always had a jovial response to all her jokes. Maybe he was on his phone.

"Come on. Tell me you'll flirt a little with Jason tonight and get him to change up the uniforms. He can't keep everything exactly like Patty had it." Her boss had inherited the diner from his late aunt. He'd been a bit too nostalgic if you asked her, keeping everything as is. The place could use some updates.

"Crypt?" Now his silence was freaking her out. She brushed her fingers through her hair, primping one last time, her motions getting slower and slower as the tingle of dread filled her veins. That bad feeling. It kept pounding away with each beat of her heart.

She swallowed, pushing the door more slightly ajar. Zoey peeked out with caution, expecting to be ambushed by thieves, but instead her porch was empty. She heard the boot stomps on her driveway and she jogged down the stairs as gracefully as she could considering the extra-large part of her body where she was growing another human.

"Hey! Crypt! I thought you were here to give me a ride to work. What gives?" She rounded the corner, not to see Crypt's motorcycle or to his truck, but a commercial diesel truck like the one her uncle used to drive. This one didn't have the trailer attached. She came up short, skidding in her tracks.

"Crypt...why are you driving a semi?"

Her mind raced, because she only knew of one family in town that had these brand of trucks. The Bradfords—one Bradford in particular. Quinn Bradford. One she'd rather avoid at the moment.

Not because of anything he'd done, but because she couldn't bring herself to face him. She counted back on her fingers. Yep. He'd had a nine-month sentence for a crime she knew he hadn't committed. He couldn't have. Not quiet, adorable Quinn. Like everything else she touched, she'd turned sweet, innocent Quinn into a felon. The reverse Midas touch.

She was cursed.

Zoey's brain told her to back-step right on into her house, hide, and wait for Crypt—but her body wouldn't obey. Instead she froze in place.

The rough, deep clearing of a male throat sent a different kind of electrical pulse through her body. Not the danger kind. The this-man-would-give-you-a-great-night kind. In bed. She always added 'in bed' mentally. That probably made her a perv.

Quinn came around the side of the truck, hat folded in his oversized hands. "Zoey." He tipped his head, glancing at her through his lashes as if looking straight at her would cause him to burn.

"Quinn—" His name was like a sigh on her lips. An endless regret of the way she should have handled things. There was too much to say between them to use words. Somewhere someone invented a language using only emotion and that would have been close-but-not-quite to what she needed to communicate.

He tapped the side of the truck. "Your friend at the garage said you needed a ride." He still wouldn't look at her. "It was an emergency or..." He let the rest of that sentence drop.

...or he never would have asked Quinn. The last person, but also the only person on Earth Zoey wanted to see. She was a walking contradiction.

"If you're not in a time crunch, I can get my dad or one of my brothers…" He stepped away from the back of the truck over to his door, reaching for his phone.

She could have waved him off—told him no big deal, she'd just walk—but instead she found herself unlatching the passenger side door. "Absolutely. I'd love a ride." She told herself that she needed to get to work, but deep down she knew it was because she needed Quinn. Needed their friendship again.

He blinked as if confused by her answer. He stumbled and recovered, springing to the driver's side and hopping in. "All right. To Patty's?"

"That's the place."

"They still have those amazing burgers?"

"Sadly, the last of Patty's famous ones were eaten from the freezer last month. Jason is still working on finding the right combination for the recipe. He's nowhere close."

Quinn hung his head. "Oh."

The rest of the conversation died. Zoey could have written it an obituary if it weren't for the fact she couldn't spell for nothing. Thankfully, it was only five miles of weird silence.

CHAPTER TWO

Quinn's heart nearly burst from his chest. He'd said more words to Zoey than he had to anyone in the last several months. He was sure of it. His throat was already drying out. His tongue swelling in his mouth.

Zoey looked exactly how he'd seen her last. Except for one very major detail. And the sight of her round, very pregnant self gave him a hard-on that wouldn't quit. He shifted in his seat. But Zoey in any form was his forever aphrodisiac.

She'd been his crush for as long as he could remember. They'd been inseparable since they were tots. She'd always been wild and he was the apprehensive one. Except for one crazy night. He lost control and he'd lost her and everything he'd built his life on. Now he wanted it back.

He eyed her stomach. Jesus. Was that kid his? He had no memory of that night. Only one: he'd told her his deepest secret. He'd told her he'd been attracted to her. She blinked back at him with a pale, lost expression. And after that? A big blank hole, compliments of too much tequila and a dollar night at the Red Saloon. He rubbed his head at the memory of the hangover.

They pulled into the parking lot and he turned off the engine. She scrambled out of her seat and slid down to the pavement, mumbling a thanks and a fast wave. Crap, he'd made this awkward. He should just come out and ask her what had happened that night. Had she been there? Did she know why he'd stolen that car?

He wouldn't have believed it himself except his prints were all over the handle and the wheel. Nobody else's. Not even Zoey's. Of course it belonged to the richest guy in town and he went after Quinn with high powered lawyers and demanded the local judicial system to act quickly with his conviction. He'd barely recovered from that hangover before the slam of the barred cell doors echoed down the concrete hallways of the pen.

He collected his wallet from the dash and set the brake.

Zoey hadn't made it to the door without having been stopped by some biker. She crossed her arms around herself, an obvious sign she was uncomfortable.

"Come on, Z. Just one night. It won't hurt nothin'. You're too far along for it to do anything. In Europe or some shit they drink wine every day."

"I said no, Trigger. I can't afford to break the rules—"

"Rules," this Trigger guy—what a name—spit on the ground. "You sound like East."

"Well, she's sometimes right."

"She's boring. Bor-ing."

He blew his smoke out in Zoey's face and she coughed and stepped back and toward the door to the diner. Trigger blocked her entry. "You gotta kiss for the toll." He leaned forward with his lips pursed.

Quinn's insides heated to nuclear. His vision blurred with a tinge of red—and he'd always thought that was an expression. His boots stomped as he tightened his fists, making it to the guy in a few straight-legged strides.

He shoved himself between them. "She doesn't want to do whatever you asked. Leave."

The guy looked him up and down. "Look who's back." He flicked his cigarette in the small space between them as if Quinn's larger size didn't faze him.

Quinn's shoulder's stiffened, unnerved that the guy knew him. Or knew of him. The heat of embarrassment flushed his cheeks. For the most part he'd been laying low. Venturing out only for the bare essentials and meetings with his parole officer.

Zoey smartly high-tailed it inside the diner, the door still ringing and swinging from the force of her entry.

"You got a problem?" The guy leaned forward, squinting.

"No problem. You're the problem if you don't leave Zoey alone."

"Zoey *is* my business. We're *friends.*" He laid heavily on that word. As if it meant something more. Trigger's lips turned up in a knowing smirk.

Quinn stepped back and held up his hands as if in surrender. He shook his head—this guy wasn't worth a violation in his parole. Zoey and he didn't have any agreement. They weren't together. Except his chest burned at the idea of her with someone else.

The pregnancy meant that whatever he'd confessed to her all those months ago, she didn't feel the same way back. She was having another man's child.

The guy, Trigger, continued to stare at him, flicking his cigarette and inhaling long, unhurried drags. Quinn changed trajectory and backed away, keeping him in sight until he reached the door and entered the restaurant.

There was a brief moment where the bright florescent lights and the clang of forks against plates reminded him of the prison mess room. The oldies music was probably a respectable volume, but inside he wanted to scream....

"Hey," Zoey's face blocked his panic attack. "Thanks for that." She hitched a shoulder. "He's kinda latched on a few months back and I can't seem to shake him."

Quinn's breathing returned to normal. He hadn't realized how much of a reverse culture shock leaving prison would be. "It's no problem. I wouldn't normally have fought your battles for you. I know you don't like it." He squeezed and rubbed his knuckles. Almost as if he wished he'd been out there beating on that guy and not in here facing something much harder. "When does your shift end?"

Her light smile faded. "Oh, you don't have to give me a ride."

"I do." He hesitated. "We have a lot to catch up on."

Her eyes flittered to her tables. "I need to…" She made a waving motion in the direction of a family who'd just set their menus down.

He nodded and she turned and scampered out of the conversation between them, nearly leaving skid marks. He grabbed a menu from the bucket at the hostess station and seated himself in one of the two-person tables against the window and across from the bar.

"It's a four-hour shift," a guy behind the bar announced. He held a glass up to the light and polished it with a cloth.

Quinn looked around, thinking the guy must be talking to someone else. Though, everyone else in the diner had been seated in the family section—a larger room with the bigger tables and sports memorabilia collected from the local schools.

"You're the cleanest guy I've seen Zoey bring in so far," the guy mused. This time he set the glass down and looked right at Quinn. "I'm Jason. Patty was my aunt."

"I'm Quinn. Bradford." He waited for the Jason to recoil or shut down all talk, probably having heard about Quinn from the town gossip. It didn't matter that he'd been a model citizen up until he'd done a one-eighty and stole a car. Not that he remembered his moment of insanity. But it didn't matter. One mistake, it tanked his entire reputation. Now he'd be doing the books and taking the haul jobs nobody wanted at his dad's trucking business for the rest of his life.

However, that brush off he'd expected from Jason never came. Instead the guy poured a coffee and brought it around to his table, setting it down. "On the house. I'm guessing you're going to stand guard for her entire shift?"

Quinn glanced at the coffee on the saucer. Black with two packets of sugar.

Jason rubbed his hands together, biting his lip. "Well?"

Quinn quirked an eyebrow. "I don't follow."

"Is it how you take it? Your coffee?"

It was actually. He ripped the packets open and stirred them into the rich dark liquid. "Maybe." He took a sip. It had even been a Columbian blend. His preferred cup. He sighed, surprisingly starting to relax. "Yeah."

Jason slid into the seat across from him. "It's my super power."

Quinn took another sip. "So, uh, how do you know Zoey?"

"My best friend sort of fell in love with her cousin. Or is it sister? She calls East her sister, but I gather they're actually cousins."

Quinn smiled wide. "Sister-cousin. That's what we always joked." He set his cup down. "Good for East. She's good people." He pulled his wallet out and set a five on the table. "And I can't let you pay for the coffee."

"Organized, like you."

Quinn paused, his fingers about to close up his wallet. "What?"

"East. She's very tidy." Jason pointed at Quinn's wallet. "You have all your bills organized, facing the same direction and in order of highest to lowest. I'm guessing that organization carries over?"

"I'm an accountant."

Jason hard-swallowed his drink, choking. "I didn't see that one coming." He wiped his mouth with the back of his hand. "Fuck, I spilled water all over me." He snatched Quinn's napkin and patted himself dry. "You looked and acted more like construction."

"Nope." He sipped his coffee, glancing out the window. The morning sun glimmering off the pavement and making him squint.

"But he did construction. To work his way through college," Zoey said, walking up to his table. Hands on her hips, she frowned. "What are you doing?"

Quinn lifted his cup. "Coffee."

She slapped down her order notebook. "No, you're not. You're pumping Jason for information on me."

"Oh, no, Zoey," Jason interjected. "I assure you I was doing all the pumping." He barely hid a smile.

She whacked her boss's shoulder. "Stop that. No flirting with him. He's straight."

"Oh geez." Jason scoffed. "I'm so glad you let me know. I might not have figured it out on my own." The sarcasm dripped off his every word. He grabbed his water and stood. "I guess I'll go back to my dungeon. Hey, I hate doing books. You interested?"

"Uh..." Quinn didn't know how to respond. That awkward moment where he'd have to explain—

"He's super good at it," Zoey pipped up, suddenly animated. "He always helped me with my math homework in school. We'd count the stars in the back of your brother's pick up truck. You remember?"

Their gazes met. Heat rose from his chest, to his neck, to his cheeks. A memory he wondered if she realized he held more fondly than her. As a teen he'd fought the urge to kiss her, their fingers grazing each other's, never fully clasping into a hold. The low, constant hum of attraction—

"Being a grade ahead really helped. You'd be smart to hire Quinn." She winked at him.

The contract of past and present hit him. He was no longer that innocent boy in the bed of a pick up truck counting stars with a strong future of possibilities ahead of him. "Zoey, I don't think—"

"I have to say," Jason rolled the water cup in his hand analyzing Zoey, "he's much more put together than anyone else I see you hanging with. No tattoos."

"No withdrawal symptoms. No collar around the neck or piercings," Zoey added to the list, her eyes rolling as if this were a daily list she'd memorized.

Jason continued as if she hadn't spoken. "He's got a clean shirt—heck, he's *wearing* a shirt."

"I'm a felon," Quinn butted in to their amusing back and forth.

The two shut up quickly at that.

Zoey's eyes went soft and watery. She quickly looked down as if she had something to be ashamed of. Jason's eyes widened, glimpsing Quinn as if he was seeing him in a whole new light.

"You should probably know that," Quinn mumbled. Great. He'd made it awkward. He gulped his coffee. It burned down his throat.

"For embezzlement?" Jason asked, swallowing.

"Grand theft auto. Apparently I made the video game a reality."

"Apparently?" Jason asked again.

"I don't remember it."

"You don't remember it?" Zoey's brows furrowed. And when the answer must have been written on his face, her features smoothed out, as if something horrible dawned on her. "Wait. You don't remember *any part* of that night?"

He couldn't help but look at her stomach. And the baby he'd been meaning to ask her about. "No. And while I'm at it...is that my kid?"

CHAPTER THREE

The baby kicked like crazy in reaction to Zoey's heart nearly falling through her chest from beating too hard. Quinn didn't have a clue how wild, or unwild, the night he'd been arrested had been. Her biggest concern, all these months, had been that he'd believe the worst of her—that she had not remained true to her promise and pact they'd made. He told her he loved her. She wanted to jump right in head first and he wanted to take it slow. She didn't react well, and he went to prison before they could really figure it out. But Zoey had kept her promise. She wouldn't date or sleep with another man until she'd given him a chance. He hadn't asked for it, but she offered it just the same.

She took a long deep breath. How to explain...

The baby wasn't his, but she'd have to delicately explain that situation so as not to breach her nondisclosure. She should ask Jason—being a lawyer before he took over his Aunt's diner—his opinion on the parents stopping paying rent to her uterus. Maybe she could break a few rules.

The zipped lips on her end had been easy with those steady paychecks. Now, a little annoyed, she was out of money and holding up the illusion she'd gotten herself knocked up. Wild, untamable Zoey, at it again. It fit the town's image of her, so most people never even asked her who the baby's father was.

"Oh, Jesus." Jason gulped his water in long swigs. "I guess I'll go see if table four's order is up."

Zoey caught his elbow before he could abandon her. "No. I'll do it. It's my job. Aren't you always grousing over my performance?"

"Zoey," Jason choked on her name and cleared his throat. "This is a little more than stealing fries off customers' plates, don't you think?" He kept looking at Quinn as if he were putting it all together.

Like everyone else, Jason assumed she had a baby daddy out there somewhere. A few of Zoey's buddies from garage had stepped up right away and offered to be daddy once it became apparent nobody would step up. Except none of them knew the truth.

Baby wasn't going to be around after birth and she'd mentioned adoption to plant the seed in their minds the last month so the men in her life would stop proposing.

What did they find so appealing about her anyway?

Jason carefully extracted her nails from his shirt and eased himself from her grip. "You can take your fifteen-minute break."

"I just started my shift." Even she could hear the desperate tone in her voice. "Quinn, you don't mind me finishing up my shift before we get all into this?"

He rubbed his forehead, took a sip of coffee and a deep breath and then meet her gaze. "Sure."

Jason jogged off, murmuring something about preventing a grease fire.

"I get off at noon." She fiddled with her order booklet. "If you want to come back."

"I'll wait."

"But it's a long wait and the seats are so hard."

He gave her a look. His lips pressed together as if he didn't buy whatever manure she'd been trying to sell.

In her mind she'd made all her comments into a dirty joke. I 'get off at noon' or 'seats making you hard'—she quickly brushed those horny thoughts out of her head. One itch during pregnancy she couldn't scratch.

She straightened her apron. "I'm not going to run off."

"Like you did that night?"

"So you do remember."

He sat back, gaze on the ceiling. "No. I took a lucky guess. We started out the evening together, but you weren't there when..." He let her finish that sentence. *When he'd been arrested.*

She sighed. "No." And then heat rose to her face. All that embarrassment coming right back and threatening to make her lose her tiny breakfast. The bell rang, indicating an order up and she ran to the counter. Saved for the moment.

Every ten minutes of her shift she'd find some reason to walk near the area where Quinn sat. Table three. Not in her section. It wasn't in anyone's section as that side didn't open up until dinner. He'd left after the first thirty minutes and she breathed with relief. Except he came right back in a few minutes later with a big rectangular book, an old-fashioned calculator, and a pencil. He rolled up his sleeves and appeared to be doing the Bradford Trucking books right there in the restaurant.

And each passing minute from that point on tightened in her chest like a screw slowing digging into an oak tree.

"There is nothing sexier than a man who does math," Jason whispered under his breath—now that he was on an early lunch break, he transformed more into friend than boss. "Tell me he concentrates that hard in bed too."

His interruption distracted her from her building anxiety. "I wouldn't know..." She let her voice trail while she tilted her head to get a better look at the way Quinn's forearms flexed as he turned the extra-long ledger pages.

"Oh, is that right?" Jason grunted, crossing his arms and tapping his foot.

Shoot. She'd meant to hint at the baby being Quinn's to buy her some time. That ball of stress rolled all around her intestines, tying them up as if it were a feisty kitten wrapping itself in string. She placed her hand there to stop it, but all that did was wake up Baby and she bounced around with it.

Zoey hiccupped as Jason guided her into his office. "Break time," he proclaimed. The door shut with a click behind them both. "So...Quinn isn't the father."

She shook her head.

"That guy with all the tats from the garage isn't the dad?"

She shook her head again, biting her lip and knowing where this was going.

"That guy that hassles you every morning, and somehow knows all your shifts, isn't either."

She shook her head.

He tapped his finger on his chin dramatically. "Zoey, I know it's none of my business, but as your employer and since it's looking like we'll be family with Ansel and East getting it on, I'm starting to care about you and your future—"

"Please don't."

"What?" He leans his butt on his desk. "Care?" He kicked his feet out, crossing one over the other, casual-like, but Jason isn't ever casual. Everything was calculated. He was a very observant guy. "I'm not sorry to say that I *do* care and I *won't* let you push this aside. At least tell me you have a plan after the baby is born."

"I do," Zoey didn't want to keep him in the dark, and she did need his advice. She opened her mouth, trying to think of how she could ask about the ramifications of the parents no longer paying her, but her nerves got there before she could, squeezing her bladder and simultaneously making her nauseous. "I have to go to the bathroom."

She rushed out of his office and toward the restroom. The door was locked but she could hear the toilet flush. A woman stood outside patiently waiting her turn and Zoey hopped from one foot to the other.

The woman gestured to the opening door. "You can go ahead. I remember what it was like at the end with my boys."

She nodded her thanks and pushed passed the older woman coming out, unable to lock the door in time before she dry heaved into the sink, barely holding back an episode of vomiting. It had been a long time since she'd had any morning sickness, but anxiety brought it right back.

Her checks have disappeared, Jason needed answers, Quinn was in town. She'd have to tell him how much of a coward she'd been and how that was the reason he went to prison—it all came to head at the same time. She heaved again. Having nothing in her stomach saved her from a full explosion. She snatched a few paper towels to wipe her face and settled on the toilet, way past the time (and weight) she could hover ungracefully over the bowl. Now she just plopped herself right down with no other choice. Toilet herpes be damned. She peed, flushed, and executed a little relaxation exercise.

She checked her make-up in the mirror as she washed. Not a single mascaraed lash out of place. Her smile flickered, gaining confidence. She opened the door to a wall of Jason.

"You okay?" His brow was furrowed, all playfulness gone.

"It's not my baby," she blurted.

He coughed, amused. "Uh, it's a little hard to play that one off, considering..." He motioned to her mid-section.

"It's being adopted." She fumbled over her explanation that seemed so reasonable when she'd practice it in the mirror in preparation for this very occasion. "I need your help with the legal.... I have a few hypothetical scenarios..." Oh god, bile rose in her throat, threatening her to barf for real this time.

The bathroom door clicked shut behind her, the woman taking her turn, eliminating that option.

A toilet flushed in the men's bathroom, maybe she could duck in there.

"If you need any legal advice, I can find you someone. I didn't practice family law, so I'm not the best—"

"It has to be you. I can't afford anyone else. This baby isn't mine to keep. It needs to go to a family that was meant to love it." Her lungs couldn't fill with enough air and she hitched each breath. Also, was she crying? Stupid hormones.

The men's door opened.

"So you want me to help with the adoption?"

"Not exactly—"

Quinn's tall form suddenly shadowed her boss. "Over my dead body."

Shit. The blood in her face drained the same way it did after a summersault. Jason turned, surprised at their new addition to the conversation.

Quinn glanced at both of them, lines around his mouth and forehead hard and disapproving. She'd never seen him so angry at her. Not even that one time.... Her stomach churned.

"The walls are thin. I could hear every word," Quinn explained. He stepped around Jason, moving toward her.

Apparently she did have some breakfast left in her, because in one heave she tossed it all over Quinn's boots.

CHAPTER FOUR

Quinn knew what a gentlemen did and it wasn't pump a sick woman for information, no matter how desperate. Before Jason could even suggest it, he'd had Zoey in his arms and out the door. He placed her into the cab with a plastic bag in case she threw up again and jogged back inside to do a quick mop of the mess.

"Hope your wife will be okay," an old woman said as she patted his arm.

"Go on." Jason took the mop as Quinn finished. "You don't have to do this. Get her home." Although the expression on Zoey's boss's face told him that he was relieved not have to clean up his employee's puke. He traded the mop handle for the Bradford Trucking accounting books. Jason had swept them all into a Patty's Diner to-go bag.

He wanted to get Zoey in bed—er, to rest of course—so he snagged the offering and hustled out to the truck, climbing inside.

Zoey clutched the plastic baggie to her chest. "I'm so gross. That was horrible. I'm so sorry."

"Come on, Z. It's not the first time."

"Right. You were there the first time I got shit faced. I'm such a terrible friend." Her face crumpled.

Crap. "No, I'm terrible. I shouldn't have compared them. You getting toasted for the first time isn't the same as being pregnant. I meant more the anxiety. I know it makes you—"

"But it was because I'd tied myself in knots over you."

He'd been about to defend her more, but her reasoning stopped him in his tracks. She'd friend zoned him. He should take the hint. Fuck, this was where he'd assure her he'd do the right thing. She didn't need to put their baby up for adoption, he'd figure it all out. Except he also didn't want to spook her into thinking he'd rush them down the aisle.

"First time I'd been drinking? It was because you started college and I was held back to do my senior year again." She twisted the bag around her finger and he wanted to tell her to keep it ready in case she'd need it again. Her color still wasn't right.

"My college was local," he countered. "I lived with my parent's right next door."

"But you weren't *there*. Not like before. And I pushed away all your offers to tutor me because I had too much pride. I didn't want you to think I was dumber than you realized."

"Zoey, you're the smartest person I know."

"Stop." She hid her face in her hands, the tears coming in big sobs now.

He didn't let her emotion stop him. Zoey and he had once been inseparable. Trouble followed her as well, but he'd been immune. What started as protective instinct for her morphed into a lot more—on only his end it seemed. This wasn't the first crying jag he'd weathered. She'd done the same for him a number of occasions. Even the last time they'd hung out—the night he'd spilled the contents of his heart and then mopped them up with breaking the law directly after. Whatever she'd said: he didn't take it well. That meant only one thing. Rejection.

He waited while Zoey composed herself.

Honestly it was a relief that she'd finally broke. The weeks he'd been avoiding her when he got back had been excruciating. His dad had said to keep a distance until she came to him first. Apparently she'd given a statement at the station. He hated he'd done that to her. Put her in a position to have to turn him in, or give the cops the puzzle pieces they needed to connect him to the crime.

"I...didn't...visit...you," she said between big breaths.

"I don't blame you. Zoey, I did something awful and I needed to be punished. And I'd pushed myself on to you—"

"No you didn't!" She sat up, indignant now.

"Yeah, I stole a car. That's a crime. I did the time."

"No." She shook her head. "I told them. I told them it wasn't you."

"That's very sweet, but our friendship doesn't include you lying to protect me."

"Oh, you don't remember." She clutched her hair and slid down in the seat. "It explains so much. I'm even more of a jerk for not being more adamant."

"Zoey, it would have been even worse if you'd lied—"

"You're going to hate me."

"I'd never hate you." He glanced over at her as she turned a few more shades of green. "Hey, get that bag a little closer. You don't look so hot."

"It's my fault. You didn't steal that car." She leaned over the bag and did that slow breathing thing people did right before they puked. "You didn't do it... and I think I know who did."

Nothing she could have told him would have shocked him. Except that.

He helped her out of the cab, both shaking. Her because she'd emptied the contents of her stomach and him because he didn't understand her confession at all. Nine months in the penitentiary for a crime he didn't commit. His entire life down the drain. He'd had plans that didn't include working for his father for the rest of his life. 'Course they also included Zoey and a couple of tikes, *after* marriage— the correct order of events was important. But everything had been turned upside down.

But his mind kept returning to the important fact that his fingerprints had been all over the driver's seat and wheel.

She held the baggie closed, her mascara smeared. "Don't help me down. I'm filthy."

He stepped out of the way. Normally he'd insist. Not anymore.

She scrambled out of the truck and wobbled to the front door, her hand on her forehead. "I thought I'd gotten over the worst of this morning sickness a few months ago. I had it bad, too."

She did have a sheen of sweat covering her skin. The concern tugged at him. He wouldn't make it his problem. Nope. Hell, he wished he could stop caring about her. He wished he could turn it off like a switch. Give her the space she needed. However, she owed him an explanation. He glanced at her stomach as she placed a hand on it, zoning out for a second. Make that two explanations.

"So on the account I could also be sick, you should go on home and save yourself from getting exposed." She nodded to herself as this were an excellent idea and dug for her keys.

He grabbed her purse from her. "No you don't."

She blinked. "Quinn. You went to jail because of me. I won't let you get the stomach flu from me too."

"Believe me, if the worst thing you've done to me has already happened, I don't think a virus will matter at this point." He unlocked the door, shoved through it and held it open for her. "Plus, I need you to explain."

She nodded as if this were her final march right before the guillotine. "All right. I suppose I do owe you an explanation."

"Please." He plopped himself on her couch.

She curled into the recliner.

There was a long pause between them. Her chin wobbled as if she were about to cry again, but she rallied and sat up straight. "I was very upset when I saw you last. I was embarrassed."

"Most people go hide under their bed, they don't steal a car and frame their best friend. I'm assuming that's what you mean by knowing who did this. It was you?"

"Okay, first of all—*I* didn't steal the car. And I don't know for sure the exact person—I was just putting together a few clues. I just know positively it wasn't you. I think you were framed."

He motioned for her to continue.

She did. "Remember Spencer Thompson? We'd seen him when we were bar hopping that night."

"That's whose car I stole."

"You didn't." She sighed. "Anyway, Thompson insisted you get in and take a look. You don't remember that part?"

He shook his head. The whole night had been one big black hole.

"He made a big deal that you had to test his steering. He wanted to ask your opinion, but you said you weren't doing cars anymore, not since you'd graduated with your accounting degree. He insisted you take it for a spin, but you declined."

"I did?" He rubbed his thumb under his bottom lip. No wonder he'd had that feeling he'd driven the car. He'd been in it. Invited. Spencer never mentioned that in the testimony.

"And later when I'd ran out of your place, after..." She turned red.

Ah, when they'd slept together. *That* he'd regret forgetting.

"The car was already there." She frowned. "We'd come home together. We'd been together up until that point and you were home for the night."

He sunk into the couch. Only somewhat closer than where he'd started. "So you actually don't know for a fact I didn't later manage to break in and take it."

"Well, I suppose when you put it that way…not really. But I know you. I know you wouldn't. Not even drunk. In fact, you'd had just the one drink. That's why we were headed home, because you started to feel it hit hard. You said over and over something didn't feel right."

"I had only *one?*" He wracked his brain to remember what she was telling him.

"I ordered one, but they got it wrong and you drank it for me."

"Zoey, I could have drank more after you left my house. *Then* stolen the car."

She shook her head. "I calmed down. I went back—right back to your house. You were passed out cold. I slept on your couch and left in the morning. I'd been so worried 'cause you were so out of it. I thought I was paying you back for the time you took care of me, by looking over you as you slept. The car was there the whole time, same spot, and I'd been with you." She met his gaze, the sincerity evident in her eyes. You didn't leave. You didn't. I told that to the cop. There was also no signs of forced entry. That was the odd part."

"That didn't come up in court."

She huffed. "No, I didn't know you'd been arrested. Not until the court date. I'd been so humiliated I didn't want to show myself." She kept on the subject at hand to avoid too many emotional details of that night. "I went down and told the cop I wanted to testify, but they said they had all the evidence and my statement wouldn't make a difference."

"They still should have talked to my lawyer about it."

"I should have insisted." She hung her head, concentrating on a spot just right in front of the recliner. "Who gets a court date two days after a crime anyway?"

"The Thompson's have some kind of pull in town." He got a glass down from the cupboard, filled it with water, and passed it over to her.

"They own a bank." She took a testing sip. Then a second when that first one stayed down. "I know because after I showed up at the court a week later our mortgage nearly got pulled. We'd apparently missed several checks. I knew I'd sent them in. I saw where I'd written them in my checkbook, but somehow they didn't cash and I never checked that closely. I know, I know, as an accountant you're probably cringing." She happen to glance at him to see he was in fact making a horrified face—he couldn't help it—and it made the corners of her mouth perk up, which in turn warmed him to see her amused. "We nearly got the house taken—I should have been more diligent. He said he'd let it slide just this once if I could pay it in a week, but I had the feeling it was a threat of some kind."

He casually opened and closed cupboards, noting her extreme lack of food. She had stale crackers, two dented cans of chili, and a mac and cheese box. All past their expiration date.

Zoey didn't seem to mind his snooping. She twisted her recliner around and kept her story going as he assessed the fridge. Also bare.

"I had to come up with a triple payment and the steep late fees at the last minute. I had to think of a way to earn some stable income. No more job hopping. And with you gone, I decided it was time to be an adult. You and East have been holding me up for too long. That's why I did this...this baby thing. A job. Adulting. Okay?"

Hence her job at the diner, he guessed. But he didn't understand how their baby played into it. She must mean the baby spurred her into action. Her eyelids hung heavy as she yawned.

"Hey, you should get some rest." He made like he was going to leave, but his feet wouldn't let him move.

She seemed to agree and kicked back the recliner and eased to her side.

"You should be in a bed, Zoey."

"Don't have one," she murmured. "Sold it."

He looked around, noticing her sparse furniture for the first time. He'd need to remedy that.

"And I have to tell you why I needed the money. Why I stayed quiet. Why I stayed away."

"All that can wait." It was obvious why she needed the money now with a baby on the way. He glimpsed the clock, the rumble in his stomach reminding him he hadn't eaten lunch. "I'll come back and check on you in an hour. We can finish our talk then." He'd also bring her some soup and proper groceries. He wiped his hand down his face. Hell, he had to stop. At some point he'd need to stop pushing himself onto her. Using their friendship to keep close to her.

She eased herself off the chair. "Don't go yet. Water goes right through me anymore. I have a pea-sized bladder." She took off to the bathroom.

He hovered awkwardly by the front door until the toilet flushed.

She only came as far as the hallway entry, biting her lip in a way that made him lose all his resolve. Her eyes rounded and softened. His breath caught in his throat.

"About that night," she said. "I kept my promise."

The words washed over him, relaxing him like a long soak in a hot shower. Her tone implied it was a good promise, so his body reacted, hardening—waiting for her to merely whisper the okay and he'd be at her lips in two strides.

He cleared his throat, struggling to keep his voice from breaking. "Remind me of that promise again."

"I haven't been with anyone. I waited for you."

He swallowed knowing what that implied. That he could have Zoey and a baby. All in one package. If being thrown in prison, even innocent—which was still hard to believe—was his price, then he'd be happy to have paid it.

She lowered her head. "Do you believe me?"

He nodded and found himself a loss for words, except a few. "Zoey, I've loved you my entire life, in different forms. I know I've disappointed you—"

"How could you? You are the good one. I'm the trouble."

"You're no trouble."

Her expression turned serious. "But there is something you should know about that night."

"I'm very sorry about anything I might have said or done. Obviously I tried to move things too fast."

"It wasn't you who went too fast. Quite the opposite. That's why I was so embarrassed. Why I ran away. I wanted you so badly and you said you wanted to wait. Go on a few dates."

He blinked, unable to process what she meant. She must have changed his mind somehow. Maybe because he was so affected by that drink? He knew he wouldn't have had the resolve to turn her down at the slightest push she would make in his direction. He was sure he would have pounced her in a second. 'No I can wait until you're ready,' he imagined himself saying. 'Let's have sex,' she'd said back. 'Okay.' He'd then stripped all his cloths and shoved her against the wall. He probably came in two thrusts. She ran out because she realized the mistake she made by trying to change his mind.

"So do you understand? Or perhaps guess…. About the baby?" She nodded as if hoping he'd connect some logical dots.

"Zoey, I know where babies come from."

"Well, there are other ways—" She trailed off, seemingly deliberately.

He ran over a few other scenarios in his head, but her gasp pulled him out of his thought bubble. She pressed her palm into her side.

"That was a strong one," she looked as scared as he felt. "Quinn, I don't think I have morning sickness." She glanced up at him, her mouth wide. "I think that was a contraction!"

He rushed to her side and propped her up as he guided her toward the door. "Let's get you to the hospital."

"It's too soon." She shook her head, digging in her heels as he gently moved them forward. "I needed to find the parents first."

He didn't contradict her. Labor wasn't a good time to discuss adoption. Or what he hoped would be a convincing argument for her to reconsider. "Do you have your doctor's phone number?"

She motioned to her purse and he snagged it off the back of her chair, holstering it around his shoulder. He kept her upright with the other arm. Time to go back out to the truck and to the hospital.

He helped her into the seat and ran back inside to retrieve the stale crackers. He figured that would be his best bet on getting a lunch anytime soon.

CHAPTER FIVE

"False labor?" Zoey sat up in the hospital bed, eyes wide at the doctor. "It felt pretty real to me!"

She'd spent the better part of the late afternoon getting admitted to the hospital. Now they were sending her home because of 'lack of progress.'

"If it was false, then how come I'd been dilating and all that other stuff?" She waved her hands to that general area on her body. For the most part, because she saw her body as rent, she'd tried not to give the birthing process much thought—mostly in an effort to completely shove away all thoughts of the experience of labor.

"This can happen sometimes," Dr. Rosenthal, the fancy LA physician the biological parents paid good money for, explained. "It appears your body went for a short test run. The nausea was likely caused by the onset of Braxton Hicks contractions. Or the Braxton Hicks could have been triggered by the vomiting—you'd said you get sick when you're under a lot of stress?"

"So it's like the chicken or the egg." She fell back into the pillows. "Did the birth parents answer your call?" She quirked up an eyebrow in hopes at least one of her problems had been solved.

Dr. Rosenthal shrugged. "I left a message. Don't worry Zoey. I'm sure they will contact us soon for more details. This is a few weeks earlier than anyone expected."

She didn't mention the lack of contact, or the sudden pause in checks. She rented out her body and was about to enter the most important part, the part where they get the baby, and they were unreachable. She wouldn't have stressed if not for the money thing.

Not many people could legitimately and legally get seventy thousand dollars, plus medical expenses covered, doing nothing but baking a baby and following some very strict guidelines. The food stipulations were one thing, but the complete secrecy was unusual. The lawyers had explained it was because Mr. Brown (a fake name they'd used to refer to themselves) was in the public eye. Mrs. Brown also had reasons to keep their transaction as confidential as possible.

The plan had been: step one find the perfect host. Young, clean, artistic, willing, pass all psychological exams. That turned out to be Zoey. What a relief to find out she wasn't crazy. And weirdly her test scores must have been switched with someone else because they told her she test very high on the intelligence quotient. Step two was pay a large sum of money for the surrogate to keep quiet and prevent the media from hounding them and Zoey. Easy enough, Zoey didn't want to be followed around by news cameras who would peek into her every misdeed. Step three equaled baby being presented to the public without her involvement being mentioned except as a passing comment in interviews.

"Zoey? Did you have any questions before you are discharged?" Dr. Rosenthal waited patiently.

"Oh, uh—" She frowned, trying to remember what she needed to ask. "Right. I can't seem to get a hold of the parents or the lawyer about...details."

The doctor closed her tablet and thrust it under her arm. "I'm sure they'll get back to you soon. I only handle the medical side of things."

"And you've been..." she carefully chose her wording, "compensated?"

"My office handles the bills." The doctor pulled the tablet out from under her arm and glanced at it then the door.

An obvious sign Zoey had been dismissed.

"If you'll excuse me, I have to make arrangements with my office to stay in the Sacramento area for the next few days to be sure your situation doesn't change. And I do have some patients here."

Of course, one of the reasons this doctor had been chosen over many others was she had a mobile office and visited the major cities. Driving an hour to her little town outside of Sacramento wasn't too much of an inconvenience. Her baby buyers were loaded, but not obscenely so.

Dr. Rosenthal left the room and Zoey stripped off the hospital gown, unclipping her clothes from the plastic bag above the bathroom door. She dug out her cell phone to call Crypt for a ride, but, damn it, she'd run out of batteries.

There was knock at her door.

"Zoey?" Quinn's voice echoed on the other side.

She jerked the door open. "Quinn!"

His gaze fell down immediately, as if mesmerized by something beautiful, then he raised his gaze, guiltily.

She looked down to discover her gown drooping over her shoulder and exposing part of her right boob. "Shit." She pulled him inside and shut the door. "What are you doing here? It's nearly midnight and you dropped me off hours ago. They said you could go."

"True, but I couldn't leave you alone and in labor. And I wanted to see the baby." His cheeks got a little flushed, and he worked hard to not let his gaze linger below where her gown wouldn't behave. "Our baby."

"Our baby..." Oh shit. Her lungs deflated of all air. She rewound her conversation with him this morning. At what point did she not make it clear they hadn't slept together. That she threw herself on him and he said they should wait and she ran off humiliated. She did return because she realized the drama queen moment wasn't her finest and Quinn needed her for once. She had a chance to pay him back for all those times he'd been there for her. She was committed to wait for when he would be ready.

She guided him to the guest couch in the tiny room. Luckily her roommate had been wheeled off for a c-section. Or, well, unluckily. At least she had the room alone to spell out the situation as best she could.

"Quinn." She leveled him with a very serious expression. "I want you to pay attention. For legal reasons I can't go into detail or even explain a bigger picture. But you could work it out, if you pay attention." She scratched her head, figuring the exact wording she could use to keep herself in the clear.

He nodded. "I know that you might have already started the adoption paperwork, but Zoey, the law states that you can change your mind at any point, even a few days after giving birth. We still have time to reconsider. And I want you to hear me out first. If you want to go forward after that, I won't stand in your way. But seeings how you want to give this relationship a go and I'm on board one hundred percent—"

"Quinn, we didn't have sex."

He opened his mouth as if he had a rebuttal but didn't quite expect that admission. He closed his mouth. Opened it again. Hesitated. Little whistles of air came from this throat as if he were trying to process the information. Then he frowned, stared at her, hard.

She held up her finger. "I told you the truth about not being with anyone."

"You've never lied to me before, but I'm finding it hard to believe—"

"Come on Quinn, put it together!"

"This baby isn't mine..."

She nodded up and down viciously. "And—and this is important—it isn't mine either." She waved her hands in a circular motion for him to complete the thought. "Advances in science and all. I needed the money." She pressed her lips together, bugging out her eyes, willing him to make the logical jump.

He tilted his head to the side. "You're a surrog—"

She jumped forward and covered his mouth. "Don't say it out loud. That's the part I'm not allowed to say."

"But I can say it. I didn't sign any weird legal documents that prevent me from saying anything."

"Except I can't confirm or deny." She let out a long breath. "East is the only one who knows because of the whole 'counselors have to keep their patient's secret' clause."

"She's a school psychologist, not a marriage and family therapist." He glared at her. "You couldn't tell me right before you signed the documents: 'Oh hey, by the way, I'm going to be pregnant and the whole town will assume it's yours, Quinn. Your parents are going to send you letters in prison about how disappointed they are that you knocked up your best friend and also committed a felony.'"

"To be fair, it was extenuating circumstances and I didn't know if you wanted to ever talk to me again. I didn't know anyone had told you about the baby while you were locked in, let alone your parents.... I couldn't keep you from getting arrested. I knew you didn't steal that car. Something isn't right. I couldn't get them to believe me and you went away for it."

He sighed, realizing he was being especially harsh. "It's not your fault Zoey. They have evidence against me. I *could* have done it. You weren't with me the whole night." He sagged in his chair. "Can we do one disaster at a time? I know I should be relieved, but I'd gotten my hopes up." His voice broke a little at the end and he rubbed his hand over his nose and pressed it into his mouth for a second. Then he shook his head looking away.

Oh god. She'd been callous. He'd thought for seven or so months that he could be a father and he'd settled into the idea. He'd even accepted that the baby wasn't his and he forgave her anyway, would have been willing to step up. Not like the other guys who'd offered out of some misplaced 1950s sentimentality, but because it was Quinn and as he'd told her all those months ago, he wanted his forever to be with her. They'd had a history of friendship as a base to make it work.

She plopped down next to him. "I'm so sorry." Her arm tightened around his tight shoulders. "It should have been the first thing I clarified. I was just all tangled up in the legal implications—"

He stood suddenly, her arm getting suddenly cold at the absence of his heat.

He moved her bag of clothes to the tray table next to her. "You should get dressed. I'll just..." he slid the curtain across to give her privacy.

She dressed in silence, except for the occasional coughs, throat clearing, and shoe scuffing sounds between them. Almost like they were communicating through awkward noises and one upping each other.

She scooted against the pleather seat and it groaned like a fart. The weird non-rebuddle made her sweat. "That was the chair!" She finally blurted.

He snorted a laugh.

She hoped they could repair whatever damage to their friendship had been done with all these misunderstandings between them. If they couldn't share a laugh at a good fart joke then all hope would be lost.

She flipped open the curtain. "I dare you to sit in that seat, wiggle around, and prove me wrong."

He hid a smile. "Don't worry about it, Z. I believe you." He said it with such conviction she knew he didn't mean the gas-passing chair.

They walked a sensible distance apart to the truck, but they at least walked there together.

CHAPTER SIX

Quinn followed Zoey inside her house, hefting a sack of groceries onto her counter. He opened a cupboard. Wiping the dried onion skins from inside, he wondered how long it had been since she'd made herself a decent meal. How long she'd been pinching pennies to keep them ahead on the mortgage.

Zoey set her purse down on the card table in the middle of the living room that served as a dinning space. "What are you doing?"

"Putting away these cans. And the milk. I can't leave the milk out it will spoil." He opened the fridge, sending her an innocent look, and did exactly that as if making a point.

"Quinn Bradford, I'm fully capable of shopping and providing for myself."

"I wondered."

She huffed. "Well, you caught me between shopping trips, is all. I was waiting for my paycheck."

"From the diner. Sure." He knew she meant the surrogacy gig, but he wanted to show he could play along. So she wasn't allowed to share that information or even acknowledge the arrangement. Although... "So," he cleared his throat, "why can't you tell anyone about your empty cupboards? They aren't going to fill themselves."

Her brow furrowed for a second, but smoothed out as she instantly caught on. "Well, these cans are Campbell soup cans. People would definitely recognize them, so I can't go opening the cupboards and showing them off."

"Ah," he stacked the last of the pantry items neatly in a row. So she must mean that the parents were high profile, or needed to remain private for some reason. "Do they at least taste better than the other soups? Do they make it worth the money?"

She took a long time to answer. "The money is worth it." There was a little catch in her voice that indicated there was more to the story there. He wouldn't push her though. Zoey was loyal and if she didn't feel comfortable sharing a secret then he knew she'd hold it back and withdraw more from him to keep herself honest.

"I'll sleep on the couch," he announced.

"Oh." She scratched her elbow. "Are you sure? You don't have to—"

"I'm guessing that little kickstart into labor was a prelude to something bigger." He tossed the throw blanket down and commandeered a pillow from the recliner. She eyed his arrangement. Then he remembered. She'd been sleeping on the chair earlier and said she sold her bed. "Or I can take the floor."

Zoey's shoulders fell. "You'd be so much more comfortable in your own bed—"

"Excellent idea. We can go there—"

"I really shouldn't..." she trailed off, not really wanting to find a good excuse.

He couldn't think of one either, but then again he was too turned on to really be the best judge. "I'll help you pack."

She didn't protest, instead she threw a few overnight items into her bag.

Getting ready for bed—take two—went a lot more smoothly now that they had more options. Problem was that Quinn's seven-hundred square foot cabin only had one room, one bathroom, and one bed. There was a small kitchen with all the basic essentials, and a very comfy couch. He and his brothers had built the place over weekends while in college on their family's property.

It had been meant to be getaway from their parents when they'd visit, but went unused after each brother married off and preferred the comfort of the big house for visits. Overall, the build had been a learning project—one of the outlets still sparked when he'd plug in the coffee maker and if he tried to run the laundry machine and the toaster, oven the lights would flicker. Although, staying there was a real smart move considering it saved him from being homeless after being released.

Zoey set her things down on the couch and they replayed the night's earlier events except in reverse. She took down the throw blanket and fluffed up a pillow, putting them on his couch.

"You're not sleeping out here, Zoey, you can take my bed."

She fiddled with the pillow, pressing it against her mid-section. "On one condition."

He nodded, waiting for her to name it.

"We share it."

He lifted an eyebrow.

She dropped the pillow onto the couch and her words rushed together. "It's just I'd feel better not putting you out and I know I'm not going to be comfortable out here." Her hand dropped to the arm of the couch. "Not that it's not a lovey couch and I know I'm...different...more ungainly...than when you saw me last."

"Don't worry about that. I like you just fine." His voice developed a husky layer he knew gave away his attraction. Did that make him a perv? Being attracted to pregnant women? Well, honestly one woman in particular.

He'd never considered it before, the idea making him freak out a bit. His brother insisted that there was nothing sexier than when his wife grew with her pregnancies. He figured it was a woman-carrying-your-child kind of buzz. Apparently it didn't need to be his child to feel that way, because that burn didn't go away. It had continued to increase with each minute he spent with Zoey.

"I have to wake up early for my shift." She glanced at the clock. "Will that be a problem? I can keep my phone volume low."

"It won't be a problem. I'll be up early for work too. Dad's been having me audit the last year of book-keeping. The person he hired might have been skimming. Not really, but dad is—well, you know how he is."

Her head fell forward, her hair coving her smile. "Yeah, I know. Tom is...Tom."

"You've always put things a nice way." He ducked into his room. "Just give me a second to get ready for the night."

She waved him on and he closed the door and rushed to work. He made the bed, yeah, kinda pointless considering, but he wanted to give her a good impression. He normally did this every morning, but after coming back from prison he'd let a lot of his good habits slide. Funny how having Zoey back changed his outlook on life. Even if this was all they ever were to each other: two friends who depended on each other; he wouldn't ever take it for granted.

He sifted through his drawers to find a pair of sweats. Thank god. He normally wore only his underwear and sometimes an undershirt if it was cold. Sometimes nothing if it was the dead of summer and not a cool breeze in sight.

He dimmed the lights. Sprayed some old perfume one of Adam's many hook ups left behind. Opened a window because that shit stunk like an overripe strawberry molding in the fridge. He coughed.

The flash of twin lights was a glimmer. Almost miss-able, if he hadn't been looking at the exact spot through the neighbor's olive orchard. He squinted, wondering. The light flicked off, as if the car they belonged to had found its place and settling for the night.

He could feel Zoey's presence before she ever entered the room. Her knock on the slightly opened door was timid and unsure. "You can come in," he said, but his attention remained out into the night. The odd lights, right where they shouldn't have been, bothered him.

"You counting stars?"

Her voice called him back into the room. Her hands brushing against his on the window sill. He let himself enjoy the touch, taking a deep breath. "Naw. I don't do that anymore."

She frowned and then her mouth hung open with a scoff. "Impossible, Quinn Bradford. How will we ever find out how many there are?"

He shook his head, moving away slightly, but the breeze chilled through him the farther away he scooted. "It's too overcast." He let his gaze drop, unable to meet hers.

Her hands fluttered as if unsure of where to put them. "All right." She skirted around the bed and toward the bathroom. "I'll just be—" She motioned and didn't finish her sentence before disappearing.

Well, damn. He'd screwed that up.

Quinn twisted the rod on his blinds to give them full privacy. In the living room he did the same above the couch while Zoey brushed passed him on her way out of the bathroom.

Her skin against his. He froze, drinking in the sensation. The initial zing and then following waves of arousal. The mysterious lights went far back on his items to care about. Zoey moved to the bed, which brought images of her moving on top—

She paused at the foot of the bed. "Do you have preference?"

He swallowed hard, willing himself not to suggest his current fantasy. "Not really. I migrate all around through the night. You?"

She went to the left side of the bed. "This has a clear shot to the bathroom."

"A sound plan." He mirrored her to the right and waited at his side. They had sides now.

She folded back the sheets and he wished he'd had more time so he could have changed them so they'd be fresh. He'd do that tomorrow while she worked.

He didn't trust himself to get in just yet, so he sat, facing away from her. "Are you sure you have a shift? As far as your boss knows you're in labor at the hospital."

"I texted him and told him it was a false alarm. He sent me a thumbs up. Since it's not a 'hey you don't have to come in for your shifts,' response I'm assuming that means I need to be there bright and early."

"Don't you have to stop working at some point?"

"I can work right up until I go into labor and since I need the money, that's what I'll do."

He wanted to ask her about her surrogacy deal, but he had to figure a way to word it. "And what about your canned food drive? What about the money you're bringing in for that?" He figured he should continue with their secret metaphor to ask about the situation.

"Oh." She folded her feet under the sheets and tucked the blankets around her waist. "That's going to the mortgage. I'm going to use the can money to

pay it off. When uncle Jake passed away we had to pay an estate tax on the property, so we would have owned it free and clear if not for that. Uncle Jake didn't have any mortgage left to pay. We had to take out another one to pay the tax. East said if I came up with all the money she'd transfer title to me. Quinn," she turned toward him, hands flat in prayer position under her head, "if I own a house, I have something when everything else falls through. I know it's a pile of junk, but I love that house."

"So it works out? Makes it all worth it?"

She didn't answer right away, like she was taking her time to come up with the answer. "I thought I'd feel different. I thought it would all be...easier."

"Cans are a difficult business—"

She squeezed her eyes shut. "I never wanted a baby. I never thought about it until now. Now all I can wonder is if she's going to be loved." Her eyes opened and were glassy with threatening tears. She didn't shed one. "I know it isn't fair. This baby has nothing of mine. Her egg, his sperm. Not a drop of me. This isn't my baby, they're just renting the space—"

He didn't answer, mostly because she didn't a question. Partly because she was talking about the baby particulars she said she'd promised she couldn't talk about.

"—then they stopped paying. So, I'm left to wonder if I'm going to get stuck with a baby that's not mine? What am I supposed to do?"

"Isn't there a lawyer or someone who set it up?"

"I called him too and left a message with the secretary. Nothing from him either." She dug herself lower into the bed. "What if this baby doesn't have anyone who wants her? I mean, I never let myself really indulge in that idea before the payments stopped. Now it's all I can think about and I'm scared. I don't want a baby." She bit her lip. "At the same time I do." She quickly moved her gaze to the ceiling when their eyes met. "After marriage and when the timing is perfectly worked out."

"That's my plan too," he said. Then he couldn't help it, he twisted to stare at her, waiting until the courage built up just enough. "I'd have been that baby's father. I wouldn't have regretted a thing."

Her hand went to her mid-section, rounding up and down for one stroke. "I know." She smiled at him.

He walked over and killed the lights and in the dark found his way back to his spot on the bed, sliding under the covers. His leg rubbed against hers.

He readjusted himself, trying carefully to not touch, but her leg met his again. He stilled. He could swear he forgot how to breathe.

She emitted a low snort of suppressed laughter.

He sighed. "Zoey, I'm trying to do the right thing here."

"The last time you did that, we both ended up in a lot of trouble."

He let himself relax against the pillows. Funny, he didn't find as much relief as he expected he would by having her close. Instead it amplified his need. That little voice in his head that had insisted for years it would be a lot better if they waited until they did things proper: dates, planning, careful discussion where they checked on each other's emotional investment.

Her fingers connected with his under the cover. She laced her pinky to his, hesitant. Zoey never hesitated. He wanted to dive in head first. How they'd swapped places in the last year.

He found her in the dark. Lips to lips. They hovered over hers as if to ask permission. She didn't make it easy. He'd have to be the one cross that last centimeter. In one motion his hand that she'd pinkie locked covered hers completely, his other hand grazed the back of her head to tilt her forward, and his mouth touched hers. First a sweep, then testing the fit of their lips like a puzzle and when she opened for him he pressed harder, changing the angle.

It had been better than he'd imagined. He eased back. "Did we do this? That night?"

She nodded. "A little. This is better." He could sense her pulling away.

He went for more kisses, wishing he could jog his memory. Something had definitely been wrong. If he'd kissed Zoey for the first time, he'd have remembered it. It would have carried him through his sentence.

She moved away again. "Quinn are you sure?"

He swallowed a deep breath, but nothing could stifle his hormones commanding him to continue with the party. "I'm really turned on right now."

She wiggled her thigh. The one that was in direct contact with his groin. "I can feel that."

Jesus, he'd been dry humping her. "I've always wanted you Zoey. I think you're right. We shouldn't have waited."

"No. I needed the time. If I'd gotten my way that night I would have messed it all up. I didn't know what I wanted until now. I needed to grow up. This surrogacy thing? Wanting the house and making a plan? That put me in a better position to step out of East's shadow. You'd taken care of me too. I never had to think for myself before. I needed this." Her hands glided down his chest. Over his t-shirt. His nipples hardened in response to her. "God, I didn't mean that you're going to prison was the best thing ever—"

He placed a hand over hers. "I know what you meant."

"Good." Her hand grazed down his arm, then away. "I have to know—I'm not fishing for compliments—

but I guess I'm needier than I'd like to admit. Why me? You could have someone smarter, prettier, someone with more going for her."

"If you really have to know, it was your tenacity." She went quiet at his admission, waiting for the explanation. "You might write it off, but I don't. In seventh grade the boys in our class discovered I was good at math. That I wanted to be an accountant and not a baseball hero, a football star, or a basketball legend. What sensible thirteen year old boy wants to be an accountant?"

"I don't think I even knew what an accountant was in seventh grade."

"Yet you defended me down to the last bully. And kept on doing it. People gravitated to you. Your confidence. You were popular. A cheerleader. You didn't talk down about others to get there, you talked them up. People were drawn to your positivity, instead of afraid of negativity some of the others would employ in the same position."

"It made me feel like a cruelty to talk about other people," she said. "I thought they'd talk about me next if I opened that door. Uncle Jake said to think about something someone does well and repeat it to them. It's the only way to make friends and prevent enemies."

"Uncle Jake was very wise."

"He was also an alcoholic."

Quinn hugged her close. "It didn't take away from his accomplishments."

"He didn't treat East, his own daughter, well, but he took me on when I had nobody else."

"He was a complicated man." Quinn shifted, attempting to relieve the pressure in his groin to no success. "Forgive me if I don't want to talk about Uncle Jake right now."

She understood instantly, as only Zoey could. She read situations well most of the time. Her touch returned, this time guiding lower. "We don't have to talk about anything."

"Let's forget about the past. I'd rather talk about our future."

CHAPTER SEVEN

Zoey's insides flipped and flopped with anticipation. She fully expected Quinn to put the brakes on things at any second. He'd realize his mistake. Decide she was too much trouble. Right now he was being powered by memories of their friendship. He thought he owed her something for keeping him from getting beat up as a teen.

Though at his size, he'd always towered over the other boys. He would never have been in any real danger. Except Quinn didn't think of violence as his answer to his problems. He would have let them throw all their punches and knowing that crowd, they'd have kept coming back for more once they learned they could dig their insecure claws in without consequences.

He slowly lowered himself to her again and she put her finger on his lips, stopping him for a moment. "I just want you to know, I'm all in. I'm loyal. If you change your mind I'll be torn to bits. I'll recover, but I'll always regret our friendship ended."

"This isn't an ending for us. I won't let it be. We work together. We always have. If anything that friendship will be a strong base for our relationship."

She let him kiss her this time. No hesitations, No regrets. She should have known that all roads would eventually lead to Quinn. In truth it must have been

what agitated her about seeing him after his release. How would they pick up from what seemed like the end of an era? In reality, that seemed like a tiny blip on their radar. If they could weather that, anything seemed possible.

Could their relationship be the one thing her Wild Winter's tendencies couldn't break? She cringed at that old nickname for everyone in their family. *Wild Winters.* Except East. She never did anything crazy until she hopped on a truck cross-country and fell in love.

He kissed down her neck to the place between her jaw and her ear. She shivered. His touch sparked every nerve ending. She'd looked up erogenous zones when she'd started having sex and giggled at the idea. She'd thought it a crock, but not now? Now with Quinn's slow caresses, she could imagine a lot more.

He breathed deep, rolling to his back. "We should stop here, if you don't want..." his voice hitched as if he didn't' want to give her the option, but being Quinn—he'd never presume.

"Oh god, Quinn, if you stop. I'll have to rub myself to relief."

His hand went to the growing mound in the sheets at his thighs. "Zoey, I'm about to burst here already—"

"Then get over here."

He gripped the sheets. "Hold on." He pressed his eyes closed and took a long, drawn breath as if clearing his head. Then he slammed open his side drawer and pulled out some condoms.

Zoey propped herself up and swung her leg over his hips. She pressed down. "Do you really need that condom? I'm already pregnant. And I know you're cautious with your partners. I bet you got tested recently too as a precaution." She held back a grin. "Am I right?"

"I'm clean." He put a hand on each side of her hips, holding hard as if attempting to still her motion with little success, instead he closed his closed his eyes and ground up against her. "But correct me if I'm wrong—

I googled surrogacy and I thought they were really careful over body fluids, namely other people's."

Zoey leaned slightly forward, as much as she could with the baby between them. A little reminder of things she didn't want to think about. "I don't think they can control my body for nine months to that degree. If you're clean then there's nothing to worry about."

He rolled the condom on anyway. "I wouldn't do anything to hurt you or the baby."

"I know. You'd never hurt anyone." She bowed to kiss him, only making it half way.

He rose to meet her and the kiss deepened, quickening. His fingers slid under her long shirt and rode it up to her chest, helping her shimmy out of it. He used the opportunity to shed his t-shirt too. She lifted herself for a moment to kick off her underwear and he scooted out of his sweats, his thick erection saluting between them. He held himself steady while she lowered herself onto him.

Quinn's head fell back into the pillow as he hissed at the contact. "I can't believe this is happening."

"Me either," she admitted. Her voice cracking, giving away to the emotions that welled up inside her.

He thrust up as she sunk down once, twice. His fingernails dug into her outer thighs. "I'm not going to make it."

"I'm almost there."

Their gazes met. Him searching for strength to keep the steady rhythm, as though he were stubborn in his resolve to let her pleasure come first. Her unable to keep herself grounded in this moment. She loved him. It wasn't just the hormones talking. She'd always loved him.

His expression grew frantic, biting his lip. "No. No." His groans edged with a horse cry as he neared.

"Yes. Yes." Zoey tiled her angle as the intense waves hit her.

Quinn may have been cursing. She couldn't have said for sure as her hearing cut out and her awareness narrowed inward. The orgasms she'd had in pregnancy were top notch. She'd explain it to Quinn when he wasn't gripping her ass and sawing his breath into her chest.

"I'm sorry."

She did blink confusedly for that. "What? I came. It was amazing. You made it back to me." She ran her fingers through his hair. Too long for Quinn, so she'd enjoy the long locks while she could.

"I'm sorry I left."

She bit off every word she formed in her head. She couldn't say it was okay, because going to prison was far from okay. She couldn't say it wasn't his fault, because she'd tried that and Quinn was too responsible to allow blame to fall anywhere but on himself. So instead she kissed his forehead and attempted to tell him with her touch what him being here now meant.

"I'd had a different idea for my future with you. I had a lot of time to think about it while I worked up the nerve to run it by you," he said. "It involved getting us out of this town and starting fresh somewhere we could outrun both our family's reputations."

"East tried that. It doesn't seem to work. The real work happens inside." She put her hand over his heart and kissed his chest. His skin glistened in the moonlight. "We can make a future anywhere. My home is wherever you are."

He watched her, as if he were processing her wisdom. "Yeah, Zoey, my home is wherever you are too." He kissed her cheek. "See, you're the smart one."

The rush of blood in her cheeks prickled. Quinn's genuine flattery would cement his place in her heart. She eased herself off him and onto her side next to him. Her head fit perfectly between his bicep muscle and his shoulder. His other arm came reflexively over to hug her closer.

"Maybe you were too perfect before, but honestly, Quinn, you've taken my tendency toward bad boys a little too far."

He half-smiled, thankfully getting her joke. "I've always been an overachiever. Teacher's pet and all." He pressed his nose against her hair and sniffed deep.

A light flashed in the dark room, headlights brightening the small space. Quinn frowned.

"What is it?" she asked.

He turned, facing the window, glaring out as if contemplating. The expression so distant and cold she didn't recognize him.

"Quinn?"

He twisted back to her. "It's nothing." Except his tone didn't indicate he believed his own brush off. "You need your rest."

She patted his shoulder to get him to release his tightening hold on her. "Let me just pee one last time. Well, in truth it won't be the last time." She was attempting to make light of whatever took his attention, but he barely acknowledged her humor.

Instead, he'd already sat up and gone to the window, pinching the blinds open.

She slipped her t-shirt back on and with a last glance wondered what had happened while he'd been serving time that meant he now kept a knife in his top drawer, still open from where his condoms spilled out.

CHAPTER EIGHT

Quinn dressed bright and early the next morning, reluctant to leave a warm sleeping Zoey while he headed out for a run. The surrounding orchards and rice fields created a morning fog that burned off by the time the sun peeked over the Sutter Buttes. So he knew he'd have to be quick to keep his cover. He wove through his parent's property, staying off the road and open fields where drivers or anyone set up camp could see him. It meant hugging close to Brant's Almond orchard.

"Morning," his friendly neighbor greeted him as he jogged past.

He slowed to catch his breath and to catch up. He'd made a point of reconnecting with his past acquaintances that were positive, a recommendation by the counselors at his brief exit interview from the penitentiary. "Brant." He waved and waited for his friend at the fence.

Brant hopped of his ladder and met him. "We got any problems?" His once close neighbor had a different spark in his eye after Quinn had returned. Still friendly, but also cautious.

Quinn had also noticed the new security cameras pointed all around Brant's house. He didn't know how to rebuild his trust with him, so he'd have to keep on proving by actions. Though he hadn't taken anything from Brant, it didn't mean Brant would welcome him with open arms after news broke of Quinn's misdeeds last year.

"Was that you driving around last night?"

"Nope." Brant shrugged his shoulders. "Kids have the flu. We were all in bed pretty early. I don't take the equipment out late at night as a rule. We got things closed up and locked once the crews leave for the day."

Message received, old friend. But the information he needed was important, so Quinn kept inquiring. "Would you mind if I check some of your gates and roads along our property line? I think we had a trespasser last night. Might have gone through your orchards as a way out. My dad wants me to look into it."

A little off from the truth, but close. He'd texted his dad last night about the car in the field. It wasn't him or one of Quinn's brothers. Nobody else has business being out here.

"Sure. I'll check our cameras too. I don't think we had anything disturbed."

Quinn didn't believe the person would have taken anything on the first scout. Perhaps if the mysterious visitor had been on foot, but in a car driving through the fields with its lights off? Pretty sure that meant he was casing the area. His time in prison educated him on all kinds of crimes and ways to commit those crimes without detection.

"Let me know if you see anything on video. I'd appreciate it. Any chance you could send me a segment?"

Brant removed his hat, scratched his head, and slid the cap back on. "If I can see anything."

"All right. I'll go check around where I saw the car."

"I'll be right here. Checking up on some pests threatening the crop. I'll be out here all morning." He went back up his ladder and back to his task, but his eyes were scanning the area Quinn mentioned he'd be headed.

Interpretation: Brant would keep careful watch over the areas Quinn would be surveying. He expected his neighbor would be calling on his dad to be sure Quinn was telling the truth before releasing any video.

He jogged to the area he figured the car must have gone. Heavy irrigation had left his muddy print—along with tire tracks. Quinn took a few pictures, following the tracks through the field and out into the main road. Someone had done a circle, stopped facing Quinn's little cabin. He stood in the spot the person would have parked. They'd have had a full view of his back windows.

Quinn decided to buy some fast growing trees and shrubs to hide the view better in case anyone had ideas of making this a habit.

It could be some local teenagers out here to find some privacy. Wouldn't be the first time the spot had been used. Road access, lining two private properties with lots of trees to shield them from the main road, yet technically still community land with all the driveways leading to the various homes. Though his gut told him it wasn't teenagers.

He took a few more pictures and then jogged back to his place to shower and take Zoey to her shift, making sure Brant saw him heading home so he could go back inside and stop worrying Quinn was attempting a heist on his nut harvest.

Quinn set up his computer and went to work getting lost in numbers and balances. Zoey sat across from him, pulling him from his hazy world where only addition and subtraction existed.

He startled, checking the time on his phone. "Is your shift over already?"

She laughed. "Wow, you really are out of it. No, four-hour shift. This is my fifteen-minute break. So, I thought I'd bring you some french toast to share. Sharon had this order up and the customer changed her mind."

He twisted around to see the other waitress and her kind smile in their direction. Jason dropped off some water to their table, murmuring for them to enjoy. He bet that a lot of orders went wrong on Zoey's shift. They kept good care of her.

"Well, it's a shame to let good food go to waste." He snagged a bite. It had a hint of vanilla. "Wow, just like Patty's."

"Don't say that to Jason, he gets a little upset when he gets it right. This was one recipe we found. Little vanilla and nutmeg added in with the egg and milk. He thinks if he does too good of a job people will think he's trying to replace the un-replaceable."

"Grief does funny things to people," he said. "Probably nobody thinks that."

"Yeah, I don't think anyone believes he's here to replace her. It's obvious he loved and admired her." Her fork moved quickly to stab several toast squares at once and she tucked them into her cheeks, making them puff out as she chewed.

He pushed the rest of the plate to her, letting her finish it off. He'd had a big breakfast, but he saw she only had a few bites of cereal.

"We should probably talk about last night," she said, finishing off the free meal. "I don't want you to think I'm not capable of taking care of myself. I've been doing good being independent and I don't want to break that streak."

"I wouldn't dream of it." He did dream of it, but he'd be good and make sure he didn't expect them to slip into their old patterns: she bringing trouble and he wrangling her out of it.

"I have a lot of stuff going on with the baby and I have to figure it all out on my own. It's important to me. It's not that I want to keep you in the dark or hide behind legal obligations."

"I don't need to insert myself into your business, but Z, I'm here when you need me. Even if that only includes a hot meal and a foot rub after a shift."

"So, even though I pumped myself up for this talk, I do have to ask you for something. I'm going to be giving birth. East was supposed to be my coach…" She bit her lip, her lashes sweeping up shyly.

"I'd be honored."

"If yesterday was any indication it won't be fun. I'll be sick, in pain, crying—"

"So basically a usual Tuesday for you."

She snorted out a laugh and snatched the empty plate up. "I got to get back to work. Two more hours."

He gestured to his work. "I got a lot to keep me occupied."

She went back to bussing tables and taking orders. Jason slipped into the seat across from him, dropping a cup of coffee between them.

Quinn set his pencil down. "I suppose you're here to ensure I'm not going to hurt Zoey, now that you know."

"The minute I saw you yesterday I knew you were different. She fretted herself into a frenzy, into labor."

"About that—why is she still at work?"

"She insisted. I told her we had someone to cover."

He pressed himself into the cushion of the seat, it groaned against his weight. "Interesting. She made it sound like you're short staffed."

"I am. I still would have covered her shift. We can't seem to get people who show up consistently. As mush crap as I give her, she's actually one of our best waitresses. The customers love her. The regulars all ask to be in her section. She remembers conversations they've had and picks right up where they left off."

"She's got a talent with people. Always has," Quinn took a sip of the offered coffee. If Jason meant it as an olive branch, he'd do his part to take the other end. "I guess we can both feel guilty with each other over our mutual harming of Zoey yesterday. Me with the coming back and seeking her out, and with you over-working her."

Jason ignored Quinn's comments on over-working. "I want to be sure that she's not getting into any tangles. I promised East—"

"Funny. I also promised East I'd always fill that role." He kept his gaze on Jason over the cup, wondering if the man had some assumed claim to Zoey. Best he understand now exactly with whom she belongs.

Jason rolled his eyes. "Relax. I'm not in the market for a woman." And to prove it Jason checked out the ass on a trucker who hitched himself onto the stool and gave the diner owner a matching fiery stare. "Excuse me. I have a short attention span." He brought his focus back to Quinn. "So, we good? Are we supposed to push each other around and grunt and stuff? I'd rather skip that part as I'm sure I can apply the effort elsewhere." He held up his finger to the trucker to let the other man know he'd be there soon.

"I think we'll do fine."

"Excellent," Jason said. "Oh, and—" he trotted to the bar and reached under it from the opposite side, pulling out a cash box, a folder of receipts, and a notebook, "—just please, please, please. I really can't seem to find an accountant at all and you're here. Also tax quarterly taxes make me cross-eyed."

Quinn arched his eyebrow. "Are you sure. Even with the, uh, record?"

"You should know I'm a lawyer. You try anything and I'll have you in court so fast you'll spin like the finale of an Olympic ice dance. But Zoey tells me that with this kind of thing you're solid. As we both know, she's good with people." Jason wiggled his eyebrows and dusted his hands, twisting and meeting his new arrival at the bar as if that was that.

Quinn unfolded the stacks of diner receipts, fearing the worst.

Not too bad—at least it was organized logically. He'd been nearly done with his work for Bradford Trucking and it's not like he were in a position to turn down work. A felony pretty much wiped out his ability to work anywhere he'd need a license. A downgrade to extra experienced bookkeeper was the best he could hope for. Bradford Trucking wasn't a full time or long term gig. It could be, but he didn't want it.

He opened a new spreadsheet in his computer and went to work creating a tidy, organized file for Jason.

The rumble of a tweaked muffler interrupted his work. A familiar sound he couldn't place, but set his hairs on edge and his teeth to grind. Glancing up he knew what must have caused his instinctual cringe. That asshole from yesterday. The one that hassled Zoey. The guy parked, honking as if he owned the parking space an older couple were maneuvering out of—a handicapped space. This jerk didn't have a special placard either. He zipped into the space at an angle, making it ineffective for anyone to use the wheelchair loading section.

Jason didn't seem to notice, his attention rapt on the trucker. The trucker's fingers were running along the back of one of Jason's hands. It were as if they were finding reasons to touch one another in those early stages of a relationship. Sort of where he and Zoey were, or he'd like to be.

Zoey glanced nervously out the window, noticing the commotion. Quinn set aside the current workbook he'd been using and made sure to calm himself before standing. No use getting his blood pressure raised over this asshole.

He waited, promising himself he wouldn't get involved unless the guy went right for Zoey. Which, of course, he did.

"Zobo hobo, let's get going," the guy called to Zoey.

Zoey shrunk in place, mid taking an order for a family of six. "And what would you like?" She couldn't kneel down to the littlest's level, but she crouched as far as she could to make him feel less intimidated.

"Zobo," the guy whistled. "Hustle."

Quinn was at the guy's side in four steps. "She's got a ride. So, if you're in a hurry, no need to wait. You can be on your way."

The guy squinted at him. "Nope. Crypt sent me. He said her shift ends today at noon."

Zoey came over, tucking her order pad into the front of her apron. "I texted Crypt to let him know I had it covered." She crossed her arms. "And he wouldn't ever send someone else. He'd let me know first."

"So? He might have mentioned you'd be off your shift soon and he wasn't giving you a ride. Here I am, at your service."

Zoey's mouth hung open and she blinked.

Quinn stepped between them. "Twiggy is it? Her shift doesn't end for another half hour."

"Trigger. Hey," he called across the diner to Jason. "Give the girl a break. Let her off early."

Jason straightened, now aware of the situation and eyeing each of them. "Zoey's got a mind of her own. If she wants to end a shift early she can ask like any other employee. We don't let customers decide that for her."

Twiggy—or Trigger—whatever, sent a look to Zoey as if she'd obey his wish merely because he desired it.

"Trigger," Zoey kept her voice even and non-threatening, as if she were a teacher calmly disciplining an unruly student. "I don't need a ride. Quinn is my ride. That's why I told Crypt I didn't need one."

"You can't go with Quinn, Zobo."

"Twiggy," Quinn interrupted. "What is your problem?"

"What's yours?" Trigger turned to face Quinn finally. "My name is Trigger. T. R. I. G. G. E. R. Trigger. Are you mental? Do you have a learning disability?" He laughed at his own joke. "Zobo, does he shutter his words when he reads, like you do?" Trigger rolled his eyes back in his head and snatched a menu from the podium. "Mu...mu. Men.. Youuuu." He tossed it on the ground, laughing and glancing at Zoey as if they shared some joke.

Zoey's face pinked. "That's not funny, Trigger."

"Oh come on Zobo. You're not sensitive. You're cool."

"Her name is Zoey, asshole." Quinn gestured outside. "Why don't we let her finish her shift and you and I go out there to settle whatever problem you have with me."

"Nothing needs to be settled. She's better off not hanging out with felons," Trigger said and then wiped his hand down his jeans. "Whatever, I'll be outside. Make the right choice or that fancy family paying for your baby bills because you're dangling an adoption might have an opinion about who you're hanging around. Might guess you're little plan to have them foot your bills."

Zoey's face paled. Trigger, having done his damage, pushed his way through the door. Quinn attempted to form the apology to Zoey in his head, but didn't get a chance to say it. She rushed off to another table, murmuring something about getting more orders before her shift ended.

Jason stood at the door. "Don't you dare go out there. He'd love nothing more than to get you in trouble with your probation officer."

"How does he even know about—" He stopped himself from speaking about Zoey's surrogacy out loud. Zoey was always careful. She signed an agreement not to share that information and wouldn't have, not even with Crypt. Trigger must have guessed an adoption, like he originally had. He must not know about the surrogacy. But how he knew about her financial situation was another matter.

"Oh?" Jason whispered, still looking shocked at the revelation of Zoey's state of affairs. "Well, it's not surprising he dug it up considering who is mother is."

Quinn shook his head not following.

"Dr. Devon. She's head of the hospital."

"Oh," he said automatically and then the connections and wheels of a small town turned over and cranked in his brain matter. "Ohhhh. That's Eric Devon. He was a snotty little brat two years below us in school."

"So that's his real name?" Jason's lips twitched. "I'll have to remember that. He always paid with cash, so I didn't know. I figured Trigger couldn't have been it, seeing how posh his mother and step-father are."

The gears were still cranking into place for Quinn. "He's best friends with the guy whose car.... The reason I went to prison."

"What did you do to the guy exactly? His friend seems to hold the grudge for him."

"I stole the guy's car."

"Grand theft auto. And you went to prison? Wow, that's someone with an intense revenge streak. Most times it's a max of a year in the county jail. But it's unfortunately one of those wobbler offenses that can be charged either way."

"I was lucky to get a sympathetic judge who only sentenced me to nine months."

"Jesus." Jason scratched his head. "That's still... odd. Zoey said you told her you don't remember a thing from that night. What was on your toxicology report?"

"My...what?"

"Did they test your blood? They would have had to, as procedure, if you looked drunk when they brought you in."

"The details are fuzzy."

"Do you mind if I look into it for you?" Jason asked. "Blacking out after one drink isn't really common."

Quinn frowned and stared out at Trigger. The guy had his arms crossed, flicking through some app on his phone. He'd really gone all the way with this biker image. Torn jeans, greasy shirt.

"Sorry," Jason said, breaking Quinn from his trance. "Guess there's no taking the lawyer out of me."

"No," Quinn forced himself to answer Jason. "It's fine. You can consider it as payment for the book-keeping organization I did for you today." He handed over a thumb drive of files. "This should get you squared away."

Jason's eyes shot up. "You work fast."

Quinn shrugged. "You were decently enough organized."

Then Jason waved him to the back office area to discuss how they were going to sneak Zoey out without having to walk past Twiggy outside.

CHAPTER NINE

Zoey brought a plate of fries with mustard instead of ketchup to the family at table three and the brother and sister dug in before the plate hit the formica.

She nervously glanced outside on her way into the kitchen. Trigger sat out there—in the only handicap parking space, no less—as if he'd won some hard fought battle, a smug smile on his face.

Quinn's truck was nowhere to be seen. Panic rose in her chest as she rushed to the spot he'd sat

through her shift. He wouldn't have left her—would he?

She should have made it clear that she didn't have any issues with his record. Trigger had no right to dig into her medical history. She worried about how much he knew. His mother couldn't possibility leak patient records. That seemed unprofessional. Illegal maybe? Zoey had no idea. People who were connected and above society, the way Trigger saw himself, didn't need to worry about consequences the same way Zoey did. Abandoned by her mother and father, taken in by her uncle who was the town drunk—she didn't have any social currency.

"Hey," Jason whispered from a crack in his office door.

Zoey startled. "Oh gosh, I didn't see you there."

"Come in." He opened the door wider, allowing her to slip in. Her belly scraping across the frame.

She nearly lost her balance, but Jason stabilized her with little effort. "I have a back door through the kitchen and Quinn is waiting out there. He made it look like he drove off, but he went around the block and came in through the ally. It was a total black ops moment."

"I'll just grab my purse—"

He placed his hand on the knob, preventing her exit. "Zoey, why don't you wait a minute..."

"If this is about the drama moment there a little bit ago, I'm so sorry. I can't control Trigger. We have mutual friends and he's been determined to wiggle his way to my side over the last year."

"I asked around and he's had a crush on you since grammar school," Jason said.

"Trigger? No." Though she instantly denied it, it did make a weird sort of sense and also explained his always appearing in the same circles as her throughout her life.

"But anyway, you'd told me about the night Quinn had been arrested. He just doesn't seem like the felon personality."

"Criminals are real people too."

Jason waved off her declaration. "Yeah. Of course. He's genuinely sorry and regretful for his actions. No excuses. That's very rare."

"Quinn is a good person. If you'd asked me who would be in prison before they turned thirty I would have raised my own hand."

Jason snorted his disbelief. "Right. So, back to your story. You *sure* he only had the one drink? He couldn't have sneaked any others by you—"

"No. I was with him. He also never drinks much at all. He never usually finishes one."

"Of course. I took all that information and did a little sleuthing yesterday. I found a few things and then I felt bad because I did it all without Quinn's permission, but I did retroactively get permission just now." He wiped his brow. "Phew." He pulled up a slip of paper. "He had a blood test right after they picked him up. He was way under the legal limit."

"It had been several hours later. He'd have slept it off."

"But wait—there's more. He also had traces of rohypnol in his blood. Did he drink any that were meant for you or another person at the bar?"

"No, he ordered his own. But he didn't drink it." But he had a drink. She did remember that.

"Did you take his drink at any point and set it down."

"I don't remember. I'm sorry, it was nine months ago and...pregnancy brain."

"Don't worry." Jason plopped down into his office chair swaying side to side. "The bigger question here is why wasn't this submitted as evidence in his case? He'd have been too drugged up to have been aware of what he was doing...maybe even too under the influence to even pull the crime off."

"They wouldn't let me testify either. The lawyers said it would do more harm than good. So I was terrified of making a mistake that would incriminate him and send him to prison or jail, except that happened anyway."

"The other interesting thing. These records are sealed at the hospital."

"Then how did you get them?"

"They were in his lawyer's file. I asked his lawyer to fax them all over since I'd be taking his case over. He sent them with glee. He'd been assigned to Quinn way by the court."

"Why didn't he submit that as evidence? Did you ask the lawyer?"

"He made it seem like an oversight and not a big deal. Made a point to explain how the evidence wasn't valid and it was all said and done anyway. But it's huge."

"I wish Quinn's dad could have gotten him a better lawyer, but he'd been so angry over the entire incident, he didn't want to 'reward' Quinn for his bad behavior, as he put it." *He'll have to lie in his own messes, Zoey bear,* Tom Bradford had told her when she pleaded with him to intervene. Something hadn't felt right about the entire event.

"Well, I looked into it and it appears that this lawyer is buddies with the father of the kid whose car Quinn stole. It's not that I relish in believing that someone who vowed to uphold the law would deliberately play fast and loose with it, but..." Jason let that conclusion hang.

In other words he believed Zoey's instincts that someone set Quinn up. And it didn't take much digging to connect the dots.

"Those assholes thought because we're lower class they could do this and nobody would object," she threw up her hands. "And nobody did!"

"And they would have gotten away with it if it hadn't been for that gay lawyer and his pregnant side kick."

"I have to tell Quinn." Zoey shouldered her purse and clocked out.

Jason pressed himself against the side of his office, smartly keeping out of her way. "Be careful Zoey. These guys pretty much figure they run this town. And they had enough clout to pull several people in on the deception. I'd be careful on where you both go from here. Don't do anything without discussing it with me first."

She waved off his words. "Of course. Of course." She flew out the exit and into the open door of Quinn's waiting truck.

She told him to take her away from there—so Trigger did not get suspicious and come looking for them—but to stop somewhere, anywhere, as soon as possible so she could tell him everything she'd just learned.

When she filled him in he hung there without much to say. After all, she'd been right—he was innocent.

Before they could do much about the new information her phone rang.

"Hello? Zoey Winters?"

"Yes," she said, attempting to place the voice.

"This is Angela Masters. You're having my baby."

The serious tone froze Zoey in her moment of celebration.

"We need to talk," the woman said.

CHAPTER TEN

Quinn waited outside the law firm where Zoey instructed him to drive. It had all happened so quickly. His finding out he may very well be innocent and framed, to Zoey then confessing she'd been waiting to hear from her surrogate parents after they'd disappeared. Her issue took precedence over his personal discovery. I mean, he'd already done the jail time—no undoing that. So now he paced outside waiting for her to emerge.

His phone buzzed. It was an email from his father: a forward from their neighbor Brant of the car that had stood watch over Quinn's cabin all night, and footage of a certain familiar someone sneaking around the fences. Trigger. Or as Quinn knew him: Eric Devon.

He'd even made a phone call, a very self-incriminating call, and wouldn't you know it—that phone call was caught on the surveillance video, which also records audio. Quinn's hands shook as he sent everything on to Jason. It was all coming together so quick, Quinn didn't have a chance to really process it. He'd been innocent all those months ago, plain and simple, and now thanks to technology he had the exact evidence he needed to get the crime expunged from his record.

Zoey had been in the meeting for over two hours and his veins were practically vibrating knowing that their future looked a lot more bright.

The throaty rumble of a car caught him off-guard. What the hell was Twiggy—or rather, Eric—doing here?

Oh, of course. He'd come in search of Zoey. He must have done something to her phone, enabled a GPS tracker, like a 'find your friends' app she didn't know about. There was no way he could have guessed she'd come here. Not even Jason knew the particulars of this meeting until she had told him where to drive. She'd only just found out herself.

As if on cue, Zoey emerged. A frown creased her forehead and she'd looked to have aged a few years.

He ignored Eric, staring at them from his car in the parking lot.

"It's fine, it's just the couple I was carrying for—" She took a deep breath. "They're getting a divorce. I had to sign all new paperwork and it looks like my payments were getting mixed up in the divorce court." She sighed. "It's just this poor baby. Not even born yet and she's going to have a heck of a start to life."

He pulled her close. "Hey look, you had a similar start and you're a really good person. It won't stop this baby."

She nodded. "Right." Wiped away a stray tear. "Hormones." She laughed off her emotional reaction.

He steered her away from a certain car and the potential drama inside, guiding her to his truck as he quickened his pace.

Eric revved his engine. "Zoey!" he called from his rolled down window. "You're coming with me."

"Just ignore him," Quinn hugged her close to his side, a zing of anxiety rippling down his spine.

If Eric knew his minutes of freedom were numbered, Quinn didn't know what the guy was capable of.

Eric jumped out of his car, door wide open, leaving it running. The exhaust billowed, the air stunk of burned gasoline. "Hands off, asshole." He yelled to Quinn.

"Get in the truck," Quinn snuck the keys into Zoey's hand and turned, blocking Eric's path to her.

Quinn held up his hands, forming his calming plea when a fist flew right to his jaw. He'd not expected that—yet it was also expected at the same time. He brought his arms up to block the next sucker punch. It landed instead on his muscular shoulder. Honestly, it kind of tickled, but he didn't laugh.

His face grew hot from the injury, a bruise probably already forming. He'd thought he'd get his life back. He'd get the sentence erased. He'd worked things out with Zoey. He didn't expect to see this guy ever again. Except now, face-to-face, he wanted to give this jerk the punch he so rightly deserved.

Another punch landed just below his ribcage. "You're a big guy. You gonna let me take you down?"

"I'm not going to give you a reason to call my parole officer," Quinn bit out, wishing he could sneak a nice nose-breaking pop right in the center of Eric's face.

The sirens whirled out at the main highway, headed their way.

"You'd better get lost. You won't get off with the minimum this time." He kicked, face red and spit flying out as he emphasized each word. Quinn had heard of spittin' mad, but never seen it until now. Eric slammed his fist down on the hood of the car next to him. "See? Property damage." He pointed at the dent he'd made as if Quinn somehow forced his hand into it. "You did it again. And this time Zoey will forget all about you. If you give her up, I'll tell the police this was all a misunderstanding. You don't and we'll put you away for a lot longer this time. You'll sign over your rights as a father. You'll do it for Zoey. She's mine."

"She's not property, asshole." He blocked a few more shoves and slaps. "And the baby's not mine. I can't sign over any rights."

He backed up a step. "Is that so?" He whooped at the top of his lungs a crazed look crossing his face. "Best news. We don't have to worry about some trucker trash's offspring messing her up. I heard she's been considering adoption anyway. A better option. We can have our own kids later on when we're ready."

This guy was insane. Quinn kept the police car in his sight as it rolled closer to the scene. The police officer assessed the situation from the safety of his car. Quinn kept his hands up, non-threatening. Eric, hands at his side, breathing heavily, pointed at a Quinn with satisfaction.

"Him," Eric yelled. "It's him."

"Don't make a fool of yourself," Quinn rumbled under his breath.

"Who do you think they'll believe? Some convict? Or the son of a prominent member of the community. Our donations to the city pay for their uniforms."

Quinn didn't doubt it. Especially as the police officer came out of his car, gun drawn. Quinn closed his eyes, unable to keep his calm with all the memories of his arrest floating back.

The confusion.

The yelling.

The officers going through his house.

His panic when he realized Zoey might have been there on his couch.

That was the only thing he'd half-remembered—most of his memories after having that drink were gone. But he had a heartbeat of a memory: perhaps Zoey coming in after she'd run off. She'd apologized and set up on the couch while she took care of him, sick, dizzy, and miserable.

Now he *knew* he'd been drugged. Those hours of his life stolen just as easily as the nine months he'd gone away.

The cold metal of the cuffs pinched like the surprise of a burn against his skin. He flinched, but held himself steady. This was protocol. Two men fighting. One has a record. Cuff the felon, especially since he's big and burly. Pay no attention to the fact he's an accountant.

"What is going on here?" Zoey appeared just beyond the officers taking statements. "I called the cops on that guy." She pointed at Eric. "He came out of nowhere and attacked my friend."

"Ma'am, please step back."

"Seriously?" She crossed her arms. "Quinn isn't the one causing problems here. He's my ride. I was walking out of my appointment and this man," she swung her arm toward Eric again, "he's been stalking me. He shows up everywhere and insists I go with him."

"It's not a crime to be concerned about a woman and keep her safe from a dangerous criminal," Eric straightened as he delivered his heroic speech.

"I've asked him to leave a number of times. We have witnesses." Another car drove in. "Ah, here's one now. My boss. I called him."

Quinn held a lungful of air. Jesus, was the whole town going to show?

Jason parked, blocking in Eric's car. He rolled down his window. "I'm this man's lawyer. Do you have probable cause to pull him into the station?"

The police officer sighed and pulled out his handcuff keys. "No, sir. I'm assuming we're getting this all wrong?"

"Yes," Zoey and Jason said in unison.

"This man attacked me!" Eric chimed in, indigent.

"Do you have a witness?" The other officer asked.

Eric's gaze swept the parking lot, meeting a number of curious gazes. He pointed to one. "You! You saw him attack me. My mother is head of the hospital. This man is the son of a trucker," he added the last awkwardly as if this proclaimed his story more true just by social class.

The man in the crowd shook his head. "This kid's been shoving and pushing the bigger guy. The bigger guy sent the lady on ahead to his truck. He didn't do a thing wrong except keep this kid from her."

The police officers looked at each other, a decision passing between them. The radio in their car crackled to life. One of them ran over to listen to the call. A few seconds later he came back, cuffing Eric.

"What is going on here!" Eric protested.

"We have a call to bring you in."

"You have to have probable cause," Eric jumped toward Jason. "Tell them! You have to make them let me go."

"I'm not *your* lawyer." Jason rolled his eyes and faced Quinn and Zoey. "Meet me at the station. We'll get this party started." His expression went soft. "You ready for this? It's not going to be an easy ride wiping your sentence." He waited for them to nod, then his car window went up, leaving them both to zig-zag their way out of the parking lot to his truck.

Zoey's eyes grew big with each step. "What? Did he say what I think he did?"

Quinn squeezed her hand. "I have a lot to catch you up on." He helped her step into the truck. She sat facing him. Their heads at the perfect height for a kiss. He held himself back. "We have the proof of the set up. with lab work and surveillance records. Twiggy—I mean, Eric—wanted you. It was your drink that was spiked with the date rape drug, but I drank your drink when you didn't like it. At the same time he'd organized for me to be framed for a crime I did not commit, just so he could get me out of your life. And the one time you didn't drink messed it all up for them. Basically, you were right—"

She took his head in her hands, her grin all-knowing. "No, Quinn. *You* were right." She kissed him and the dread and fear from his brush with the law a few minutes ago vanished. "We were meant for each other and you were the brave one to say it."

"God," he said, his forehead resting on hers. "I hate that that was the worst night of my life, but to be truthful, it was probably the drugs they slipped me that gave me the courage."

Her face crinkled in confusion. He barked out a laugh. "Like I said, a lot to catch up on. Let's get this out of the way so we can go star counting tonight."

She swung her legs, as gracefully as an eight-month pregnant lady could, into the truck. "I can't wait to get on with our lives. Maybe more trouble free this time?"

"Don't count on it," he said and closed the door shut on her giggle.

Two years later...

The baby, wide-eyed, her head tilted toward the doctor, emitted a tiny squeak. The doctor wrapped her arm a little tighter into the folds of the burrito wrapped blanket. "There, there little one. You have plenty of time to learn to run and jump and play. Why don't you stay close for now."

Quinn gently held the baby's head, cradling it close to his chest. "Oh god, I'm going to break her."

"You know how to do this, daddy," the doctor answered him. "You've done it all before."

Quinn's expression went blank, a small half-smile on his lips giving away the mixed emotion how he felt about the first time. It had been hard for Quinn to let go of his desire to be the father of Zoey's first pregnancy.

Zoey sat up in the bed. "She looks exactly like you, Quinn."

He propped her up closer, facing her. "She does?"

A short knock at the door had everyone in the room sweeping their gaze to see who'd waited to visit the new member of their family.

A two-year-old girl came bounding in, blond curls bobbing and cheeks like full plump apples. "Sister. Sister!"

Her mother, wrapped in a scarf and sporting oversized sunglasses, strolled in after her. "Now, now, we talked about this. Baby Bradford isn't technically your sister."

"We shared a tummy." The little girl patted her own stomach as if to emphasize her understanding of the situation.

"Grace," Zoey's grin deepened, her focus intent on the little girl. "I'm so glad you could meet Ava."

Quinn knelt down, presenting the baby to Zoey's surrogate daughter. It had been a long two years filled with fighting to have his sentence overthrown, marrying Zoey, getting a new job as a CPA at a local accounting firm, planning this pregnancy. It was like a full lifetime had passed since Grace had been born, instead of two years.

Grace's mouth fell open at the sight of the baby. She poked at the infants chest gently. "Oh, Ava. Pretty baby."

"That's right. Just like you were," Grace's mother said, adjusting her sunglasses over her head. It revealed her famous face. After her and her husband divorced it had been a rocky year of custody battles. Quinn and Zoey had stepped in to help with Grace's child care—keeping a very low profile. None of the media outlets had figured out the connection.

"She has black hair." Grace frowned.

"Just like her mommy," the doctor explained. "Daddy's got some brown hair." She pointed to Quinn.

Grace analyzed the two parents as if processing the coincidence. "Okay." She nodded and marched to her mother, grabbing her hand. "Cupcakes!"

"Right. Of course. I promised her we'd stop at Patties for their famous milkshakes. She calls them cupcakes. We're working on it."

And with as much fanfare as they entered, they left.

"She's getting more independent by the day." Zoey's gaze trailed out the door as if Grace were still there.

"She knows herself." Quinn propped one leg onto the hospital bed, bringing the baby between them and laying back with a smile. He'd never want to be anywhere else right now. "Like someone else I know." His eyelids lowered, heavy from the all-nighter labor they'd just pulled. Whoever promised a second labor was easier had lied big time.

He jerked a little as he felt the baby shift from his arms. Zoey had taken the baby. He sat up, alert. "Come on now, I was just resting my eyes. You need your rest."

"And so do you." She plopped out one nipple, the baby latched on after a few tries. "Ava has to practice breastfeeding anyway."

Quinn shifted back, resting his head into the pillow. "But just for a minute, then she's mine again."

But another knock on the door kept that hope for a nap from happening. East and Ansel came in.

And after that Jason. Then Crypt. Then Quinn's parents.

Hours later, after the nurses had declared visiting hours over, Zoey had passed out in the hospital bed and Quinn dimmed the lights. Quinn scooped Ava into his arms again, taking her to the rocking chair and staring out into the twinkle of stars. She heaved a long breath as if she'd been waiting for this moment of solitude as well.

"We're going to have a lot of fun together. But first things first. Ground rules." He waited as if she'd answered. "No, not about painting your room hot pink, or black if that's your thing—I'm talking about your math skills. Let's start by counting the stars."

And they both gazed up above and started counting.

Copyright © 2018 by Christina Smith.

Our columnist, Julie Pitzel, has been a receptionist, radio DJ, bill collector, telemarketer, administrative assistant, community college instructor, and an expediter (aka professional nag). She's been involved in the Houston writing community for many years including two years as President of a local Romance Writers of America Chapter. She writes paranormal fiction from a geodesic dome south of Houston, where she lives with her husband and a pair of cats. Most recently, her story "The Dance" was published in The Death of All Things *anthology.*

YOU READ THAT?: DIVERSITY. DIVERSITY. DIVERSITY?

by Julie Pitzel

Diversity and inclusion are the current buzzwords. We hear them used in regards to corporations and politics. They're selling points for toys and games. It's the subject of blogs and articles. Movies and television shows are dissected, and the types of characters counted and compared. And then we have the romance industry, one of the few places where women dominate. We must have that diversity thing under control.

But, of course we don't.

One of the first published authors I met years and years ago was Anita Bunkley. Anita self-published her first novel in the 1980's, long before self-publishing was acceptable. Although the editors who saw her novel liked the writing and the story, they wouldn't buy it because "black women didn't read" (seriously, someone said that!) and no one else would be interested in a historical romance with black protagonists. She proved them wrong by selling books out of the trunk of her car, which led to a contract.

Today it's difficult to believe that a publisher would make those types of assumptions, or at least difficult to believe they'd admit to them. Though publishing has opened up to people of color as well as other marginalized groups, it needs to include more—especially as editors, publishers, and other positions of power.

Lack of diversity and issues of exclusion are found throughout the publishing world. The main difference with Romance is that we're biased towards white women instead of white men. The bias isn't just a casual observation. For those who aren't aware, Romance Writers of America (RWA) recently had a dustup regarding their RITA Awards, the top honor for published romance fiction. In the RITA's thirty-six year history, no black author has received the award. And only about one half of one percent of all finalists have been black. That's a problem.

Yes, people of color are statistically in the minority, but not by that large of a percentage. We can't boil books down to just a numbers game, but at the same time, it doesn't make sense numerically for zero black authors to have won the award. It's especially questionable when they *have* won the Golden Heart— RWA's contest for unpublished writers. Other than the published/unpublished thing, the main difference between the two contests is that Golden Heart entries are anonymous and the RITA's are not.

As a straight, white woman, I'm part of the majority. With the current system, if I ever get a novel published, (butt in chair, stop reading Facebook and playing computer games) my chances of winning accolades are greater than my POC fellow authors. So why would I be concerned about diversity and inclusion——other than basic decency?

For the same reasons we should *all* care. We live in a diverse world. Every single one of us is different and can be singled out for some reason. If not for skin color or sexual orientation, it could be age, hair color, or because we like pineapple on our pizza (yes, it *is* a viable topping!). Bias exists, but we don't have to accept it. And when we see it happening, we should actively work to erase it.

The other reason we should care about bias with awards such as the RITAs, is because they are supposed to exemplify the best romance fiction out there. If a significant percentage of books are not represented, are not lauded as the best, are not even given the opportunity to be judged, then how do we know we're getting the best?

And maybe most readers aren't aware of the RITAs, but publishers, book buyers, and critics are familiar with the awards. Authors who can claim a RITA nomination or win are going to be given better coverage and consideration. It could be a critical career boost and the difference between readers finding a book on the shelf in the nearest bookstore, or not.

When we talk about diversity, race and sexual orientation are generally the main focus, but other marginalized groups are underrepresented in fiction as well. We don't see many stories about people on the autism spectrum or with disfiguring illnesses. Main characters rarely have a permanent disability. A writer I know with mobility issues noticed that in the park evacuation scene from Jurassic World, there were no wheelchairs. Most events and parks we go to have accommodations for disabled people. Disney provides wheelchairs. But this major attraction had none. She felt excluded.

There is a welcome trend to label stories with ownvoices. It's an indication that the protagonist shares a marginalized identity with the author. For instance, both might be trans or hearing impaired or Muslim. The label can help readers find stories with voices similar to their own. The hashtag started as a way to recommend diverse kids' books, but it's grown to encompass adult books as well.

There are some who believe all stories about marginalized individuals should be told by members of that particular group. In other words, only a Native American can write stories with a Native American hero. Only an individual with Down's syndrome can write a story from that point of view. A Latina heroine should be written by a person of Latin American descent. Otherwise, they consider it appropriation, theft.

I understand this position to a point. So many of the characters we see in books and movies are caricatures, cardboard cutouts with labels. No one wants to see their heritage or religion or disability portrayed as clichés. Another point is if we are going to read stories about marginalized characters, the people intimately connected to those stories should get the contracts and acclaim. But I also think most fiction coming out today should include minority, LGBTQ, and disabled characters. Not because it's politically correct, but because they are our coworkers and neighbors and family. If I were to write about only straight white women in Houston, it would be as false to the setting as describing rolling hills and low humidity.

This column has been difficult for me to write. I struggled with finding an angle that didn't make me sound preachy or clueless or both. And I don't want to sound like I'm bashing the romance industry. I do believe romance fiction is leaps and bounds above most other genres when it comes to diversity and inclusion. No one can deny that there are problems, but they are being addressed.

And I do have to admit to being part of the problem. Most of the authors I read look a lot like me. I don't step out of my comfort zone very often, which is kind of stupid. I'm limiting myself and missing fun and engaging stories because they are unfamiliar.

One of the main reasons I read is because it's an escape. It allows me to explore new worlds or historical places as a variety of different characters. I can—fictionally——walk a mile, dance a quadrille, or run a marathon in someone else's shoes. It's time I worked on diversifying my own reading habits; try on some different shoes for different journeys and exercises. Maybe we should all do that.

Copyright © 2018 by Julie Pitzel.

C.S. DeAvilla writes award-winning science fiction, fantasy, and romance under another pen name. She has been a romance fan since she sneaked a peek at her mother's massive historical romance bookcase and fell in love with all the characters. She reads every romance genre—as long as two people are falling in love, she'll give it a read. Her favorite authors are Jennifer Crusie, J.R. Ward, Darynda Jones, Suzanne Brockmann, Sarah MacLean, and Kristan Higgins. But she always has room for one more.

RECOMMENDED BOOKS

by C.S. DeAvilla

Title: ***Song of Blood & Stone***
Author: L. Penelope
Publisher: St. Martin's Press
ISBN: 1250148073
Release Date: May 1st, 2018

Song of Blood & Stone grabs readers right in the gut at the very beginning and doesn't let go, not even at the end. L. Penelope's strong voice and imaginative world are only two of a long list of excellent attributes of this novel. *Song of Blood & Stone* opens with Jasminda, our main character, as she's asked to sign away her heritage and questioned about outstanding taxes. Then, threats of war send her on a long journey with mysterious stranger, Jack. There are several opportunities for the characters to prevent a lot of *big bad* from happening, but they're foiled at every turning point. But don't worry dear readers, Penelope delivers us right where we need to be by story's end. At the beginning of each chapter there's collected folktales that set the mood and add a level of emotional depth to the coming events. There was at least one twist involving Jack I didn't see coming (no spoilers!), but it sure does pile on the tension between Jasminda and Jack, and well, just about everyone else. This is a book that is sure to delight fans of fantasy who like a side of just-the-right-amount of romance in the plot and shades of Sarah J. Mass and Anne Bishop for style.

Title: ***Trouble Brewing***
Author: Suzanne Baltsar
Publisher: Gallery (Simon & Schuster)
ISBN: 1501188313
Release Date: September 25, 2018

Getting a sneak peek at books set to release later in the year is a special treat. I'd gotten an early copy of *Trouble Brewing* during a reader's conference in the spring and from the title and cover it already had me curious to flip to the first page. Piper Williams is attempting to survive as a master beer brewer, in a world dominated by men and good ol' boys clubs. Her newly developed beer and brand "Out of the Bottle" is everything she's worked for and she's given up a lot to accomplish this much. Spending two years in Germany and enduring an emotionally abusive relationship, Piper won't let anything else stand in her way. Except Blake Reed plants himself directly in her path. Being the first venue to offer her beer on tap, she can't let their easy chemistry steer her away from her goal. If they start up a relationship or even if a hint of their attraction blows in the direction of the other beer brewing society in town, her reputation will be ruined. She'll only be known as the female brewer who turns tricks for favors from bartenders. She'll never be taken seriously. Blake, however, isn't going to allow Piper to slip past him too easily, despite his desire to want her to succeed as well. This novel is filled with characters you feel like you might know in real life and might have chatted-up at a local bar or pub. Their chemistry sizzles off the page, and Piper's concerns about making it on her own in a man's world are relatable. This is one debut that's sure to stand above the rest of the pack this fall.

or smart couple is sometimes the exact right fit for my reading mood. Melody Gage in *Remedial Rocket Science* was that nerd hero I didn't know I needed. The storyline starts while Melody is attending college in Boston and meets Jeremy. The two hit it off and fall into bed, even though both know it can never go anywhere. Melody needs to finish school, Jeremy lives across the country in California. But, a few years later when Melody is in Jeremy's hometown for a job interview she remembers that one night and decides to contact him after years of silence. They become fast friends, but timing for romance once again isn't ideal. Jeremy is engaged and Lacy (his fiancé) becomes Melody's best friend. Drama and emotional rollercoasters ensue. Nix delivers characters that keep readers engaged in the story and a style that keeps it humorous but touches on some more serious topics. A female in a STEM field is also a major plus for the book—we need more bold heroines like Melody!

Title: **Remedial Rocket Science**
Author: Susannah Nix
Publisher: Haver Street Press
ASIN: B0721MYNL5
Release Date: August 21st 2017

Title: **Sinner**
Author: Sierra Simone
Publisher: Self-Published
ASIN: B0799G4SDF
Release Date: March 15th, 2018

If there's one super fun niche romance genre, it's nerd romance. An intelligent hero or smart heroine

I've developed a fascination with this series of books. First with *Priest*, now with *Sinner*. I'm still wrapping my mind around an inspirational, erotic romance. Two romance genres that seem to be on opposite ends of the spectrum, but Simone has managed to have the two play nicely together—adding on a pile of compelling conflict. In *Priest*, Father Tyler is defrocked after falling in love with one of his parishioners. In *Sinner* we get the inverse of that, Sean, Tyler's brother, falls for a nun. Well, not quite a nun yet. She's a postulant (in training) and hasn't taken her final vows. However, the head nun is slightly unconventional in that she's tasked Zenny with the assignment to go experience life and love. The head nun, unsure of Zenny's young age and commitment, would like to see how the trainee will hold up to temptation. Who better to recruit to that task than her older brother's best friend, Sean. Some of the fascination on my part might be due to my catholic upbringing and knowing how taboo love is within church ranks. Readers who love stories that have high conflict scenarios that are un-put-down-able reads will find *Sinner* a must read.

I'll be honest, Ward had me by the throat through this entire novella. No vampire pun intended. Silas appears in Ivie's life while she's explaining an odd job interview to her cousin at a bar. She can tell right away he's part of the vampire aristocracy, so what in the Scribe Virgin could he want with her? His instant charm cuts through Ivie's usual cynical nature. He invites her on a date and she immediately declines. Except her curiosity over his genuine interest leads her to show up anyway. The couple hit it off and forge an immediate friendship with attraction as a bonus—although the relationship does come with an expiration date since Silas will be moving overseas in a month. However, midway through the novella, right about when I'm planning the happily ever after, readers realize nothing is what it seems, and that expiration date is more real than Silas is admitting. I thought I'd been duped into reading a story that would end in tragedy. After all, Ward's books do not come with guarantees (as I've learned). For readers who are waiting on this one until they know for sure it will end happily—then feel confident in buying a copy today. Ward runs readers through the emotional grinder on this one, but she will leave you satisfied.

Copyright © 2018 by C.S. DeAvilla.

Title: ***Dearest Ivie***
Author: J.R. Ward
Publisher: Ballantine Books (Random House)
ASIN: B0796F4874
Release Date: March 13th, 2018

Susan Donovan is an American author of romance novels and women's fiction. Her novel Take a Chance on Me *won the 2003 Best Contemporary Romance Award Winner from* Romantic Times. *Two of her novels—* The Kept Woman *and* Not That Kind of Girl *were selected as RITA Award Finalists by the Romance Writers of America. Before writing her novels, she was a journalist, and studied at Northwestern University's Medill School of Journalism. She lives in New Mexico with her family and labradoodle.*

Celeste Bradley is the New York Times *and* USA Today *bestselling author of more than twenty Regency romance novels and has twice been nominated for the RITA Award by the Romance Writers of America. Before becoming a writer in 1999, Celeste was an artist who specialized in pottery and ceramic sculpture. Although originally from the South, Celeste now resides in New Mexico. "It is one of the last habitats of the Free-Range Human." She is very fond of food that someone else cooks, animals of all sorts, painting, jewelry making, reading, and grandbabies.*

An excerpt from
BREATHLESS

by Celeste Bradley and Susan Donovan

Brenna Anderson is a Harvard sociology professor known for her study of human sexuality in art. Much of her research has been about the mysterious Siren Series, erotic paintings by an unknown European painter of his luminous muse. Fitch Wilder is an art investigator who's unearthed another painting in the series and was just hired by an eccentric collector to track down the remaining canvases. They cross paths in London and realize each holds an important piece of the historic puzzle. Will they be able to put aside their differences for the sake of art?

"Shall we?" He opened the limousine door for her.

"We shan't." Brenna planted her feet on the sidewalk and crossed her arms over her chest. There was no point. She would be in Barcelona the next morning, seven hundred miles away from Fitch Wilder. She could forget all about this series of distasteful coincidences.

"Have you had a chance to enjoy your hotel's traditional afternoon tea? It's something worth doing while in London."

She ignored him.

Fitch let go with a rich and leisurely chuckle and leaned against the car. With him all stretched out and relaxed like that, it was obvious to see how some women might find Wilder appealing. He was long and lean. His wrists had an elegant turn to them, the muscle and bone etched in his tanned skin. His shoulders were exceptionally broad, and his waist slim and solid. And those complicated eyes….

It was difficult not to stare. But she managed.

"No? Then we should have tea together. That way I can tell you all about the underpainting I found beneath the sixth Siren portrait."

Brenna's spine stiffened in alarm. "The *what?*"

"Here's my proposition, professor—I'll show you mine if you show me yours." The look on Wilder's face was pure amusement. He was enjoying this!

She was not.

"I have no interest in 'yours,' Wilder."

"Don't kid yourself. You know you do."

"Mine is far more significant than an underpainting."

"You don't know that for certain—mine could be a pretty big deal, too."

She narrowed her eyes at him. "What I have changes art history."

Fitch's smile widened, revealing a set of white, straight teeth. He raised up from the car. "Yeah? What I have is a love poem from the artist to the Siren. Mine doesn't change history, it *is* history." He wiggled an eyebrow as he gestured for her to take a seat in the SUV. "How about that cup of tea?"

A few minutes later, the driver had turned into London traffic. The two of them sat quietly in the back seat, their eyes locked in a dare. Brenna's muscle and tendons were pulled so tight she heard her cells strumming. She had to remind herself that this guy was no more than an arrogant con man. She couldn't believe a word he said. And yet…the notion that Fitch Wilder knew anything more about the artist and muse than she did made her see stars.

He didn't intimidate her. Not in the least. But a love poem? She had to know what it said. The only way to deal with Wilder would be to offer him a crumb in exchange for the poem, and then walk away and never look back.

She nearly hissed at him. "Game on, Wilder."

"You got it."

"Tell me about the poem. Now."

"At tea—much more civilized."

It wasn't long before they sat at a dining table overlooking the rainy, early spring English garden. The linen-covered table had been set with a small bouquet of fresh flowers, bone china, heavy silver, and crystal. A three-tiered silver tray had just been placed between them, laden with a colorful tea-for-two. An assortment of finger sandwiches and delicate sweets was displayed on white doilies.

Sharing high tea with a cowboy swindler seemed surreal, to say the least.

Frankly, Brenna was surprised the *maître d'* had let Wilder into the dining room in the first place. He was still wearing those jeans and battered cowboy boots. No tie. Not even a collar this time—just a generic charcoal gray T-shirt. And it didn't appear he'd taken the time to shave since she'd seen him four days before. When he took a dainty sip and set the fragile teacup back in its saucer, it looked like a child's toy in his beefy hand.

And yet…she'd had to stifle a laugh when Wilder ordered a pot of passion fruit Darjeeling as easily as she imagined he'd order beer in a saloon. Then he'd peered over the tray with wide eyes and said, "Yes! I love clotted cream!"

She sat back against her chair now and studied him. It occurred to her that she had no idea who this man really was. Half of what had transpired between them had obviously been pure farce.

"Who the hell are you, Wilder? Really?"

Fitch had just shoved a scone into his mouth. His large green-gray-gold eyes went wide with surprise as he swallowed. "Mmm?" He dabbed at the corners of his lips with a linen napkin. "I was just being the man you expected me to be."

Brenna eyed him skeptically. "You're a con artist."

"And you're so freakin' easy to mess with, professor, that I couldn't resist. Besides, you deserve it."

She squirmed in her seat, her breath shallow and fast. She kept staring at his lips. A smile quivered at their corners like an actor waiting for his cue. And those eyes…so intelligent and playful that she had to look away.

If this guy were anyone else—*absolutely any other man on earth*—she'd drag his chiseled ass to her bed and make him her plaything.

Women likely lined up for blocks to give themselves to Fitch Wilder. Not Brenna. She was an expert on the human psycho-sexual experience. Every one of her lovers, to a man, would insist that they won Brenna through skill and dogged determination, but only because Brenna wished them to think so. In truth, she was always the seducer and never the seduced. Without exception.

But she had standards. She never seduced a man she did not respect.

"You haven't even tasted your oolong." Wilder gestured with a half-eaten scone. "Why not loosen up, professor. Let your hair down. Get your tea on."

She laughed in disbelief. "You think you're the best thing to happen to women since sitting on the dryer, don't you?"

Wilder coughed. He covered his mouth with his napkin in an effort to stifle the hacking sound now echoing off the dining room walls.

Brenna sipped her oolong and tossed her hair. She was proficient in the Heimlich maneuver, and if absolutely necessary she would save him from death by scone. She wasn't a horrible person. In the meantime she selected a pretty little smoked salmon sandwich and took a nibble.

Fitch eventually stopped coughing. The appalled dining room guests returned to their refreshments and conversations, and Brenna sat across from him, clearly pleased with herself. He poured himself a fresh cup of tea, envisioning the lovely Brenna Anderson riding a front-loaded Kenmore, her head thrown back in permanent-press rapture.

Not a chance. A woman that gorgeous would never have to turn to household appliances for a good time. Despite her frosty disposition, plenty of men would risk hypothermia for just one taste of her.

"I got another proposition for you, professor."

She concentrated on spreading a thin layer of cream on her scone. "We haven't dealt with the last one. I'm still waiting to see the poem."

Fitch relaxed into his chair and threw an arm over the back, appraising her. Brenna had elegant hands. Though she could benefit from a few minutes of sunshine, she had nice skin. Her hair looked especially bright in the warm tearoom light, and he wondered how silky the long strands would feel between his fingertips. She wore a tight gray skirt and a floaty top that shimmered like mother-of-pearl. The skirt would have shown off her legs were it not for the D'Artagnan-meets-Madonna leather boots.

Fitch wondered if he'd ever get to see the porcelain knees, calves, and ankles she kept tucked away in there.

He stifled a smile. Yeah, he had to be nuts to admit it, but he liked Dr. Brenna Anderson. She was growing on him. Fitch was intrigued by her complexity and her intelligence, and planned to find out what existed beneath that prickly-pear exterior of hers.

"Professor," he said. "How about we clear the air between us before we trade Siren secrets. I'll sit here all proper and silent while you open a can o' Ivory Tower whoop-ass on me. Go on. Tell me every single thing—big or little—that you despise about me, no matter how long it takes."

Brenna checked her watch. That made him chuckle.

"Fine." She set her knife upon her plate and met his gaze with calm, cool blue eyes. "You claim to be an art expert yet you have no degree."

"That's correct. What I have instead is a lifetime of experience working with my father in art appraisal, investigation, and sales, and I apprenticed with the country's foremost authority in technological applications in fine art."

"Oh really? And who was that?"

"Edna Abrams at Carnegie Mellon. Ring any bells?"

A look of surprise flashed across her face.

"Don't hold back on me." He raised his teacup. "Continue with the whooping."

Brenna lowered her chin and steeled her gaze before she spoke. "All right, Wilder. Your father was a notorious New York art forger and convicted felon."

"You're correct." He returned his cup to the saucer and leaned forward. "He took a plea and agreed to become a consultant to the FBI's Art Crime Team, a job he held until he died. He also moved to Santa Fe to become a highly respected businessman. I happen to be very proud of the man my father was."

Her laugh was dismissive. "Santa Fe?"

"Yes, Santa Fe, a world-class center for art collection and home to one of the highest concentrations of artists anywhere on earth."

Her eyes narrowed, a sign that she was about to get to the nitty-gritty. "You plagiarized my dissertation during that TV interview. Maybe you're more like your father than you'd like to admit."

Fitch leaned even closer, careful to keep his voice low. He moved his plate to the side so he could fold his hands on the tabletop. "You know what, professor? I did credit your work during that interview, but they edited it out to shorten the segment. I was about to call them and insist they do a correction when I saw your tweet. And then I thought, *well, to hell with that.*"

The delicate skin of her left eyelid began to twitch. Otherwise, she remained unflappable, even in the face of the uncomfortable truth. He had to admire her resolve.

"And just so you know, I can find my ass with both hands just fine. In fact, sometimes it only takes one."

Her mouth pulled tight. "I apologize."

"Apology accepted."

"Great. So now that we're BFFs, how about you show me the poem?"

Fitch nodded. He wanted the details of her courtesan theory, and this was the only way he'd get them. He reached into his pocket.

Just then, Brenna's phone rang, and she began digging in her bag like she expected to find pirate treasure. Her eyes flashed in surprise at the caller ID and she looked up at him. "I need to take this." She turned away in her seat.

Of course he listened. How could he not? It couldn't be classified as eavesdropping if she stayed right there at their table.

"*Claudia?* Wait. Slow down. I can't understand—"

She took a furtive glance Fitch's way, but he pretended to be reading a pamphlet on the history of the hotel's afternoon tea. She went back to her call.

"Letters? Really? But what kind of…? *What?* Oh, my God! I don't believe this. Hold on."

Brenna turned all the way around in her chair so that her back faced Fitch. She shielded one side of her face with an open hand and lowered her voice to a whisper. "You faxed one *here?* Why only one? All right, all right. I understand. I'll check with the front desk but…" She stood up, grabbed her bag off the chair. "Just a second, Claudia."

Brenna turned toward him, her resting professor face back in working order. "I have to go. Excuse me." She began walking away.

He called after her. "We haven't finished our game of show-and-tell!"

"Hold on, Claudia." Brenna spun around on her Musketeer high-heels, her eyes narrowed. "I've changed my mind. I don't want to play anymore. Goodbye, Wilder."

He watched her swish her fabulous ass across the dining room, letting the finality in her dismissal sink in. Whatever the subject of that call had been—and whoever this Claudia person was—Dr. Anderson had just accelerated to overdrive. Fitch watched her make a beeline for the lobby, no doubt on her way to the front desk to pick up her fax. *Damn.* He still had no idea what she was up to.

There were always ways to find out.

When Fitch got the check a few moments later, he engaged the waiter in a friendly chat, all the while conspicuously counting out cash. "I find my-

self needing a little special assistance with something here at the hotel."

"And what would that be, sir?"

He continued stacking the bills on the table, one after the other. "Something off the books, so to speak."

The waiter nodded in the affirmative, his face contorted in alarm at the pile of money. The young man then glanced around the dining room, making sure no one was watching.

Fitch handed him the check—along with the ginormous tip. "That's just to start," he said.

He stayed behind to finish his pot of Darjeeling, mulling over his next move. Brenna claimed she didn't want to play anymore, but he didn't believe that for a second. He raised the teacup to his lips.

"Game on, professor," he whispered.

…End of Excerpt

CLOSING EDITORIAL

by Tina Smith

I hope readers don't mind a slightly different closing for our August issue. See, usually we reserve our closing to treat readers to a sneak peek of what's to come in the next issue, but we have so much awesomeness planned for you all through to the end of the year, I can't hold it all inside. I might burst with excitement!

First of all, we do expect a return of Gracie Wilson, a newcomer in this issue, along with even more stories from our regular writers, Kate Pavelle and Petronella Glover. We know L. Penelope is writing a longer piece for us, and Lezli interviewed more fan-favorites at the RWA2018 conference, including bestseller Brenda Jackson.

We have been delighted to hear at the conference that *Heart's Kiss* is creating a buzz, and so we hope to continue bringing you those scrumptious stories and delicious surprises by partnering with very well-known authors you know and love. A little cupid whispered to us that one of the queens of paranormal fiction is penning a non-fiction article for an upcoming issue and Brenda Novak will have some more recipes for us to fall in love with, so the future looks great for our magazine.

Speaking of secret projects, we have also been planning a special treat for our last installment of the year. A holiday issue where we explore winter holidays as a backdrop to some amazing romance tales of all genres. Reading for the special issue has caused both Lezli and I to pine for the colder months and our mugs of hot tea by the fire. Isn't it funny when summer is in full swing we want the winter back and when it's cold we want our beach weather? There is just no satisfying us—except with a good romance. We will never complain as long as our inboxes continue to fill with wonderful untold stories of love.